FLORENCE
AND THE
HIGHWAYMAN

ANGELA RIGLEY

ISBN **9798532613270**

Copyright belongs to the author

Published by Angela Rigley
www.nunkynoo.yolasite.com

Chapter 1

"Oh, Lizzie, I know not what to do." Florence Fisher slung her soft, faded kid gloves onto the settee.

Her sister, Eliza, pushed back a wayward brown ringlet from her heart-shaped face. "You mean Lord Head? Has he repeated his proposal?"

She nodded, staring into the fire. "For Mama's sake I ought to accept, but I do not love him. I have not the slightest liking for him. In fact, he nauseates me. I cannot help but shudder at the thought of lying in bed with him."

Her sister winced, blinking her brown, heavy-lidded eyes. "I agree. But he would solve our problems. He has ten thousand pounds a year, so they say."

"Mm, yes, I know. It's the only thing going for him. That and his full head of thick, black hair."

Eliza laughed as she pulled the bell for the maid. "And doesn't he just love showing it off?" She pranced around the room, cupping her hands around her hair. "It is not as if he has any meaningful conversation," she added when she stopped. "He must be the most boring person in the whole of Cumberland."

Florence nodded in agreement as she took off her bonnet and shook out her curls. "Where is that maid? I am fair parched."

Her sister rang the bell again. "I hope Mama has not laid her off. Surely, we cannot be in such dire straits?"

The door opened and the maid appeared, her eyes red, as if from crying.

"Ah, Lilian, tea and biscuits, if you please." Eliza grimaced at Florence over the maid's head as the girl bowed and backed towards the door.

Florence asked, "Is everything well? You seem unlike your usual ebullient self."

"Yes, ma'am, sorry ma'am." She went out, without divulging the reason.

"I do hope Mama has not given her notice," gasped Eliza. "How will we manage? But I did hear tell she was found canoodling with the footman last week. Perhaps she is up the duff."

"Eliza, please, do you have to be so crude?" muttered Florence, her blue eyes flashing a warning as the door opened, revealing the maid with the tea tray. She placed it on the side table and withdrew without speaking.

Florence poured out the tea and handed her sister a cup. "Are we accepting the invitation to Lord March's ball next Saturday? There will be plenty of beaux there, so I am reliably informed."

"But that does not solve the problem of Lord Head of Black Hair." Eliza's tinkling laugh filled the room. "Do you not find that funny? Lord Head of Black Hair, or rather Lord Hairy Head?"

Florence shook her head. "I'll indulge you. But I just wish he would go away and leave me alone."

"But he is so enamoured of your big, beautiful, blue eyes, and your...what does he call them? Your 'little pink rosebud ears'. I heard him tell his friend—he didn't know I was listening, of course—that your ears have the most exquisite lobes he has ever seen. His friend did give him a peculiar look, I must admit, and when he saw me he winked. I don't know if he realised who I was but I turned and left, blushing to my hair roots." Her face took on a dreamy expression. "He was very handsome, this friend. So if you were to accept Lord Hairy Head, it might throw me in his path more often."

"Well, dear sister, I am sorry, but I am not accepting him just to provide you with suitors. And stop calling him Lord Hairy Head. I shall be unable to look him in the eye, the next time I see him, without thinking of it and grinning."

"So, there will be a next time? Make sure it's when he's with this friend, and that I am with you."

"Of course there will be a next time, even if only to decline his proposal once and for all. But how am I to know which particular friend you mean? He has so many."

"Oh, I'm sure you will recognise him. He has the dreamiest, blackest eyes I have ever seen, oh, and a teeny-weeny little scar on his chin."

"You were that close?"

"Oh, yes, and the most kissable lips I have ever seen."

"Eliza! I am shocked. A well-brought up young lady should not think in such a fashion." Florence brushed a biscuit crumb from her new violet and white striped dress and walked over to the window.

"Oh, no, it's raining again. What a good job I returned when I did. I wish these incessant showers would go away. I wanted to take a walk in the garden and pick a few flowers. The blue of the cornflowers matches the décor in this room so well, and Mama told me we have orange dahlias near the lawn."

Eliza cleared her throat. "Well, I cannot tell a tulip from a primrose."

"Maybe not. You are more talented in the artistic sense. You play the pianoforte with much more skill than I ever will, and you sing like an angel. I muddle along, fudging my words, but it comes so naturally to you. I envy you in that respect."

"Do not make me laugh, Flo. You, envy me?"

Florence smiled at the incredulous look on her sister's pretty face. "Yes, believe it or not."

The door opened and their youngest sister, Felicity, ran in, surrounded by three puppies and the mother spaniel. "Hello, you two." She tumbled onto the couch, her fair ringlets bouncing up and down, the puppies jumping on top of her.

"Fee, you should not allow them onto the furniture."

"But they're so cute. How can you resist them?" She tried half-heartedly to dissuade them. "See, they won't obey me."

Florence scooped them up and put them on the carpet. "Then you will just have to teach them. They need discipline or they will never learn. How many times do we have to tell you?"

The little girl's bottom lip jutted out.

"And do not give me that face."

The nine-year old put her arms around her big sister's waist. "Don't be cross with me."

She kissed the top of her curls. "I am not cross. If this rain clears up later, maybe we could take them outside and let them release a little of their energy. Has Mama said if they are allowed out yet?"

"I'll go and ask her now." She ran to the door. "Come on, pups. Let's find Mama."

They ran out, jumping and cuffing each other, their mother following at a more leisurely pace.

Eliza also turned to go. "I wonder where I left my embroidery. Have you seen it?"

Florence shook her head. "The new one with the intricate scene of a ship on the high seas?"

"Yes, I am beginning to wish I had not started the thing. But I will not let an inanimate object like a piece of silk better me. I shall finish it or die."

Florence laughed. "Well, I am going up to change. This new frock chafes my neck." She rubbed her finger under the neckline, trying to ease the seam of the soft, woolly material.

"That is a pity, because it suits you," rued her sister. "I wish I could wear violet, but it does not suit my complexion."

"Hopefully, it is just the stitching. I dare not complain. It is the first new one I have had this year. I shall ask our maid to take a look at it." She picked up her bonnet and gloves and made her way upstairs.

Changing out of the itchy dress, she called her maid, Sybil, to re-pin her long, fair hair. She didn't need ringlets during the day, but liked them.

While the maid chatted about this and that, she thought more about the proposal. Her mother kept telling her she should do the right thing, and accept. Since her father had died in a riding accident the previous year, finances had become very tight, almost to the point of desperation. She already had to share her maid with her sister after Eliza's maid had upped and left a few weeks before, to marry one of the local farmer's servants. A step backward, in Florence's opinion. The maid must have been very enamoured to take such drastic action. But then, love was supposed to be blind. Not that she had ever experienced it herself. At the ripe old age of nineteen, she had yet to meet any man she could say she fancied. No, Mister Hairy Head would have to be given the brush off, much as she would invoke her mother's wrath.

"Not everyone marries for love, my dear," her mother had said. "I know from experience."

"But you did grow to love Papa, didn't you?" she had replied. "And I am sure he loved you."

Her mother had turned away with a non-committal reply of, "He had a funny way of showing it, if he did," leaving Florence with a confused image of her father. Her parents had been civil to each other, but, looking back in hindsight, they had never had much physical contact, had not held hands or hugged. She would want more than that in her own marriage.

Dear Papa, he had always shown his love for his children, even her brother, Frederick, who, to put it mildly, could be somewhat erratic. His gambling had been the main cause of their downfall. Maybe he had gone to the dogs from grief. He had adored his father, so perhaps she should not judge him.

She thanked the maid and dismissed her, making sure she took the dress to mend. Then she went to the window. Still raining. "I won't be picking any flowers today," she told her raggy doll that sat on the pink flowery bedspread. "I shall have to find a different activity to occupy my time."

Embroidery not taking her fancy, she remembered the book Eliza had lent her. Her sister had received it as a birthday present, but had said she could not concentrate long enough to enjoy it, not being bookish. The shelves searched, and even the underneath of the bed, she smiled at herself for being so silly, when she recalled she had been reading it in the library the day before. If her mama did not need her for a more pressing task she would go there and finish it, as long as she did not bump into her on the way, and receive orders to the contrary. Not that she did not want to pull her weight. She hated chores. Since they had fewer servants, sometimes she had to clear the table or put things away. Things she had never had to do when her father had been alive.

She sidled downstairs to the dark, fusty library and closed the door behind her, muttering as she looked around at the shelves, many full of brown books, but many others empty, the valuable tomes having been sold. "Now, where is it?"

"Who are you talking to?" asked a voice from an armchair to her left.

"Oh, Frederick, I did not realise you were there. Why are you sitting in the dark?"

"It's the only place I can find solitude."

With a laugh, she faced him. "That's why I am here. Are you reading anything interesting?" He lit a candle and turned the book over to show the spine. "It's 'A Christmas Carol' by Charles Dickens. Most of his stories are in serial form, but this one is a full-length novel."

"Is it exciting?"

He shrugged. "Not really. It's time someone wrote a gory book about a bloodthirsty murder."

"Ugh!" She shuddered as she turned to the table where she thought she had left hers. "I could not read such stories without feeling sick. They would not be good for your disposition."

"A book is just an escape from the reality of our mundane lives, nothing else."

"I suppose so. Ah, here it is." She found her book, hidden under a magazine. "Are you staying in here?"

"I had intended to do so. What are you reading?"

She showed him. "It is by my favourite author, Jane Austen, about a family of girls who lose their father and have to move to a smaller house." As she turned to walk away, the thought occurred to her that they could be in such a position, if their situation did not improve. "Frederick?"

"Um?" He had opened his book once more and didn't seem to be listening.

"Are we really in trouble, financially, I mean?"

He put down his book and took off his glasses. "Well…"

"You can tell me. I'm a big girl now, you know. I'll soon be twenty." She sat on the arm of his chair, patting one of his wayward curls.

"Hopefully, it won't be as bad as Mother makes out. The other day I leant of a new investment that should save us."

"Not like the last one you tried, is it? That one almost bankrupted us."

His eyes opened wide in surprise. "How did you know about that?"

"Ah, I am not as foolish as you think. I heard you talking."

"I've never considered you to be foolish, Flo, not at all. You're much more cognisant of the world than any of the gals in my circle of friends. But, no, this one is a much safer bet."

"So a gamble?"

He puffed out his cheeks and let out his breath in a whistle. "Not so much a gamble as a…what can I call it?"

"It is a gamble, however you coat it. Please, Frederick, do not ruin us. Mama would never recover. You know she is not in the best of health."

"I have to try. I cannot let things ride. So, trust me. I'm your big brother."

"Um, that's just it. But could I not do something? I have savings."

He held out his hand. "No, sis, really. Don't worry. Things will work out, you'll see."

She had to be content with that, so went to the armchair near the window and opened her book, soon becoming absorbed in the comings and goings of Elinor and Marianne Dashwood

The following week, unable to resist the pull of another ball, Florence and Eliza and their mother stepped out of their carriage and looked up at the bright windows of Lord March's mansion. "I hope Mister Hairy Head is not here, Lizzie," whispered Florence as they entered the large hallway. "I still have not told him I do not wish to marry him."

"But his friend…now that would be a different matter."

Florence grinned, handing her coat to the servant. The autumn air had a chill to it, so she had come well-wrapped. "Don't disgrace yourself tonight, little sister."

Eliza's eyes lit up with a mischievous twinkle. "Maybe I will, and maybe I won't. But I'll try not to do so in front of you."

"You had better not," retorted her mother, giving a discreet wave to one of her friends on the other side of the room, then hurrying over to her.

Florence straightened her yellow dress, the same one she had worn only a few months before, but altered with extra lace around the bust line, and on the end of the three-quarter length sleeves. She hoped it would pass off as a new one. Eliza had done the same to her blue outfit.

Once their names had been announced, they mingled, arm in arm, until Eliza saw one of her friends. "There's Betty over there. I really must go and find out about her latest amour. I'll see you later, Flo." She hurried over to the other side of the room, leaving Florence on her own, waving her fan in front of her face, trying to look nonchalant.

Who could she talk to? Who would be the most interesting? A group of young bucks caught her attention. One of them glanced at her and said something she could not hear, causing the others to look her way.

Pursing her lips, her head high, she turned to face the opposite direction, hoping it had not been anything defamatory.

"May I have the next dance?" a voice asked from her right.

She turned to see the young buck she had seen earlier. He sported a very dashing moustache, and had twinkling eyes. Maybe the night would turn her fortune.

"I thank you, kind sir." Closing her fan, she held out her hand and they cavorted around the room with the other dancers.

"You are very light on your feet, sir," she commented when one of the other men stepped on his partner's toes.

The gavotte ended and he showed her to a seat next to some elderly ladies, who were chatting as they fanned their red faces. He bowed, kissed the back of her hand, keeping hold of it for longer than a man should.

She looked up into his laughing green eyes and blushed. Then he spoke to each of the ladies in turn, kissing their hands also.

Once he had walked away, one of them, a French lady, Madam Orgée, turned to the others. "What a very splondeed young man, I must say. Do you not agree, mesdames?" They all nodded, watching him weave his way through the crowd. She turned to Florence. "You would do well, Mademoiselle, wiz zat one. Ah, zose eyes!"

Florence laughed. "But you do not know anything about him, Madame. He could be the most rakish fellow imaginable."

"Ah, but who would care, when he looks at you like that? Eh, bien sur?"

Eliza nudged a path across to her. "Who was that divine person, Flo? I've never seen him before."

"Oh, not you as well. Madame Orgée here has just been singing his praises, although she does not know the slightest thing about him. He didn't give me his name. And, anyway, he's dancing with Flora Thoms now, so he's forgotten about me already." She waved her fan briskly in front of her face, watching the young man's every step over the top of it. He didn't tread on that lady's toes, either.

For the next few dances Florence partnered various young men, many of whom had at one time expressed their love for her in some way. Although pleasantly complimented, she had never taken any of them seriously, knowing they would have been appalled if she had done so.

She noticed Eliza had the fortune to dance with the fine-looking one. Afterwards, she raced across. "Oh, Flo, I'm in love. Isn't he the most handsome man you have ever encountered?"

"I must admit he is rather attractive, but not really my sort." He hadn't asked her for another dance, so could not be interested in her, so why should she be in him?

"Oh, he is mine, one hundred per cent." Eliza twisted around so she could see him. "Oh, my goodness. Is he?" She slumped, letting out a loud breath. "No, he isn't. I thought he had been about to come and ask me again, but...would you believe it? Just look at that! He's asking Flora Thoms. That weasel-faced harridan. That's the second time. How could he prefer her to me, or you, even? It doesn't make sense."

Florence smiled, pulling her sister away. "Ignore him, Lizzie. He's a rake, a scoundrel of the worst kind."

"No, he isn't. You're just trying to make me feel better. And don't tell me you aren't the teeniest bit interested yourself. I've seen you peeping at him."

"There's no harm looking at a personable face."

"Especially one with eyes so sparkling, eh?"

"Come on, let's find some refreshment. Mister Sparkly Eyes can dance the night away with as many young ladies as he pleases. We will not be bothered, will we, Lizzie? Not bothered at all."

Her nose in the air, Eliza took her arm. "No, sister, not in the least. Although, would it not be the greatest pleasure if he saved the last waltz for one of us? "

Chuckling, they tucked into the fine food and drank a glass or two of punch.

"This is potent, isn't it?" asked Eliza a while later, as they took their drinks onto the balcony for a respite from the steamy, smoky atmosphere in the hall.

"Yes, it is, so you had better not have any more after that one."

"I agree, and anyway, we're wasting time out here. We should be inside, marking our cards for the remainder of the evening."

"You go. I think I'll stay here a while longer."

Eliza stepped towards the door. "Are you sure? I don't like leaving you on your own."

She urged her through. "Yes, I have a slight headache. Nothing serious, so don't worry. But I think the fresh air will ease it."

Breathing in the evening atmosphere, her arms wrapped around her body to keep warm, Florence became aware of company, as the scent of cigar smoke wafted over to her.

"Lovely evening, is it not? A lovely evening?" asked a familiar voice.

Oh, no, not Mister Hairy Head! She took a deep breath, holding her ear lobe so he could not see it. "I had not...I did not know you were coming tonight, sir. I had not seen you dancing."

"I have been watching you and your sister, drooling over that young man."

"We were not drooling, sir. How can you say such a thing?" *And what business is it of yours,* she wanted to say. *You don't own me yet.*

"Just an observation, my dear, just an observation."

And why does he have to repeat everything? I'm not deaf or stupid.

She shivered. "I think I might be catching the chill. I had better return to the warm. Good day, sir." She bobbed a curtsy and, without waiting for a reply, made a swift departure through the open door. How could she marry such a bore? She debated whether to go out and tell him, there and then, but another handsome man grabbed her hand as the next dance began, and she lost the moment.

Her card soon filled up, the only empty space being the last dance. Not inclined to wait for it, she considered finding her sister to ask if she minded if they left early, but the opportunity did not arise. As she stood chewing her nail, the young beau from earlier came up to her.

"May I mark your card for the last dance, if it is not already spoken for?" he asked, bowing low.

"Oh, I…um…I had not intended…"

He raised his eyebrows as if in a challenge.

"Thank you, I would be honoured."

He bowed and walked away.

She bit her top lip. Eliza would be so jealous.

Her sister hurried to her. "Has he asked you? Has he? Oh, he has. It's not fair."

"Calm down, Lizzie. Is your card marked for the last dance?" At her sister's nod, she continued, "I had intended leaving early but, in that case, we cannot, so I may as well honour his request. If it had not been marked, I could have asked him to dance with you instead." She shrugged, a smile creeping over her lips as the realisation of standing close in his arms swept over her.

She turned her back as she saw Lord Head heading in her direction. "Don't turn now, but Mister Hairy is coming our way."

Eliza did exactly what she had told her not to do. "I thought I saw him earlier. I wonder why he hasn't invited you to dance. Do you think he has an inkling you are about to refuse him?"

"Hopefully, then I shall not have to tell him face to face. Much as I dislike him, I don't want to hurt his feelings."

"I doubt he has any."

With eye and head gestures, Florence tried to warn her—for she had turned to face her—that he stood behind her.

At his cough Eliza's mouth dropped. "You should have warned me," she mouthed silently.

He bowed. "Miss Fisher, Miss Eliza."

They nodded in tight, polite movements. "Lord Head." Florence could feel a bubble of hysteria looming up inside her at the nickname they had given him, and dared not look at her sister, for she could feel her shaking already, most probably with the same thoughts.

"May I see your card, Miss Fisher?"

She wondered why he had become so formal. Lately, he had taken to addressing her by her Christian name. Perhaps he had come to realise. She showed it to him.

A severe set on his mouth heralded his disapproval. "I see. I might have thought you would save the last one for me, seeing as…" He looked her directly in the eyes.

She opened hers wide. "I apologise, sir, but someone else has forestalled you."

"And who is this…?" He peered at the signature more closely. "A. N. Other?"

"What?" She grabbed the card from him. "Oh."

Eliza leant forward to peer at it. "Let me see." She stood up, a puzzled expression on her face. "A. N. Other? How can someone have a name like that?"

"I don't know. Ask him."

Her sister frowned. "I will, when I see him again. Or you could do so, when you are in his arms, waltzing around the room to the slow, dreamy music." She looked at Florence's would-be fiancé out of the corner of her eye.

He said nothing and stalked off.

Florence poked her in the ribs. "You did not need to say that."

"Maybe not, but it rid us of him, didn't it?"

"Mm, but at what expense?"

"Never mind, let's enjoy the rest of the evening. Here's my partner, oh, and yours."

Florence's nerves took over and she found herself going the wrong way more than once during the next few dances. Finally, she heard the last one being announced. Perhaps Mister Sparkly Eyes had left early. She had not seen him in the previous gavotte. But he had not. He stood before her, unsmiling, holding out his hand. Should she break into conversation, or wait for him to do so?

He pulled her close, his warm breath on her cheek. Her heart fluttered. She drew back. Nobody had ever had that effect on her before. She did not even know his true name. It could not possibly be Mister Other, surely?

She plucked up courage to speak. "Excuse me, sir, but what is your real name?" There she had said it, rather bluntly, but she wanted, desperately, to know.

"I beg your pardon."

"Your name, sir? You signed the card as 'A. N. Other'."

"And why do you think that is not my real name?"

She made no reply as he pulled her close again. Her steps were as light as feathers as his adroit steps led her around the dance floor.

All too soon the musicians stopped. She opened eyes she had not realised she had closed, and stepped back.

He bowed and, after showing her to the side, walked off, leaving her feeling somewhat foolish, for her feet would not move.

Eliza came over to her, her eyes shining. "Well?"

"What?"

"Did you find out his real name?"

She shook her head.

"What did he say? Did he ask you lots of questions about yourself, or tell you anything about him?"

"No, actually, he hardly spoke at all."

"How disappointing."

They collected their coats, found their mother, whom they had barely seen all evening, and went outside to find their carriage, Florence in a dream.

"Are you in love with him?" asked Eliza on the way home.

She sat back and wiped her hand over her mouth. "In love? Do not be so silly, Lizzie. How can one be in love after a chance meeting?"

"Well, I am sure I would be if he had danced with me like that, so close you could barely put a hand between you."

Sitting up straight, Florence stared through the window at the blackness outside.

"Everyone, and I mean everyone, noticed, dear sister," continued Eliza. "I heard one or two remarks, especially from that Madam Orgy or whatever her name is. She thought it was obscene."

"Pah, I would bet she has been more intimate than that, from what I have heard about her shenanigans in France before she came to England. Someone told me she performed at an infamous theatre in Paris."

"That's impossible. She's too old."

"She has not always been old, you silly goose. She must have been very beautiful in her youth."

"I suppose so. But, back to you. Did he say he would see you next week, or anything?"

Barely able to see her sister, she could imagine the look on her face. "No, my dear, and please, stop going on about him."

She looked across at her mother, who appeared to be asleep, and whispered, "You had better not mention it to Mama, either. You know she'll have a fit of the vapours, especially as she is still hoping I'll accept Mister Hairy Head. She'll go on and on, about responsibility and all that stuff."

She sensed her sister sitting back. "Oh, I wish it had been me. I never attract the good-looking ones. It isn't fair. Mister Hairy's friend didn't even come. You know - the one I fancied. I'm sure I could have attracted him. I know you are much prettier than I, but could you not leave one for me, now and again?"

"Lizzie, I am not much prettier than you at all. In fact, I consider myself to be very plain, with my little nose and…"

"Rosebud ears."

They both laughed.

Florence continued. "Your features are more classical, with your heart-shaped face, high cheekbones, large eyes, even though they are brown, clearly not as appealing as my blue ones."

"Ha-ha, Florence Fisher. At least, I know I am a true daughter of Papa's. His eyes were brown. You could be anybody's. Even Mama's aren't as blue as yours."

"What a shocking thing to say. Of course, I am Papa's daughter. Why would you say such a thing?"

They drew up in front of the house. Eliza patted her arm. "I did not mean it, sis. I would know if you were not my true sister. I am sure I would."

"But I am. I shall ask Mama."

"No, please do not do that," Eliza hissed as they alighted from the carriage. "I really did not mean it."

"Relax, I am jesting. I would never embarrass her in such a way, especially if were to be true. Can you see her face? She would have an apoplectic fit."

"Are you talking about me?" their mother asked, sleepily.

"No, Mama," they replied with one voice.

Lying in bed later, Florence thought back to the evening. Could she be in love already? The beau did have a wicked gleam in his eyes at times, and he had held her close, so close other people had noticed. She had never had such intense feelings for a man, so could not be sure how to manage them. In any case, she might never see him again.

Leaning over to blow out the candle, Eliza blew her a kiss. "That is from your Mister Other. I bet you wish it were a real one. Umm, can you imagine being kissed by those luscious, full lips?" She made smacking sounds with her lips as she lay down.

"Stop it. How would you know what it feels like? You have not been kissed yet."

"Ah, but maybe I have."

Florence sat up. "You have not, have you?"

"That is for me to know, and you to find out, dear sister. Goodnight."

"You're just teasing me, as usual."

She tried to think who her sister could have kissed. The only one she herself had received had been a snatched peck in the woods, when they had been playing hide and seek some years before and Lawrence Bowen had grabbed her when she had been unawares.

She fell asleep, not having come to any meaningful conclusion.

Chapter 2

"Why don't you want to go, Flo? I wish it were me." Eliza peeped out from beneath the bedclothes. "If only I had not caught this infernal cold, it would have been."

"I suppose it is only for a few days. I love Aunt Enid, but all those children. They are so noisy. She never reprimands them, and they run riot."

"Little Eddie is so sweet, though. He will have grown since we last saw him, won't he?"

Florence tied her bonnet ribbons. "Poor Sybil, she hates young children, but I cannot travel all that way on my own so she has to accompany me, whether she likes it or not."

Eliza snuggled down under the covers. "Please would you ask her to bring me something for this blasted headache before you go?"

Florence checked her appearance in the mirror and then stroked her sister's hair from her forehead. "You are rather hot. Are you sure it is only a cold?"

"I hope so. I have people to see and places to visit before my eighteenth birthday, and I don't intend spending long in my bed. Anyway, it hurts too much to talk. My throat feels as if it has been cut, so farewell. Enjoy yourself at Aunt Enid's."

Florence covered her sister, tucked in her sheet and went downstairs.

Her mother sat sewing in the lounge. She looked up as Florence entered. "Ah, are you ready, dear?"

"Yes, Mama. I'm worried about Eliza, though. She's burning with fever."

"Is she? Oh my goodness. I had better call the doctor."

"Do you not think I should stay and help to look after her?" Ready to take off her bonnet if she received an affirmative reply, she twiddled with the ribbons.

"No, my dear." Her mother put down her sewing and stood up. "This visit has been arranged for so long. We have put it off and put it off. Your aunt will think we do not have a care for her, that nobody wants to see her and her unruly children."

"Mama! That is precisely why I am…well, not unwilling, but I would much rather not go."

Her mother patted her arm. "I am sure you will enjoy yourself, once you are there. You rub along well with your cousins, the older ones, at least, do you not? And the views around Cockermouth are stunning. You loved them last time we went. Maybe it will put you in the mood to write some poetry, to be inspired by that poet…what's his name?"

"William Wordsworth."

"That's the one. I love that poem about the daffodils, 'I wandered lonely as a cloud…' What's the rest?"

"Mama, I do not think the atmosphere will be inducive to writing poetry, not with all those children, running around me, screaming and shouting."

"Inducive? Is that a word?"

"Is it not? Well, it should be. I am sure I have heard it before."

The butler came in. "Your carriage is ready, Miss Florence."

She sighed. "Ah, well, I shall try to glean some sort of positivity from the visit." She kissed her mother on the cheek.

"There you go again, inventing words." Missus Fisher smiled, taking a hair off Florence's shoulder.

"Now what have I said wrong?"

"Never mind. Off you go, and try to have fun."

"Yes. Mama. Oh, I nearly forgot. Eliza would like some pain relief. Do you have any laudanum or anything?"

"I shall wait until the doctor arrives. Now, shoo." She ushered her out the door.

Sybil appeared, and they climbed into the carriage.

An hour or so later, having nodded off, she jolted awake when the carriage pulled up sharply.

The driver shouted, "Whoa, there, steady on."

She put her head out of the window. "What's the matter, Henry?"

"Nothing for you to worry about, ma'am." Then he fell silent.

Anxious, she looked at her maid.

"Stay still, ma'am. I shall find out what's happening." The maid jumped up to open the door, but the carriage started again at an alarming pace. She yanked it closed, falling onto the seat, almost on top of her mistress.

"Henry, slow down," shouted Florence, trying to poke her head out again. "For goodness sake, man, you will kill us all." But they hurtled onwards, even faster, the two ladies clutching onto each other for dear life. Either Henry had gone berserk, or he had fallen off and the horses had bolted. What other explanation could there be?

Within minutes her worst fears became reality. The wheel hit a large rut in the uneven road, and they overturned. She landed on top of her maid, sprawled out in a most undignified manner, her skirts way up past her knees.

It proved impossible to stand at such an awkward angle. Her foot hit the window, smashing the glass. It scattered all over them.

A low moaning sound came from her maid.

At the top of her voice, she yelled, "Sybil, are you hurt?" A scream rose from her mouth into the still air on seeing the maid's face covered in blood.

With raised arms, she tried to open the door above them, but did not have sufficient strength, so banged on it, calling, "Help! Is there anybody out there? Please, help."

How were they to escape from the confined space? They would both die in the cold, probably starve to death, as well. As she opened her mouth to yell once more, the carriage shifted. The top door opened, and a face appeared.

"Henry, oh, thank goodne...but you're not Henry. Who are you, sir? Have you come to rescue us?"

The man reached in, shielding his eyes with an over-accented gesture as she tried to cover her legs. "Luke Lancaster at your service, ladies."

She clung onto his arm as he lifted her out into a glade, surrounded by trees. "My maid seems to be hurt. Please save her," she begged as she adjusted her dress and pulled on her bonnet.

One of her shoes had fallen off, so she did not know where to put her stockinged foot on the leaf-covered ground. Placing it on top of the other one, she lost her balance.

Strong arms righted her, and she looked up into the most exquisite pair of deep-set blue eyes she had ever seen. They seemed to be mocking her.

"Th...th...thank you," she stammered, pulling away.

He lifted her as if she were as light as a feather, and carried her over to a tree stump, where he dropped her most unceremoniously.

Her arm throbbed, whether from the indignity of being treated so callously, or from the accident, she could not tell. Before she could complain, the haughty man had stalked over to the carriage, and she watched him reach inside and lift out—what seemed to be—the body of her lifeless maid.

"Is she alive?" she called. "Please do not say she is not. I could not bear it."

He did not reply, merely laid Sybil gently on a soft patch of green grass.

She could not just sit there, not knowing, so, uncaring of her shoeless foot, she limped across as Sybil gave a low moan.

"Oh, thank God," Florence cried, bending to her. "Sybil, can you hear me?"

Another moan.

"This kind gentleman has saved us. We shall be home again in no time at all. Please be brave." Not knowing what else to do, she took the maid's hand, stroking it as if she were a kitten or a puppy.

The man gnawed at his knuckles, his brown coat awry, hat missing, fair hair sticking up at the back.

Florence turned to him. "We were on our way to my aunt's house near Cockermouth, sir. Do you think you could take us, or would it be quicker to return home?"

"That depends where 'home' is, ma'am."

"Oh, you do speak, then," she added sarcastically. Without waiting for a reaction, she continued, "Home is in Ambleside. Do you know it? Not far from Lake Windermere? In fact, it's on the shores of the lake. A very pretty village, except when the tourists come and drop litter." She grew conscious of rambling. What did this stranger want to know about her home?

"Yes, ma'am, in fact I have taken a ride on the new steamer."

"Oh, good, so you can take us?" Peering past him, she continued, "Where is your carriage, sir, or were you on horseback?"

One of her own horses had righted itself, and stood munching grass, but the other could not be seen. She hoped it had not gone far, or had not been hurt, lying in some ditch, bleeding to death.

Sybil gave another groan and tried to sit up. "Where am I? What happened?"

"I do not really know, but this gentleman has rescued us from our speeding horses. I am afraid I don't know what's happened to Henry, though." She gave a glance around. "I cannot see him." Turning to the man beside her, she asked, "Did you see our driver, sir, when you arrived?"

He raised his eyebrows as if he did not understand the question.

She repeated slowly, as if she were talking to a deaf person or a young child, "Our driver, Henry, did you see him?"

When he made no reply, merely stood biting his lip, she continued, "Oh, dear, that means he must have fallen off when we…when we… I do not know what happened to us. It's very strange."

The man bent to help the maid to her feet, mumbling, "I have to admit I caused the accident, ma'am."

"What? Did I hear you right? You mean to say you caused us to plunge headlong into a ditch, and turn upside down and be all but killed? Why on earth would you do that?"

The thump she gave him almost lost him his footing. Regretting her impulsive action for the briefest of seconds, she put out her hand, but pulled it back. He ignored it, anyway. "Pray tell me, why would you do such a thing?" she repeated.

He shrugged.

"Is that all the response I am to receive? A shrug of the shoulders? You, sir, are a blaggard, a reprehensible… Oh, words fail me."

"Well, that must be a first." He gave her an enigmatic look from beneath his eyebrows.

"Sybil…" She grabbed her maid around her waist' "Come, we shall have to find our own way home."

The maid could only take a few steps before slumping to the ground. "I'm sorry, ma'am."

Glaring at the man, she stormed, "Help her to stand, you deplorable, amoral, disgracible excuse for a man."

His mouth tweaked into a grin.

"What is so funny?"

With a shake of his head, he sneered. "Dear lady, if you must insult me with long, abusive adjectives, then please use ones that are in the English language."

"What? What on earth are you talking about? Just get us out of this glade. I have had enough. Your little prank is over. Please, return us to… Ouch," she squealed with pain when he took hold of her elbow.

"Did you hurt yourself?" he asked, suddenly solicitous.

"Much as you care, sir, but yes, my leg also."

She turned away from him, brushing away the tears that had filled her eyes at the pain. It would not do to reveal weakness. Not knowing why she had been put in this predicament, she had to show strength against the man.

He whispered in her ear, "Then, I apologise."

"Pah, it's rather late for that. Pray tell me what your intentions are."

"That, dear lady, I ask myself."

Standing back, she surveyed her surroundings, still trying to work out what could have happened. Had the man deliberately set on them with the intention of robbing them? She clutched her side. What had happened to her reticule?

"If you intend to rob us, sir, then you will be unlucky. I have no money to speak of, and I am sure Sybil has not, either."

The maid shook her head in agreement.

She sidled across to the upturned carriage, to look for them, but he took her bag from inside his coat. "Is this what you are looking for?"

How could he have picked it up without her noticing? She reached out to grab it, but he pulled it away. Hands on hips, she glared. "Pray, sir, return my property before I…"

"Before you what? Call a constable? I do not see any around here, do you?"

She reached up again, but his greater height rendered it impossible to grab. Nobody had ever considered her small, but this man must have been well over six feet tall, with long arms, to the bargain. The attempt brought her in contact with his hard body. A shock wave ran through her, making her jump back, aghast.

One raised eyebrow mocked her.

Her shoulders sagged in defeat. The hateful man had them at his mercy. What could she do about it? The maid could barely stand, let alone walk, and her own leg had swollen to the size of a large marrow, so the possibility of her running away on her own had been reduced to nil.

"I give up." Stretching out her arms, she sighed. "Do with us what you will."

His face turned severe. "That is it. I do not know what to do with you."

"What do you mean? Just take us home."

"How? Your carriage has lost both wheels."

"You could ride the horse and find help."

"Uhuh." He shook his head.

"Why not?" When he stared at her she continued, "I shall, then. I have never ridden bareback before, but I am sure I could manage if it means escaping from you."

"But what about your maid? Are you not worried I might…?" Again, the raised eyebrow.

"Might what? Oh, you cannot mean…? Surely you are not such a rake as to abuse a poor, defenceless maid who is, not only injured, but…but…a virgin."

A gasp escaped the young woman sitting on the tree stump. Florence ran over to her. "I'm sorry, Sybil. I don't know whether you are or not, but it was the first thing that came into my mind. Pray, forgive me for being so bold."

A chuckle came from behind her and he whispered in her ear, "As you are, I hope."

Forgetting her injury, she stamped her foot, sending pain searing up her leg. "Sir, the state of my…my intactness is none of your business," she retorted through gritted teeth. "And any well-bred gentleman would not refer to such a delicate subject, especially in the company of a maid."

Luke stood before her, hands on hips, his short, fair hair sticking up above his right ear. "Ah, but I never claimed to be a gentleman."

"Obviously, you are not." Florence tossed her head and turned away. "And, anyway, there is no way I am telling you."

"Ah, but you are at my mercy. I could easily find out, if I felt so inclined."

"You…you will do nothing of the kind."

"Try my patience much more, and we shall see."

"*Your* patience? For goodness sake, man. Do you expect me to take this impertinence lying down?" The implication made her change tack. "I mean, without any retaliation? I have never been treated in such a way in my entire life. Do you realise who my father was?"

"Was?"

"Yes, he died last year." All energy left her at the memory of her dear father, lying in the road, his back broken. Not that she had seen him, but she had envisaged it.

"I offer my condolences. My own father passed away but a few weeks ago, so I share your pain."

Maybe he had a soul, after all.

She did not know what to say. She glared at him, but he stared back, seemingly daring her to look away first. Determined not to do so, she stood her ground, grinding her teeth in the effort. He won. Of course, as she had known in her heart of hearts he would. How could she, a mere female, stand up to him?

Silently cursing inside, she took another look around the glade.

They had left the main road and were on a cart track, so there would be no chance of a passer-by coming to their rescue. She did not recognise the place, though, so had no idea how far away they had strayed.

Maybe it led to a farm? She could struggle along it and find out. But, as he had said, she could not leave her maid.

Bending over her, she whispered in her ear, while pretending to brush some leaves from her coat. "Sybil, are you very badly hurt? Do you think you could walk?"

Her face covered in bloody scratches, her hands too, the maid lifted her skirt to reveal her cut leg and whispered back. "I cannot put any weight on it, ma'am. What shall we do?"

"I do not know why you are speaking in such hushed tones, ladies, for I can hear every syllable," announced their abductor. "I have an acute sense of hearing. My mother always says it will be my downfall, one day."

"'Eavesdroppers never hear anything good about themselves' is what my mother says, sir. It is very impolite to listen in on a private conversation, so pray skedaddle over in that direction while we discuss our options."

A loud chortle echoed around the glade. "Your options, dear lady? I do not see that you have any."

"Of course we have options. We can merely wait until you are asleep and creep up on you and…"

"And?"

"Oh, pray, do not dally with us any further, sir. Tell me what you are going to do. If you intend to murder us, then do so now. Put us out of our misery." Her hand squeezed Sybil's shoulder at the maid's intake of breath.

"If I intended to murder you, as you think, I would have done so long ago, madam." He stroked the little goatee beard she had been looking at earlier. "The truth is…the truth is I have no idea."

She walked over and looked him in the eye. "What? You do not know what will happen? Pray tell me, fine sir, why did you kidnap us in the first place?"

"It was a dare," he muttered, turning away. "A dare that went horribly wrong."

"A dare?" she shouted, causing several rooks to fly squawking from the trees above them. "Why on earth would anyone dare you to kidnap us, two defenceless ladies, whose acquaintance you have never had the honour to gain?"

Incensed at the revelation, she stamped around the little patch of grass until her swollen leg would take no more punishment. "I thought you to be a highwayman, at first, although I know such villains no longer exist, but what other explanation could I give? Somehow or other, a dare did not enter my head at all." Her eyes wide open, she glared at him. "I wonder why?"

"You asked for the truth. I gave it. Now we need to find a solution to our problem."

"You hear that, Sybil? We are now a 'problem'. Before, we were a 'dare', now we are a 'problem'."

The maid's shoulders slumped, her face full of pain and her eyes filled with tears.

Florence hobbled across to her. "Please, do not weep, Sybil. We will find our way out of this predicament, somehow. Do not give up hope. Do you have a handkerchief?"

Sybil shook her head.

A hand appeared, bearing a clean, white handkerchief, with the initials 'LL' embroidered in the corner.

"Take this," a gruff voice ordered.

She snatched it and handed it to the maid, who dabbed the sides of her eyes, blew her nose loudly and offered it back. He waved it away, so she tucked it up her sleeve, still sniffing.

Florence turned to Luke. "Well, sir, have you come to any conclusion? Are we to stay here all night? Dusk is fast approaching. The only option I can see is for you to ride the horse and find help. That is the only sensible thing I can think of."

"Well, I…I would, but…"

"Surely you are man enough to ride without a saddle? My brother, Frederick, can occasionally."

He shuffled his feet, looking embarrassed. "I incurred an injury some time ago, and cannot ride."

"What? At all?"

She looked down at his trouser area as he covered his private parts with his hands. A laugh welled up inside her. "That takes the biscuit. We are kidnapped by an impotent highwayman who cannot even ride a horse. Wait until I tell my sister, Eliza. She will be so entertained."

"I did not say I was impotent, ma'am, merely unable to sit in a saddle."

He turned at her laughter and grabbed her, kissing her with such ferocity she felt sure her lips must be bleeding.

He pushed her away and she stumbled. "Well, sir," she uttered a moment later, "I hope you will apologise for that outburst of uncivility."

She brought her hand down from her mouth, showing she had been correct in her earlier assumption. "My lips are bleeding from your onslaught." Wiping her sleeve across her mouth and, shaking with anger and indignation, she went across to her maid. "Sybil, I care not in how much pain you are. We are leaving. This man is a monster. We are not safe in his presence."

The maid tried to stand, but could not. "I am so sorry, ma'am, I cannot go anywhere."

"Then I shall have to leave you to his mercy. I am not staying with him a moment longer."

She picked up her bonnet that had been trodden into the mud and plonked it on her head.

"You still have trigs in it." The wretched man grinned, reaching out to remove them.

She jerked her head away, overbalanced and fell headlong into a muddy puddle. "Damnation," she

41

cursed as her hand banged on the ground. "Hellfire and bramstone and everything else."

He reached down and helped her stand. "My dear lady, your bad humour does not improve your vocabulary, I see. I should not laugh at another's sorry predicament, but…"

"You are going to, anyway."

"You make it very difficult for me not to do so."

"Huh! I am so glad to be the but of your merriment, sir, but pray let go of me."

He looked at his hand, still holding her arm, and jerked it away, as if he had been scalded.

Her mood changed. He had not needed to pull away so sharply, even though she had ordered him to. "In which direction should I start?" she barked.

"That depends where you want to go."

"I know where I would like you to go."

"Oh, my dear, I have already been there, and come back from it, so your rantings do not bother me."

She hobbled to the edge of the glade, but could see no sign of a road.

"How did you steer us in here?" she called, looking for wheel marks to see how they had arrived.

"I do not remember," he called back. "To be quite truthful, the horses had become difficult to rein in." The remaining horse nickered, as if it knew they were talking about it.

She went and patted its neck. "You should take off this broken harness. It is chafing its neck," she called, bringing him over to examine it.

"You're right. How remiss of me not to have noticed." He unticd the harness and, holding onto the horse's mane, asked, "What do you propose I do with it now?"

"Do not ask me. I do not know how to look after a wild beast."

"A wild beast?" he sniggered. "This is the most docile animal I have come across in a long while. Even with sore withers it isn't creating as much fuss as a certain young lady."

"Fuss? Fuss? You deride me for creating a fuss? But then gentlemen with no feelings do not care about causing mayhem to others. And if this horse is so tame, pray help me onto its back."

With a raised eyebrow and a shrug of a shoulder, he cupped his hands for her foot.

"Pray, look the other way while I lift my leg over," she ordered.

With her leg halfway in midair, she heard a scream from her maid over on the other side of the glade. Losing her concentration, she fell once more into the mud.

He pulled her up and made sure she stood, before he hurried across to the maid, followed by a limping, bedraggled, muddy mistress.

"What is it, Sybil?" she yelled.

"A spider, ma'am, a spider just ran across my leg."

With eyes closed, and biting back a retort, she pulled up. "A spider? Is that all? I thought you were being attacked by a lion or tiger, at the very least."

"But, ma'am, you know how afraid I am, and it was an enormous black one, with at least ten long hairy legs."

Sybil took out the handkerchief and blew her nose again, a look of abject fear on her face. She would quake at the sight of a little money spider, and would run out of the room whenever one appeared, no matter what task she had been performing. "Please find it and kill it."

"It will be long gone by now, I am sure. Perhaps our intrepid hero, here, would find it for you. You know how loath I am to kill anything."

She turned to him, but from the look on his face—it had turned grey, and his eyes had almost glazed over—he would not be much help.

She laughed out loud. "Don't tell me you are also an arachnophore, sir? How hilarious! Oh, something else to tell Eliza, once I finally arrive home. This is becoming better and better. What a merry time we will have, giggling and laughing at everything. She adores a funny story even more so than I."

"Arachnophobe, dear lady."

His face returned to its normal colour, but she could see his eyes darting around the ground near the maid as he pulled his purple waistcoat about his body.

"Whatever you say, sir," she scoffed. "At least I am not afraid of a poor little defenceless creature like a ssppiiddeerr." She made movements with her hands in imitation of one. "I cannot believe that a grown man could be so afflicted."

He grabbed her arm. "Enough. It is not a..." he could not even say the word, "that you need to be scared of, ma'am. You have tried my patience too far this time."

From the manic expression in his eyes, she did not trust him to stay sane. She struggled to pull away as he yanked her out of the glade, and into a clearing. "Please, sir, don't hurt me. I didn't mean to make fun of you. Please," she begged as he pulled down her bodice and kissed her breasts.

With an almighty kick, she wrenched herself away and, holding up the bottom of her ripped, muddy dress, she ran, not caring if he followed.

Chapter 3

Uncaring of the pain in her leg, and full of shame that she had left her maid to the advances of the maniacal Luke Lancaster, she ran until she could run no farther. The branches of a large, overhanging oak tree gave her shelter as she gasped for breath, taking in a huge lungful of air, and clutching her side at the aching stitch. She glanced behind to see if he had followed. At one time she had been sure she could hear his breathing, but could see no sign of anyone. Not even a bird's song broke the silence in the woods as she slumped down onto a pile of leaves.

A small, reddish-coloured deer walked past within yards of her, soon followed by two larger ones. Not wanting to frighten them, she sat still, admiring their sleek bodies and the majestic antlers of the buck. They ambled off, leaving her once more to her thoughts, sucking her thumb, a habit she thought she had given up years before.

Through the trees she could see the mountains in the distance. They gave her comfort. If she could only find the right direction to follow, she knew she could reach home. The mountains would direct her. They were her background, always there for her. She loved them, and a feeling of contentment crept over her whenever she saw them.

Full of purpose, she took a deep breath and stood up, grimacing at the pain in her foot.

She brushed the wet leaves from her dress, shaking her head at the scolding she knew she would receive when she returned home with it stained and bedraggled. Shivering, she tried to wrap her coat around her. If only she had found her shoe before she had taken such a headlong departure. Her stocking had completely disintegrated and she bent down to remove the prickles from her bleeding, swollen foot.

"Oh, what a predicament. Eliza will surely find it so amusing when I tell her about it, but it certainly is not now," she muttered, tying the lace on her one remaining shoe. "What should I do? It will soon be dark." A shudder ran down her spine as she looked around for inspiration. Since she had been a little girl she had never liked the dark, and would never step onto the bedroom floor in her bare feet, imagining snakes living under her bed, ready to pounce on her naked flesh as soon as she became unwary of them.

Maybe Luke Lancaster had regretted his assault on her body. Would it be safer to find him and Sybil, and take her chances with human company, rather than risk being attacked by wolves, or bears, or whatever other vicious animals dwelt in the forest? She hobbled over the field, hoping it was the same one she had crossed earlier.

Darkness descended quickly and a fear more intense than she had ever experienced overcame her. Even

Luke Lancaster's assault of her earlier had not frightened her as much. "Please, God," she prayed, "please let me find them. I will take up charitable works and do anything you ask of me, as long as I am not left alone this night."

"I am glad to hear you praying," came a voice from her left.

She ran to him and wrapped her arms around him. "Oh, thank you, God, thank you so much."

He held her tightly for a moment and then, gently pushing her away, in the little light that remained, she thought she saw solicitousness in his eyes. "I have never been called 'God' before," he growled.

She blew out her breath in a loud 'phew'. "I did not mean you. I…"

"I was worried about you, not knowing how far you had gone, so I came to find you."

"Where's Sybil? You haven't left her on her own, have you?"

"It was either her or you, and I thought you to be the more important. Your maid will not be going anywhere. I rigged up a shelter, using a blanket I found in the upturned carriage, and she is quite comfortable."

They set off, with him supporting her. Branches and brambles catching at her weary legs, she prayed he would find his way in the twilight, for she could barely see a few yards in front of her.

"Oh, so what will I shelter beneath?"

He did not reply at first, and then said enigmatically, "My dear Miss… I do not even know your name."

"What does my name matter? It's a bit late for formal introductions."

"I agree, but I must address you somehow."

He stopped and she assumed they had arrived at the glade. "Sybil, are you there?" she called, peering through the murk.

"Oh, ma'am, thank goodness you're safe. I was so concerned for you. Where have you been?"

"I…um…I…" What could she tell her? She did not want to alarm her maid with the fact that the man at her side could very likely rape them both during the night, and leave them to die, even if he had sustained an injury.

"I am sorry to have distressed you after all you have already been through. I am here now. That is the important thing. How is your leg?" She hobbled over towards the voice.

"Not good," replied the maid. "But I'll bear it, knowing you're near."

Unable to see what she was doing, she dislodged the blanket and it fell on top of them. "Oo," she yelled, trying to extricate herself.

"Lie here with me," Sybil pleaded. "We can share the blanket, wrap it around ourselves."

"That's a good idea. Yes, we shall do that."

She snuggled down next to her and pulled the cover over them both, adjusting her dress so she did not lie on the wet patch.

"How will *he* keep warm?" Sybil whispered, once they had found a comfortable position.

"I do not know, and I do not care," she replied. "He can freeze to death for all I heed."

His voice came from right beside them. "And I most probably will, so good night, ladies. If I am dead in the morning, I wish you a speedy return home."

"You need not try to make us feel guilty, sir. You created this situation."

"True."

She heard the rustle of leaves as his footsteps became fainter, and wondered where he would spend the night but, as she had told the maid, she cared not.

After tossing and turning for ages, she finally fell into a fitful sleep, her maid's snores behind her somehow soothing. She marvelled that Sybil could sleep, when she must have been in so much pain.

A howl awoke her some time later. She grabbed Sybil's hand. "What was that?"

"It's only a fox," came the deep voice of her abductor. "Go back to sleep."

"How do you know I have been asleep?"

"Your snores told me so."

"I do not snore, sir. And, anyway, Sybil was the one doing that." She sat up, all thought of returning to sleep leaving her.

"Even your maid cannot snore in two different keys. No, it was most definitely you as well."

Sensing him coming towards her, she shrunk back towards her maid. "Keep away, sir. Please, do not repeat your atrocious behaviour of before."

"I have no intention of harming you, my dear. I apologise for my actions. They were reprehensible."

She relaxed, her mouth as dry as sand, and licked her lips in a bid to moisten them. "I could do with a drink. I don't suppose you have one handy?"

"I have a flask of brandy, if that would help. But it will probably only increase your thirst."

"I shall take my chances." She felt a hard, smooth object being placed in her hand. How he could see where her hand was, she could not fathom, for even though her eyes had adjusted slightly to the pitch blackness of the night, she could only see vague outlines, nothing specific. She took off the stopper and sipped the pungent liquid. Drinking it too quickly, she coughed.

"I knew I should not have indulged you," he retorted.

Sybil rubbed her back, crying, "Mistress, are you all right?"

Once she had recovered, she took another swig and then handed it to her maid. "You must be as parched, Sybil. Have a taste."

"I do not like brandy, ma'am," said Sybil but Florence heard her swallow.

"Hey," yelled Luke, "leave me some."

The maid gave her the flagon and she passed it to him, her fingers brushing his in the process. It almost fell as she pulled her hand away.

"Am I so abhorrent?" he asked in a low voice.

"What?"

"Did not your governess, or your mama, teach you not to say 'what'? A well-brought up young lady should not use the word."

"Do not start lecturing me, sir, on good manners, after the way you have treated us. I do not know how you have the gall to do so." She turned to her maid. "How's your leg, my dear? Do you think you will be able to walk as soon as first light appears over the horizon?"

Luke sat down beside her. The warmth from his body transferred to her leg. Should she move away? But it was so comforting. What an odd situation, sitting talking in the dark, as if they were enjoying an evening's get-together. She could not wait to tell Eliza about it.

The maid tried to shift position.

"No, I don't think so, ma'am. I'm sorry to be a burden on you like this."

Seething inside, but not wanting to show her disappointment, she patted her arm. "Do not worry. We shall sort something out."

The screech of an owl made her grab the nearest thing—his leg. She heard his quick intake of breath as he moved away. Should she ask him the same question he had asked her? Was she so abhorrent he could not bear her to touch him?

"Ah, look." He stood up. "The first fingers of dawn. 'Hark, hark, the lark at heaven's gate sings'."

"That's Shakespeare." she replied. "I learnt that poem years ago. 'Hark, hark the lark at heaven's gate sings, and, and...' Oh, I cannot remember the next line. Something about Phoebe, isn't it?"

"Phoebus."

"I did not take you for a poet, sir. You surprise me."

"Why should my love of the bard surprise you? I had a good grounding in the arts. I am not an ill-bred layabout, with no social skills or breeding."

"No, no, I did not mean that. I can tell you are not." *I had better not upset him,* she thought. *I need him to get us out of here.* "Pray, tell me, which school did you attend?"

In the first faint light, she could just make him out, drawing back, and imagined his eyebrow raising.

"Pray, tell me, ma'am, why the change of tack? I am sure you are not genuinely interested in my background."

Sybil gave a groan behind her and she turned towards her. "Oh, my dear, I had not forgotten you." The anguish on the maid's face told her how much pain she must still be suffering. "But I am helpless, you understand. Our fate is in the hands of this gentleman." Forgetting her vow of a few minutes before, she said the word with such a scornful expression, she wondered he did not hit her.

"And this 'gentleman' has thought of a plan." Luke pulled her up. "Now it is almost daylight, and we can see, you can find some water while I light a fire."

"Light a fire? Whatever for?"

"Well, that is what Robinson Crusoe did, did he not, in the novel by Daniel Defoe?"

"Are you trying to prove a point here, sir, to say you are more learned than I? I have to admit I have not read that particular book, although my brother, Frederick, loves it. It is one of his favourites, in fact."

"No, ma'am, I am just trying to make the best of a difficult situation."

"The best way out would be for you to find help, sir, not light a b..." She bit her lip to stop herself swearing. It would not do to lose her temper in front of the man.

"Which I shall do, once it is bright enough. Now, are you going to obey me?"

"Obey? Who do you think you are, telling me I must obey?"

He breathed in deeply and let out his breath in a loud sigh, as Sybil groaned again. "I would appreciate some water, Mistress, if it is at all possible."

"Yes, of course, Sybil." She would have to curb her bad humour if they were to escape. "I am on my way." She turned to Luke. "Pray tell me, sir, in which direction I should go."

Cupping his hand to his ear, he looked around. "Can you hear running water? I think I can, from over there."

Screwing up her face, she concentrated and leaned forward as she listened hard. "Yes, I think I can. Why did I not hear it earlier?"

"Too busy arguing," she thought she heard him mutter, but ignored it as she made her way in that direction. But then she turned back. "What am I supposed to fetch the water in? I will not be able to bring much in my cupped hands."

"Oh, yes, let me think, um…"

Sybil suggested, "I have just remembered, ma'am, I had a bottle of water in my bag. Maybe that has survived the accident."

"Why did you not tell us before? We could have…"

"Do not berate the poor woman, Miss…," began Luke. "I still do not know your name. Did you intend to never tell me?"

She shrugged. "I had not thought we would be together long enough for you to need to know, but it is Florence Fisher. Satisfied?"

"Ah, I have heard tell of a loud-mouthed, belligerent… No I did not mean that. I am pleased to make your acquaintance, ma'am."

Bowing, he held out his hand.

Should she take it or ignore it? Her upbringing overcame her reluctance, and she offered hers. He kissed the back, bowing deeply once more, and then turned it over and kissed the palm.

Pulling away, she exclaimed, "There is no need for exaggerations, sir. Once would have been sufficient." A sudden thought occurred to her. "Anyway, if you kidnapped us for a dare, how come you did not know my name? You might have grabbed the wrong person. I might be here on the brink of death by mistake."

"No, I knew exactly whom I was to – not kidnap. That's the wrong word."

"Oh, save your explanations for later." She moved towards the upturned carriage. "Where's that bag? And where's mine, for that matter?"

Luke's breath on her neck made her jump. "Did you say you were going to Cockermouth, Miss Florence?"

"Miss Fisher to you, and, yes, we were on our way to my aunt's house in Dovenby, near Cockermouth, before we were waylaid by some highwayman, some brigand who kidnapped us for I know not what reason. But, I forget, you knew all that."

"I told you…but what's the point? Come on, let's find this water bottle. I hope it is not smashed."

They found the cases in the dirt, hers open, revealing her fine dresses and intimate underwear, lying there for all to see.

She tried to shove it back inside before he could spot it, but his chuckle told her he had already done so.

"Pray, do not be embarrassed on my account. I have sisters of my own, and am used to seeing delicate items of lingerie drying on the clothes line."

"But that's different."

"Why? Lingerie is lingerie, is it not, although…"

A leering expression appeared on his face. He removed it, but not quickly enough to allay her earlier fears.

She jumped across to the other side of the case, and picked it up, still half open. "That one's Sybil's," she said, gesturing to the green tapestry bag, lying upside down in the leaves. "Please would you take it to her? I do not think she would be very happy at you rummaging about in her underwear."

"But how do you know I do not have a fetish for a maid's nether garments? Maybe…?"

"Now, sir, I can see you are attempting to tease me. It is not working. It just vexes me."

"And a vexed woman is not one to trifle with. Is that what you are saying?"

Nose in the air, she stalked behind the carriage, so he could not see her rearranging the contents of her case, and peeped to see if the bottle he handed to her maid had remained intact. It had. Thank goodness for that.

Still vainly trying to stuff her clothes in, so the case would close, she watched as the other two drank from the bottle until the tiniest portion of water remained. "What about me?" she yelled. "I would like some."

"But you are going to find the stream. You can quench your thirst there," he called back, handing it to the maid, who looked at it hesitantly, and then at her mistress.

Finally securing the clasp, she dropped her case near the carriage. There would not be much point lugging it over to them.

She wouldn't need it, although she could do with changing her filthy dress but, hopefully, they would be leaving very soon.

Sybil held out the bottle to her but she shook her head. "No, my dear, you finish it. Mister Lancaster is right." She took the now empty container and, sucking in her cheeks to produce saliva, she prayed that the water she found would be palatable.

"I'll be off, then. If I am not back in half an hour, send out a search party," she called, after recovering her lost shoe from the carriage. "Oh, there isn't one, is there? How remiss of me to forget."

His usual chuckle followed her as, pushing aside brambles and small trees, she shuffled towards the sound of the water. It gradually became louder until she emerged into a large clearing. The little stream she had envisaged flowed into one of the lakes for which the area was so renowned.

What a beautiful sight! She staggered to the water's edge, placed the bottle carefully on the grass, so as not to break it, for that would cause a fate worse than death, and scooped up a handful of the clear blue water, swallowing it down in gulps. Her stomach rumbled, reminding her she had not eaten for the best part of a day. No wonder she had been so grumpy. One of her worse traits was being grumpy when she was hungry. Eliza always told her that.

Thoughts of her sister overcame her as she sat at the water's edge. Eliza would not even realise she had not reached her aunt, although her aunt would surely have sent a message to find out if she had been delayed or even changed her mind, so maybe both households would be in uproar. Her mother would be weeping into her embroidered handkerchief, and her aunt would be looking up and down the road, wishing for a carriage to appear. If only she could deliver a message to let them know she was safe. Well, relatively so.

Reluctant to leave the beautiful scene, the mountains in the background—her mountains—reaching up to give a wonderful backdrop, she sat with her knees bent, her arms wrapped around them, thanking God for giving her an appreciation of beauty.

After a while she lay back on the grass, listening to the birds twittering in the trees. Peace descended upon her and she closed her eyes.

A nymph, dressed in leaves and with a band of flowers around her head, came out of the forest and beckoned her to follow. At the end of the path stood a handsome man, with eyes the colour of cobalt, and hair as black as a raven's. He took her hand and kissed it, then put his arm around her waist, and they danced around and around, until her head spun, her eyes almost coming out of their sockets. Then he stopped and put his cold hand on her cheek. She shivered, but he enfolded her in his arms and kissed her neck. She wanted him to kiss her all over, her lips, her eyes, to take off her dress and…

"There you are," barked a familiar voice. "I had begun to worry for your safety. But I find you here, fast asleep, careless of the thirst of your maid."

Rubbing her eyes, she jumped up. "Oh, was I asleep? What a pity. I had been having such a delightful dream." She blinked and looked at him, so close, she jumped as she realised the face of the man in her dream to be one and the same.

"What a charming view." He took her arm, uninterested in her dream. "I think I may have been on this lake before, on the boat."

But she wanted to remember the feel of her lover's kiss on her lips. Surely it had not all been a dream? Leaning as far away as she could without him noticing, she murmured, "Which one do you think it could be?"

He scratched his head. "Well, it is not Lake Windermere, I know that. It is probably…"

"But do they have steamers on the other lakes?"

"I did not refer to the steamer." He put up his hand to shield his eyes from the rising sun. "What a beautiful day. Just look at that blue sky, and those puffy white clouds at the tops of the mountains. And there's a falcon."

Amazed once more at how lyrical he could be, she looked up to where he pointed. "It's a red kite, isn't it?"

His turn to be amazed, he stared at her. "I did not take you to be a connoisseur of wild birds, Flossie. You seem more like a..."

She yanked her arm away. "Please do not call me Flossie. Nobody calls me that, not since my grandfather died. It was his pet name for me."

"Ah, I have found a raw spot, eh? I knew there had to be one in that icy exterior you try to convey. Very close, were you, to your grandfather?"

Happy memories flooded her brain. Memories of sitting on his knee while he told her stories of his life at sea. How he had conquered the mighty waves in tempests likely to have capsized any other boat, and survived to tell the tale. Cuddles, when he would brush his wiry beard against her soft cheek and tell her how much he loved her. "Yes, very close, and I still miss him so much."

Tears filled her eyes and his arm closed around her. He held her until they stopped, and then kissed the last one from her cheek.

"I'm sorry you have had to experience suffering," he whispered. "Death is never pleasant, especially when it comes to someone special."

Wanting to remain in his embrace, she tried to reason why her heart beat so erratically and why her legs had turned to honeycomb. She took a deep breath. "Have you…? Oh, yes, you said yesterday, your father died."

He delved into his pocket and grinned. "I'm sorry, but I gave your maid my handkerchief. I shall have to carry more than one in future, in case a young lady might have need of them."

"I should hope you will not be abducting any more young ladies, sir. That is, of course, unless you make a habit of it. Maybe it is your usual occupation. My first thoughts were that you were a highwayman. Perhaps that is how you gain your livelihood, preying on the rich? And where you have the money to sail your own boat?"

"Ah, dear lady, I did not say it was my own boat."

She took another drink of the water in the lake, as did he, and filled the bottle. "So you are not denying the other, then?"

He gave her an enigmatic smirk but made no reply, leaving her still confused as they wandered back.

A while later, still not having reached their base, she began to worry. "I hope you're not leading me around in circles. I have already seen that mushroom growing on that tree twice before."

He stopped and looked around. "I am sure it's in this direction. The sun is behind us so we are going west, but, I must admit, it did not take me this long to find you."

They could have been going north, south, east or west for all she knew. Direction had never been her strong point. The bottle shifted to her other hand, she peered at the sky through the trees, as if she knew what he meant.

A faint moan alerted them. "Is that my poor Sybil?" She turned towards the sound. "Hold on, my dear, we're coming," she called.

A low fire glowed red in the clearing. He hurried over to it. "I wondered why I could not see the smoke. That was why I couldn't find our way back straightaway. I should have put more kindling on. It's almost out. Pass me those bits of wood, if you would be so kind."

After giving the maid the bottle, she gathered an armful of twigs and small branches and the fire soon burned once more.

"What do we need a fire for, sir? It is not as if we have anything to cook. We have no food at all, let alone anything that needs a fire," she sneered, as she picked up more wood. As she aimed to throw it all on, he grabbed her arm to prevent her, and it dropped in a heap at the side.

"We do not want to set the whole forest alight." He tidied it into a neat pile. "And to answer your previous question, I shall see if I can catch a rabbit or something."

Amazed, she stared at him. "A rabbit? If you think I am going to eat a little bundle of furry rabbit, you can think again."

A shrug was all she received as reply.

Sybil still lay where she had been all night. She had not even opened the bottle.

Florence felt her forehead and gasped. "She's burning up. We have to take her to a doctor." She poured the water into her mouth and, if she did it slowly, the maid swallowed a few drops. Then she put some onto a clean patch of petticoat and dabbed her red face. It seemed to sooth her, and she closed her eyes and fell asleep. "We have to do something, Luke. We cannot just leave her here like this."

His eyebrow rose at her use of his name, but he came across and looked at the maid.

"I agree. When I have caught something to cook, I shall try to find a way out. In the meantime, you could pick some berries. There should be plenty of blackberries around at this time of year, and hips and haws."

"Hips and haws? What are they?"

"Rosehips, you know, those little red oval-shaped berry-type fruits from the wild rose?" When she looked vacantly at him, he shook her head. "No, I suppose not. Do you know what blackberries look like?"

"Of course I do. My sisters and I often pick them in the hedgerows around our house."

"Good, then find some."

Once he had left, she opened her tapestry bag and took out a dress with which to cover her maid, to make sure she did not catch a chill. In her condition, it would be so easy to do so.

"I shall be as fast as I can," she told her, although she slept too soundly to hear.

What can I put berries in? she wondered. Rifling through the maid's clothes, she held up a white apron. *This will do if I bunch it up into a pouch.* Satisfied that her plan would work, she set off.

Several brambles grew at the edge of the clearing, so she did not have far to travel. Large, juicy blackberries. Many did not make it to the make-shift pouch, they went straight into her mouth. *Why did I not think of this earlier, on my way to the water?* she rued. *They are delicious.* Deciding she had better take some for the others, although she did not consider that Sybil would be in any fit state to eat them, she filled the pouch and made her way back.

Luke had not returned, so she put more wood on the fire and sat down to await him. *How on earth will he catch a rabbit?* she wondered. *He cannot just chase one, even if he finds one.*

Several deer wandered through the trees in the distance. Now, venison, that would be a different prospect. She laughed at herself. Why was she aghast at eating a rabbit? They had rabbit stew occasionally. She would quite happily eat a deer, although, when it came to the actual act of how it would be done, she did not think she would be so eager.

Meat would be nice, though. She thought about the large plates of food served every day at home. Sometimes, barely half of it would be eaten, and it had never occurred to her to wonder what happened to the rest of it. She assumed the servants ate it.

Bored with waiting, she wandered over to the upturned carriage. The horse neighed as she approached. Luke had offered it water and there was plenty of grass for it to chomp.

"Not like me," she murmured as she pulled its ear. Her stomach growled, and she grimaced. Eating so many berries had probably not been such a good idea.

The damaged wheels of the carriage lay bent on the ground, half of the spokes broken. She turned one over, wondering if it could be mended. Her brother, Frederick, would have been able to do so. He could turn his hand to anything practical. Maybe Luke would. But he would not have any tools. Even a handyman needed tools. Even Mister High-and-Mighty Lancaster would not be clever enough to work a miracle. Why had he been gone so long?

She rummaged inside the carriage and found a parasol and a pair of gloves. Equipped for all weathers. If the sun became too hot and unbearable, she could put up the parasol, and if she grew cold, she could wear the gloves.

She put them on, anyway, just for something to do. Anything else? Maybe she could pull out the seat and have something to sit on. She yanked at it, but it would not budge. If she righted the carriage, though, the seats would be in the correct position. That proved futile as well.

"Ohhh," she moaned, using her sleeve to wipe her brow, sweating from the unusual activity.

She decided she may as well find a book in her case, reading being an activity her body could cope with.

"If I ever reach my aunt's house, I shall not have anything decent to wear," she rued as she took out her clothes one at a time, cursing at their creased condition, and then folded them and laid them on top of the maid's bag. The last item removed, she stood up and arched her back. "Where's my book, then? I'm sure I packed it in my case. Hell fire and damnation." She covered her mouth, glancing around to make sure nobody had heard her use such profanities. A well-brought-up lady did not swear. Not in company.

Her maid slept on. If her injuries were so severe, surely she would be unable to sleep? Her brow was still hot. The only solution she could think of was to wipe her brow now and again with cool water. The bottle soon emptied after performing this task a few times, in between taking a sip herself. More water needed.

Lifting her skirts, she made for the direction she had taken earlier, hoping she would find her way back more easily than they had done that morning.

The lake looked as peaceful as it had done on her previous visit. Birds glided past, moorhens, mallards, coots and a pair of swans. How majestic they looked, with their wings folded upwards. Three brown and white cygnets followed in their parents' wake, trying to look as regal.

She grinned, catching her breath as a heron flapped its wings and flew off. "I could stay here all day and watch you. But I need to return to my maid. She's poorly, and I don't know what to do about it. I cannot leave her here to find help, and our abductor, Mister Almighty Luke Lancaster, seems loath to do so, so I am stuck. Any suggestions?"

Squawking loudly, a pair of ducks came in to land feet first on the shimmering surface of the lake. "I am afraid to say I don't understand duck language, but thank you for your suggestion."

You stupid fool, she told herself. *Fancy talking to birds.*

Well, I see nobody else around with whom I can make conversation, so birds it has to be, whether they appreciate it or not.

The way back was easier to follow. She just had to look for the broken branches, but the glade still contained only Sybil. Should she call out to see if he could be close by? She cocked her ear to listen for any cracking of underfoot twigs or footsteps. Nothing. No point calling out, then.

Dropping another branch onto the fire, she decided she had better find more wood. The fire seemed to be eating it. How could it burn away so quickly? Sighing, she went into the woods and came back out with an armful. "Just slow down. I trust this will keep you satisfied for a while," she told the fire.

Sybil stirred.

"How are you, my dear? I am so sorry to have put you in this predicament. I know I keep using that word, but it is so apt. No other word accurately describes the situation, does it?"

The maid put out her hand to her mistress. "Pray, do not be concerned for me. I worry about you with that awful man." She coughed, so Florence gave her a drink of the water. "That awful person. Has he told you why he abducted us?" Coughing again, she lay down, leaving Florence flapping her hands. The last time she had tended anyone had been Felicity, when she had caught whooping cough, and that had only been for five minutes until her little sister had been sick all over her. She would never make a good nurse. Too squeamish. She thanked the Lord that Sybil had not cut herself badly. The sight of a lot of blood would have been too much to bear.

"Not really," she replied, once the cough had abated. "He said something about a dare, but that was all. I wonder where he is. He left hours ago. I'm starving. I dare not eat any more blackberries. They gave me stomach ache earlier. Would you like some?"

Sybil shook her head. "No, thank you. Another drink would be welcome, though, and then I need to...you know?"

"Mother Nature calls, you mean? Me, too. I hid behind a bush earlier, hoping against hope that his highness would not return just as I did so. Now, even though I'm desperate, and would be mortified if he realised where I had gone, in a funny way, I wish he would come back. I would be too scared to spend another night here, just the two of us."

She helped Sybil crawl, practically dragging her into the bushes, where they both performed their ablutions, not an easy task with the volume of material in their dresses. Then, making her as comfortable as possible, she wrapped her in the blanket and dress once more.

Determined to find the book she knew she had brought, as soon as the maid fell asleep again, she rummaged through her bag. Still no book. What else had she brought? Her reticule, of course. But would it have fitted inside that?

She went to the carriage, remembering stuffing the book inside it, in case she wanted to read it on the journey. The bag nowhere to be seen, she searched around the ground near the carriage, and there and behold, almost hidden by a pile of leaves, lay the book.

"Hoorah!" she yelled. "I've found you, slightly curled up at the edges, but in one piece. Now, I can read, and forget that his majesty still has not returned, and has…" A horrible idea formed in her mind. "What if he's abandoned us? Left us to fend for ourselves against the vicious beasts of the forest? Oh, no, that thought had not occurred to me. I assumed he would be returning. But, what if he does not? How will we protect ourselves?" The horse whinnied. "Do you know something, Dobbin, or whatever your name is? We used to have a rocking horse called Dobbin. Anyway, are you saying you'll look after us? If only you could transport us back to civilisation, as if by magic, by waving a wand, like those magicians do." It whinnied again, making her smile.

Patting its neck, she rested her forehead on it, and gave up a prayer that her fears would be unfounded, and that Luke Lancaster would come waltzing into the clearing with…a constable? No, he would not do that. He would be arrested, once she told the policeman about the kidnapping. What reinforcements could he bring, then?

But he had only gone to find a rabbit, not help. Shoulders slumped, she found the most comfortable-looking tree stump, fetched her maid's other clean dress—she would not be needing it for a while—and made a cushion to sit upon.

The book could not hold her interest, though. Her concentration wavered, and her stomach kept rumbling. *What else can I eat, besides berries? If only I had not led such a pampered life, I would know what would be safe to eat and what not. But I never envisaged finding myself in the middle of a forest, fending for myself.*

A foray into the woods did not reveal any clues. Her father had told her never to eat the bright red-topped toadstools, and she could not tell the difference between the others and a mushroom. "Beech nuts!" she exclaimed. "I remember collecting them one year. They are edible. Are there any beech tress around?" But no beech trees could be found in that part of the forest, and she was too afraid to explore any further.

Returning to the clearing, she yelped with joy, when she saw Luke Lancaster entering from the other direction. She ran across and hugged him. "Oh, I never thought I would be so pleased to see anyone," she squealed. "I thought you…"

The amazement on his face made her smile. "Well, that is the second time you have given me such an exuberant welcome. Maybe I should go away again."

"Oh, no, please do not. I have been beside myself with apprehension, thinking you would not be coming back."

A wounded look came into his eyes. "How could you think I would leave you?"

"Well, I do not know your character, sir, do I? A man who could take two defenceless women hostage could be a mass murderer for all I know."

"My dear," he gently disentangled himself from her clutches, "I…"

"Never mind that, did you find us anything to eat? I've kept the fire burning."

His mouth turned down as he shook his head. "I'm sorry, but, no, I did not. Did you find any berries?"

Disappointment filled her as she pointed to the messy, purple-coloured apron. "Help yourself."

"How's your maid?" he asked as he popped one into his mouth. "Mm, these are sweet."

She flopped down onto her tree stump. "Still very unwell, but I think the fever may have abated somewhat. We really ought to take her to a medic. Maybe we could concoct something to drag her in, a sort of stretcher-type thingamy. The horse could pull her."

"And what do you propose we use?" He ate the rest of the fruit, and wiped his mouth and fingers with a clean part of the apron.

She looked towards her case. Sacrifice her lovely clothes for the sake of her maid? What about Sybil's own dresses? Would they make a suitable base for a sling?

"We could try, I suppose," he conceded after a moment's hesitation.

"How far did you wander?" she asked as they emptied the bag, not daring to look at his face as he held up a pair of large, white, frilly knickers. "You were gone a long time." She snatched them from him. "Maybe I should do this on my own. Poor Sybil will be mortified if she knew…"

"Yes, ma'am?" a squeak came from behind her. "Did you call?"

She burst into hysterical laughter.

Trying to contain it, she replied, "No, my dear. I'm sorry to have disturbed you."

The hilarity would not leave her, though, and she doubled up once more, her sides aching, while Luke guffawed beside her.

"Stop it," she cried, nudging him in the ribs. "It's not funny."

"I know, but I was not the one to start."

"Then be the one to finish, for I cannot." She bit the inside of her mouth, but that did not work. The knickers pushed underneath the dresses, she thought she might stop if they were not in full view, but then he held up another pair. How long had the maid been thinking they would be staying away, to need two spare pairs? Did she have an incontinuence problem? The idea of that made her laugh even more. She felt very uncharitable, but even guilt would not bring the giggles to an end.

Her stomach aching more and more, she tried walking around the glade. Eventually, wiping the tears from her cheeks, she pulled up beside the stricken maid. "I am so sorry to find hilarity in your underwear, Sybil. It is unforgivable of me." She took her hand. "Pray do not be distressed."

"No, ma'am, not at all. It pleases me to be the object of your hilarity."

Florence looked at her closely, unsure if she were being honest or sarcastic.

"I was just wondering why you were going through my clothes."

"To see if anything would be appropriate for making a type of hammock that we could pull you along in."

"Oh, ma'am, no, please do not try anything like that, I beg you."

"But it might be the only way we can find our way out of here." She turned to Luke, who had been building up the fire. "What are you doing that for, if we have nothing to cook?"

"Just in case. You never know, something might turn up."

"Oh, yes, like a rabbit might come hopping in here to see what we are doing, and give itself up?"

"Sarcasm does not suit you, Flossie."

Between gritted teeth, she hissed, "I asked you not to call me that. I told you why."

"So you did, so you did."

"Does that mean you will not do so again?" She walked across and looked him directly in the face.

He stepped back, as if scorched, raising his arms. "I surrender, General. Please do not shoot."

"I didn't know you had been in the military."

"I didn't say I had. I merely used one of the terms my grandfather would often say when I was a little boy. He devoted his entire life to the army, worked his way up the ranks to be a general. And, for that matter, you do not know anything at all about me."

With a flick of her hair, she turned away. "No, sir, and I have no inclination to find out. The sooner we escape this hell-hole, the better. The less time I spend in your company, the happier I shall be."

"Ha! Not that long back, I seem to recall you running into my arms. And there was me, thinking you cared for my safety."

"No, sir, do not flatter yourself. It was my own, well, mine and my maid's safety I had become concerned for, not yours."

"Shame."

She looked back at him.

"Maybe I should find some way to make you want to stay with me." Before she could stop him, he grabbed her arm and pulled her towards him, latching his mouth onto hers with a ferocity against which she had no resistance.

The impact would have knocked her off her feet, if he had not held her so closely. Her heart beating at twice its normal rate, she succumbed to the intense pleasure of his lips against hers.

It did not last long, though, for he flung her away and she landed in a heap. Confused, she watched him walk to the other side of the glade, his hands ruffling through his fair hair. With the sun shining on it, it looked blonder than Felicity's.

"No gentleman," she muttered, trying to stand on her wobbly legs, "would treat a lady in such a way."

He did not turn around.

"I thought you promised," she yelled, in case he could not hear her, "you would not try anything again. You are sorely lacking in credibility."

He still did not reply.

Unused to being ignored, it irked her that he would make no comment. Her lips still tingling from the kiss, she marched over to him. Was his reluctance to speak because he felt abhorrence for her? If so, why had he kissed her? Although, it had been more of an onslaught than a caress, so technically could not be called a kiss.

"What are you doing, sir?"

"Um?" He looked up.

"Did you not hear me calling you?"

The eyebrow rose and she felt sure his lips twitched as he continued with his task.

Outraged at receiving no polite reply, she yanked at the sleeve of his greatcoat, once probably of very fine quality, but now covered in smudges and stains. "I am speaking to you, sir."

"So?"

"So, it would be polite to reply." Arms folded, she glared.

He stood upright. "What would you like me to say? If you want polite conversation I could begin with 'Good day, ma'am. How are you this fine afternoon?'"

"Of course I do not want that sort of exchange." She shielded her eyes from the sun. "Have you thought of a way out yet? Would it not be a good idea to go back the way we came and find the road and ask for help? That seems to be very logical to me. Does it not to you?"

"If you want to try it, go ahead"

"Not me, you idiot, you."

Her outburst did not attract the sort of attention she had envisaged. He bolted upright, his eyes blazing.

She stepped backwards, rueing her words. "I mean…that came out all wrong. I did not intend to use that word. I apologise. My sister always says I should think before I speak."

With a shake of his head, he pulled the roof of the carriage and eased it away from its supports.

"To answer your earlier question, I am trying to make a shelter."

"So, you did hear me?"

"I did not say to the contrary."

"No, but…"

The infuriating man walked into the woods.

"Now, where are you going?"

"For goodness sake, stop all the questions. Just let me finish the job in hand. Here, take this and put it next to the roof."

When she hesitated, he added, "If you would be so kind," in such a sneering way that she turned and left him to carry the long branch himself.

"I still do not understand why you cannot go to find help. We would have no need of a shelter if someone rescued us. Or…but, I know why you cannot. You are in trouble with the law. Am I right?" Of course, he did not deign to reply. "I am, aren't I? I must be. That is the only explanation."

Pleased for solving one quandary, it provided her with another. If the law were looking for him, he must have committed some heinous crime. She and Sybil would definitely not be safe in his company. But what could she do? As she had told herself many times already, she could not leave her maid in his clutches. But was she prepared to sacrifice her own honour, in order to save Sybil?

She crept over to the maid.

"Sybil," she whispered, shaking her awake, rather more violently than she had intended. "Sybil, do you think you could walk yet?"

"Mama, where am I?"

"You're in the middle of a forest, and I am not your mama, I am your mistress, Florence Fisher. Surely, you can tell the difference?"

"Where's Papa?"

Another shake. "Sybil, wake up. It's me, Miss Florence."

Luke came across. "She's hallucinating," he observed in her ear. "You will not be able to move her today."

"Grrrrr." Pulling at her lips, she stomped off, uncaring of the pain in her foot, as far away from him as she could, without actually leaving the glade.

Not realising he had followed, she jumped back when his voice came from just behind her ear. "You will have to accept your situation, my dear."

"I do not *have* to do anything, sir. In fact, if you will not find the road, then I shall do it. Pray look after my maid while I am gone. I may be some while."

"Suit yourself, ma'am, but if you go that way," he pointed in the direction she had begun to take, "you will merely end up at the foot of a mountain. Why do you think I was away for so long this morning?"

"I know not, sir. You did not enlighten me, as usual. Pray, which way should I go, then?"

"If I knew that, I would have found it myself."

She stopped, looking all around.

Memories of the gorgeous eyes of the man, Mister A N Other, who had danced with her but a few days before, wandered through her brain. It seemed like a lifetime ago. He would not treat a lady so, she knew that. Tears threatened, but she brushed them away with the back of her hand. She had to stay strong. No point in crumpling.

She looked up at the sky and offered up a prayer to her grandpapa to give her some advice. *What should I do, Gramps? Should I stay or should I go? Leave Sybil and try to find help, or stay and be assaulted by the murderer over there.* She glanced across at her kidnapper. He had taken off his jacket. His white shirt sleeves clung to his arms and stuck to his sweaty back. His muscles could be seen through the thin material. He stood up and brushed his hair from his face, defying her with his eyes to go against him.

Well, Gramps, do you have an answer for me?

With pursed lips, she spun around in a circle, her eyes closed until she could spin no more; if she faced the glade when she stopped she would stay and take her chances, or if she faced the outside, she would go.

Twizzling round and round, a kind of ethereal peace descended upon her. Bird song mingled with other sounds in her head, and she felt as if she was floating, floating in a sea.

"What do you think you are doing?" A gruff voice halted her as dizziness overcame her and she fell into the arms of the man she had been trying to escape from minutes before.

"I do not know," she wailed. "That is the trouble. I do not know what to do."

The tears that had threatened before, spilled over, but, instead of remaining in the haven of his embrace, she pushed him away and ran. Ran as fast as her swollen ankle would allow, through the thorny brambles and sharp branches of trees and saplings, ran until her lungs were bursting.

Had he followed? She could hear no echoing sound of pursuit. That decided it. She would continue.

The answer to her prayer had been solved. *Well, Gramps, I don't know if that was what you meant, but that is what's happening, so please, watch over me and help me find a way out.*

81

Chapter 4

A while later, with still no sign of a road, she sat down on a fallen tree trunk, piggling at a large tear in her dress. What if darkness fell and she had not found a road, or a cottage, or anything? What had Luke said that morning? She had not really been listening. Her legs were scratched and bleeding, as well as her arms. Her tangled hair hung in rats' tails around her neck. What a sight she must present! She would be unable to look anybody in the eye, even if she did find someone.

A loud, braying scared her. Through the trees she could see a clearing. *Dare I go and see?* she pondered, scratching her leg. *But what if it's a wolf?*

Don't be so stupid. They don't run wild in this area.

Are you sure? She argued with herself for a few minutes, before jumping off the tree trunk. Ants swarmed all over her foot and up her leg. Yelping, and squirming, she brushed off as many of the insects as she could. "Go away," she yelled, running from the nest towards the clearing. "You're not having me for your supper."

Satisfied she had removed the little creatures, she stopped in awe at the sight before her. Two huge stags, their antlers interlocked. Twenty or so smaller deer—presumably their does—ignored them, munching the grass. Even though one of the stags had blood flowing down its neck, it seemed determined to carry on, lowering its head and charging. Eventually, the other one slunk off, clearly beaten, and the victor gave a roar of triumph.

"That must be what I heard earlier," she muttered. "Thank goodness it wasn't a wolf." The stag walked towards her. "Oh, heck, it's probably just as dangerous." Turning, she went back into the woods, desperate for a drink of water, having seen a stream running down the mountainside opposite.

Maybe she could skirt around the clearing. The trees seemed closer together to her right, but the other way looked passable. Hitching up her skirts, after knocking off two more ants she had missed, she followed that direction. Her legs itched, but she had to grin and bear it. That water beckoned. Her mouth felt too dry to ignore it. The stream in her view all the time, she pushed her way towards it. "Water, water everywhere, nor any drop to drink," came to mind. Her governess had instilled in her a love of poetry, and had made her learn Samuel Taylor Coleridge's 'Rime of the Ancient Mariner' by heart.

Her favourite poet was William Wordsworth, though, especially as she felt an affinity, with him living nearby. The governess had told her and Eliza all about him and his sister Dorothy. What good was poetry, though, in the situation she now found herself? *Well, maybe I could write a poem about my experiences when I do, finally, return to my family. I could ask*

Felicity to help me. Eliza would not do so. She would rather do anything than put pen to paper.

After a while she eventually reached the stream. Making sure the stag—or any of the others she could see dotted about—was not looking her way, she dipped her hands in the cool, clear water and scooped some up to her mouth. How delicious it tasted. Not like water at all. She washed her face, sat down on a big stone and lifted her skirts to examine her bites.

"Oh, my goodness," she exclaimed at her leg and foot, covered in raised, red lumps, each trying to vie with its neighbour for the title of the most irritating. She scooped up more water and soaked them, but it did not help much. It was so hard not to scratch them. When she and Eliza had caught chickenpox their nurse had told them if they scratched the spots, devils would erupt and invade their souls. It might not apply to ant stings, but she did not want to take the chance.

"Oh, Gramps," she yelled, looking upwards. "Surely you did not send this plague upon me. I asked for assistance, not to be eaten alive."

Another ant walked innocently across her skirt. She picked it up and looked it in the eyes. "You are going to die," she told it through gritted teeth, and squashed it between her fingers so hard her fingertips turned white. "And if I find any more of you little pests I shall do the same to you, even if you are God's creatures. I do not feel any guilt whatsoever, so beware."

Her frustration eased by murdering the ant, she took another drink, hitched up her skirts and waded into the water. The coolness eased her discomfort a little. As she stood there, she looked at her surroundings. The stream ran down the mountain like a silver thread through green material. White blobs of sheep wandered in and out of the rocks, some with black faces. One gave her a questioning look, as if asking why she dared to invade their territory, and then resumed its eating, clearly satisfied she posed no threat.

Wishing she had not been so rash in her flight, she wondered if Luke Lancaster had finished concocting the shelter. Why did he seem so reluctant to find help? Maybe he was in debt to someone and needed to stay out of their way for a while? Was that why he had abducted her and Sybil? He gave no appearance of cowardice, so evading a duel did not seem likely. Whatever his problem, did she have the courage to find her way back to him, and suffer the consequences of his actions? After all, his kisses had aroused her in a way she could never have imagined. She had thought herself to be falling in love with Mister A N Other, but he had not made her feel so alive, although, of course, he had not kissed her. The other alternative would be to stay out in the wilds on her own. Not a very pleasing proposition.

The water chilled her so, shivering, she stepped out and examined her leg and dress once more, to make sure she had not missed any more creatures.

The deer had calmed down, munching, so she decided to risk going back. But which clump of trees would lead her there? Halfway across the clearing, she stopped, uncertain. Fortunately the deer scattered as she came close to them.

"Gramps," she shouted, "I need you again."

Scanning the semi-circle of trees ahead, she thought she could see movement inside. Treading stealthily, she stared at it. Now, what danger awaited her? Probably only more deer. The dark figure grew larger. She stopped, ready to turn and run back if need be.

Luke Lancaster appeared from the trees.

Relief, but also anger vied with each other in her head. Relief that he had found her, but anger that he had followed her. Should she run to him or ignore him? But he must have left her maid alone. Maybe he had come to tell her Sybil had died? How would she bear it, if her maid had died because she herself had not had the courage to stay and face the man?

Head high, nose in the air, she ambled over to him, trying to look nonchalant. "To what do I owe this honour, sir, that you should come looking for me?"

He grabbed her arm. "You stupid girl, you could have been killed by those rutting stags."

"But they came nowhere near me." She yanked her arm away, turning back to see if the deer had followed, or where close. "See, I am perfectly safe."

He gave her a look from under his eyebrows.

"And, anyway, how did you find me?"

"Find you, my dear? I never lost you."

"But… You mean, you followed me, and have been watching me all afternoon? I do not believe that."

He shrugged and took her arm, leading her through the wood. "Believe what you want, ma'am."

"How is Sybil?"

She tripped on a protruding branch and gripped his arm, but let go once she had regained her balance.

He marched on ahead, clearing the browning ferns and other various plants for her easy passage.

"I asked how my maid fared?" she called, once she had come to the conclusion he had not heard.

"I know as much as you, my dear. I have been away, making sure you were safe."

"Oh, my, so she has been alone all afternoon? Oh, poor, unfortunate thing. What if she is calling for me, or needs assistance? You should have stayed with her, sir."

He pulled up. She ran into his hard back. His face as thunder, he turned and barked, "*I* should have stayed? What about you?" Hands on hips, he glared at her. "She is of no concern to me. She is your affair, your maid, not mine."

Her eyes lowered. Of course, he was right. Wild horses would not drag the admission from her, though. She remained silent for the remainder of the way, concentrating on keeping the wet material of her dress from sloshing against her legs.

Before long they arrived at the glade. It had taken twice as long to leave it. How had they returned so quickly? He would not have the satisfaction of telling her, for she would not ask. In fact, if she could manage it, she would not speak to him ever again.

Sybil lay in the same position. Florence hurried over and touched her forehead. It still burned, her cheeks clammy. She dabbed the maid's brow with the remainder of the water. His shelter seemed no nearer completion than when she had left. He must have followed her straightaway. How come she had not heard him?

The fire had reduced to embers so she poked it with a stick, trying to coax the last few red cinders to burst into flames.

A strong arm crept around her waist. "It will need more kindling," he said in her ear.

With a jerk, she broke free and threw on a few twigs. They just lay there, resistant to the heat. He gathered dry brown leaves, placed them in the embers and, when they caught, he pushed her twigs on top with a long stick. Silently, she gathered small pieces of wood and added them. Then she went further afield, found larger ones and took them back, trying to ignore his questioning look. *I will not give you the satisfaction of knowing you were right.*

Luke went back to his shelter. She ought to help him, for he was struggling, but she stalked off to refill the bottle. On her return she managed to squeeze a few drops into Sybil's mouth.

Her legs on fire, she sat down to take another look at them, somehow resisting the urge to scratch.

Luke came across. "They look nasty. Try rubbing them with these dock leaves."

"Wha…?" *Whoa, do not give in.*

"They work for nettle stings, but those are bites, if I am correct?"

Determined not to give way, she pressed the leaves onto the bites.

"They would not be mosquitoes, as they do not usually feed during the day. My guess would be ants?"

She rolled her eyes. Mister Clever Dick. If he had been stalking her all afternoon, he would have seen them.

Don't be so silly, Flo, how could he see such minute creatures?
Well, he sees everything else.

The dock leaves did not help, so she stood up and shook out her dress, embarrassed at him examining her legs.

He shrugged. "Please yourself. I see you have taken a vow of silence. Well, it does not bother me. I am quite happy to remain in a state of peace and tranquillity. Quite happy, indeed." He stomped back to his

89

handiwork, as Florence felt something fall on her arm. A raindrop? Surely not.

She peered up at the sky through the orange and yellow leaves above. Black clouds scudded towards them. Not something else to contend with. Had Luke noticed? He seemed to be working with more vigour than before, so maybe he had. They needed to cover up her maid, even if they themselves were left out in the open.

She crept across and pushed in a piece of leather he had been trying to put into a hole. He looked up at her, but she would not meet his gaze.

"We need to complete this urgently, now," he told her. "I presume you've felt the rain?"

"Yes." What would be the point in continuing her silence? It did not bother him, so she was the only one being affected, and that adversely. "What can I do?"

"Hold this, if you please." He handed her a long branch. "If I—I mean, we—can raise this on top of four equal poles, it would, at least, stop the rain pouring down directly on top of us."

They worked together until the shelter took shape.

Wiping his brow, he put his arm around her shoulders. "Now, we need to drag your maid underneath it. She is our priority, don't you think?"

"Those are exactly my feelings, sir."

Sybil made hardly a murmur as they dragged her and her blanket into the dry area.

Luke rubbed his hands together. "Are those chestnuts roasted?" he asked. "I'm starving."

"Chestnuts?"

"I brought back pocketfuls from our soirée earlier, and put them in the side of the fire while you fetched the water. They should be well and truly roasted by now."

"Oo, how exquisite. I love roasted chestnuts."

"There's no need to thank me. It was a purely selfish act. If you had not returned with me, I would have eaten them all myself, for I think your maid would not be able to consume them."

"Oh. Yes, of course."

"Do not take me so seriously, my dear. I jested. Of course, my first thought had been for you." He took her hand and kissed it. "Come, let us find them before they burn to cinders."

Most of the nuts had survived, although some were indeed cinders. Luke found thick, big leaves to collect them, and they dashed back to the shelter with the pouch Florence had made with her pinafore. Eagerly waiting for them to cool down, she tried not to be aware of his closeness as they sat with their knees under their chins, their arms wrapped around them.

After a moment or so, he picked one up. "Let me try it. I know I should allow you the first one, but I would rather suffer the consequences if it is too hot." He peeled off the brown skin, looked at the yellowish-white nut inside, and then popped it into his mouth.

Her mouth watering, she watched him chew it with deliberation. She grabbed one and did the same. "I'm sorry, but I cannot wait," she squealed. Rolling the nut between her teeth, she thought it to be the tastiest thing she had ever eaten. Her eyes closed, she savoured the moment, but opened them when she felt his firm fingers put another one in her mouth. With no resistance, she let him draw down her lip and push open her teeth to pop it inside. Tempted to bite his finger, she thought better of it as she smiled into his mocking, blue eyes. Her heart gave a peculiar leap.

"Nice?" he asked in a gruff voice.

"Um, heaven."

He peeled another and held it towards her.

"No, it's your turn. I don't want to be greedy."

He wavered, before popping it into her mouth. "You are in more need than I." They shared the rest equally. "How's your leg?"

"You mean the ant bites or the swollen ankle?"

"Both."

Uncertain if she should lift her skirt while so close to him, she felt up her shin. "Still quite bad."

"May I take a look?"

"Um…"

"I'm not going to ravish you, my dear, if that's what you're thinking. I'm not in the habit of seducing young, virginal maidens."

He reached over to touch the soft silk of her dress, now ripped and filthy.

"You do not give that impression, though, sir, when you grab me as you do."

"Like this, you mean?" His hand cupped her cheek.

Helpless to stop him, she closed her eyes as his lips touched hers, so softly, but the fire they created consumed her whole body. If she came so alive from one tender kiss, there was no hope for her if he tried anything further. She pulled back as he raked his fingers through his hair. Her earlier thought struck her again. Had he been repulsed by the touch? Was that why he had bestowed such a soft kiss, and now seemed indifferent?

If Florence had read Luke's mind, she would have been very surprised. The touch of her lips had affected him as no other female had ever done. He put it down to their extraordinary circumstances. She had pulled away but he knew he could have taken her there and then, and probably would have at another time. The girl was different, though, not like his usual bed mates and he felt confused at his reaction.

"What shall we do about my maid?" she whispered. Sybil's brow seemed less clammy, but she did not stir as Florence dabbed it. She felt around for the water bottle, intending to wet the cloth again, but could not find it. When she stood up she almost knocked over one of the supporting poles.

"Steady on," yelled Luke. "Where are you going?"

"The bottle, where is it?"

He shifted his position.

"We must have left it out there when we moved her." She peered through the gloom, for evening had advanced, the rain making it darker than normal. "I shall have to find it. We need a drink as well. At least I do, even if you do not."

She ran out to the spot where the maid had been lying and found it, covered in mud. "Ugh," she groaned, looking round for something with which to wipe it. Some of her clothes had fallen out of the case and lay bedraggled and damp in the mud. She used a pair of pantaloons, cringing at the thought of the man over the way seeing her undergarments.

How long had they been lying there in full view? Maybe she would find it funny when she related the story back to Eliza, but did not find it so at that moment.

With rain running down her neck, she hurried back to the shelter. "There's not a lot left, and I don't fancy going to fill it. It must be your turn, sir."

He grinned at the sight of her hair, plastered to her face. "And I thought you were being so efficient."

"What?" The wet material of her dress clung to her, and she tried to ease it away from her back, twisting and turning in the confined space.

"Stand still, woman, or you'll have the whole thing down on top of us."

"It's all right for you to sneer, but I am wet through, and most uncomfortable."

"Then take it off."

"Do not be so bold, sir. As if I would."

"You have clean dresses, I am sure, in your valise. Change into one of them."

Would any of them be any drier than she one she wore? Going out to find the case would mean getting wetter, but maybe it would be worth it.

"Well, if you are fetching the water, sir, you could bring me my case before you go, and I could change while you are gone. That would solve the problem, would it not?"

Feeling smug at her good idea, she smiled sweetly at him.

"Oh, and what will I change into when I return, wet through? I do not have any spare clothes." Hands on hips, he glared.

"And whose fault is that?"

"I had not intended needing fresh shirts when I set out yesterday morning."

"No, and you still have not told me what you were intending." Florence shivered and wrapped her arms around her midriff.

"We won't go into that now. You're cold." He nipped out and fetched her case. "Maybe I could wrap myself in something out of here."

Dresses and undergarments flew out of the portmanteau as he rifled through it. "Do you not have a shawl?"

Hysteria welled up inside her again at the image of him wearing her clothes. "No. I do have a clean petticoat, but I don't think it will fit you." Laughter bubbled over and she held her sides. His lips twitched and he joined in also, guffawing like a donkey, making her laugh all the more.

The noise disturbed Sybil, who groaned. "Ma'am?"

"Pray, do not stir." Florence pulled herself together and patted her arm. "We...that is..." She could go no further for the hilarity returned threefold.

Luke put a mobcap on his head.

"That's not mine," she gushed. "How did that get in there?" She reached out to pull it off, but he clung onto it, and they fell in a heap, her on top of him, still laughing.

He stopped, his face changing to a frown, and eased her off.

The mood altering, she moved away from his hard, lithe body, as eager to put distance between them as he obviously was.

"I had better go," he mumbled, stepping outside the shelter.

"Take something to cover you, Luke," she called after his retreating back. "You'll be soaked to the skin within seconds..." Her voice tailed off, realising the futility of continuing. The rain seemed to have abated, anyway.

In the process of lifting her dress above her head, she thought she heard his stern voice, and peeped out from the folds.

With a face like thunder, he stood before her. She quickly pulled down the dress as he cleared his throat and reached inside. She stepped back and almost fell on top of her maid.

"I forgot the bottle."

"Oh." She blew out her breath in relief. For a moment she had felt…what? Excitement, or dread?

Not daring to look him in the eye, she watched as he picked up the glass container and left once more. She plonked down on the hard ground. Luke had concocted a makeshift carpet from the seat covers, making the interior of the shelter not too muddy, but still hard on her bottom, especially as her petticoats had ridden up, so giving her no padding.

What had she expected him to do? More to the point, what had she wanted him to do? A stranger, an unknown force. How could she be having thoughts about doing anything with him? She had only known him a day.

Lord Head had been her acquaintance for several years, since she had been a child, almost, and she still could not contemplate doing anything like that with him. What had happened to her? Had she turned into a promiscuous harlot overnight?

She changed into drier clothes before Luke could return and find her half-naked again. Had he taken her semi-nudeness as an invitation? No. If he had, he would not have walked away. He would have acted there and then, surely? Not if he found her repulsive, as she had thought earlier. But, in that case, he would not have been so in tune with her laughter. He would have folded his arms and given her the glare, not joined in with it.

Her wet clothes folded up, she rolled them into a bundle and put them outside, but decided they would make a good pillow, so brought them back into the dry.

Darkness had fallen and he still had not returned. Guilty for sending him, she peered out, praying he had not lost his way. If only she had a candle. *Why did we not take the ones out of the lanterns on the carriage?* But she did not have any matches. Would Luke have any? He had not smoked while they had been there. In any case, he might have matches in his pocket. He had to have had something with which to light the fire. She peered out once more, but could not see beyond her hand. He would never find his way in the dark. What a thoughtless idiot she had been.

Luke stalked off into the forest. The song of the birds in the trees calmed his nerves. He stopped and took a deep breath. How could the girl have had such an impact on him? Never in his life had he ever felt such passion flowing through his whole body.

He'd had plenty of females, many of them satisfying his needs quite pleasantly, but none could be compared to the girl behind him. Oh, she put on an act of bravado and innocence, but he could have taken her there and then, with no resistance. Why hadn't he? Had he suddenly become moral? He could not answer his own question.

He stumbled on, becoming wetter and wetter, barely taking notice of his way.

Florence took a few steps outside. "Luke!" she called. "Can you hear me? I'm over here." With her hand to her ear, she listened for a reply. Nothing. She called again, "Mister Lancaster! This way." Still no answer. "Oh, heck, what am I to do?"

The horse whinnied from her right. "Is that you?"

"I did not think I would ever be compared to a horse," his voice came from the other direction.

She ran to the sound, stumbling into his arms, and punched him in the chest.

"Why did you not answer me when I called?"

"I did not know if I would be welcome."

"You stupid man, why would I be shouting you, if I did not want you?"

"Want?"

"I mean, want you to…to…" What did she mean? "To be safe."

"Oh."

"Did you find the stream?" She felt down his side for the bottle, but came into contact with his empty hand. He linked his fingers with hers, so she squeezed them, feeling protected. The rain has ceased and in the glow of the moon emerging from above the trees, she could just make out his eyes, smiling at her. She smiled back, and his face blotted out the light as he bent down to brush her lips with his. She had no hesitation as she pulled his head closer. Revelling in the sensations, she kissed him back with fervour, until he pulled away, his breath ragged.

"We must stop meeting like this," he tried to joke, but she wanted more, and pulled his head down again. A low moan in his throat betrayed his emotion as he ran his tongue along the inside of her lower lip. She opened her mouth to allow better access and his hand came around to cup her breast. She pulled back, not trusting her own feelings. Breathless, she turned from him and slid inside the shelter.

"Pray forgive me," he hissed as he followed.

"No, it was my fault. I should have stopped when you wanted to, but..."

"I hope you were about to say you were enjoying it too much?"

Opening the bottle, he handed it to her. She took her time with her drink, not wanting to admit he was right, in case it gave him the inclination to go even further. Better not to say anything at all. She handed it back, her eyes downcast.

He took her chin and raised it. "There is no shame in admitting feelings, my dear Flossie."

This time she did not mind him using her pet name. "There is when you are practically engaged to another man."

He let go as if scalded. "Oh, I had not realised."

Maybe she had told a little white lie, having already come to the conclusion that there would be no way she could marry Lord Head, but she could not enlighten this man. Her pretend betrothal would provide a buffer between them, to stop any further lovemaking. Her burgeoning feelings made her too aware of him, and she might not be able to stop him if he became too persuasive with his gorgeous kisses. Better to be safe than sorry, as Gramps had often told her.

An uneasy atmosphere grew between them, but she made no effort to ease it, as they made themselves comfortable, using clothes from the case.

She covered Sybil, who had fallen asleep once more, and tucked in the red dress which Luke had chosen as a cover, smiling to herself, wanting to say how the colour suited his features, but reluctant to recreate the intimacy they had shared earlier.

Lying awake, listening to his heavy breathing, she wondered if her family had been made aware that she had not arrived at Dovenby. The best scenario would be if her aunt had assumed she had changed her mind, so her mother and sister would be none the wiser, but she feared it would not be the actuality, her aunt being a stickler for correctness and punctuality.

She would probably have sent off a letter within two or three hours of her non-arrival, and she could imagine the chaos that would have ensued. Her poor mama. Smelling salts would be waved under her nose, but they might not be sufficient.

And Eliza, her darling sister, what would she be doing? Knowing her, she would probably have summoned a carriage forthwith, and could very well be scouring the neighbourhood. Hopefully, not in the dark. With any luck, she would be tucked up in a warm bed in a coaching inn, maybe the Fleece Arms, that lovely inn in Kendal. They had once stayed there for a night. She loved Kendal, a hilly but beautiful town, right on the edge of the Lake District. But that would be too far out of the way.

A movement in front of her made her start. She had been facing Luke, not trusting him behind her. He rolled over, but even with pins and needles in her hand, she determined not to turn.

"I cannot sleep," he groaned. "I am unused to taking to my bed at such an early hour. Tell me a story."

"You sound like my little sister, Felicity. She loves a bedtime tale, even though she is almost ten years old."

Leaning up on his elbow, he asked, "What stories do you tell her? Ones about goblins and witches? I used to love my father telling me them."

"Your father? Did you have a happy childhood?"

"Yes, very happy."

Tempted to ask more details of his life, she resisted, not wanting to know, in case knowing drew her closer to him, so she replied, "She prefers fairy tales, and I have recently discovered a book by a Danish poet and author—I forget his name, Hans something or other. The stories are exquisite, they all show virtue in the face of adversity."

"Oh, I shall have to look for that one. If you remember his name, you must let me have it."

"Well, they are supposed to be for children, but I enjoy them as much as she does."

She did not add that once they were out of there, she had no intention of ever seeing him again.

Lying so close to him was taking all her reserve not to want to know him better. How could she see him, anyway? Their paths had never crossed before, so why would they again? From his accent, he probably lived further south, maybe London or Brighton, places she had never been, but had heard of in general conversation.

"Tell me one of these tales, then."

"Oh, very well." She related her favourite, the Little Mermaid, not really thinking he would be interested in the story of a mermaid, he being a strong, manly gentleman, but he made no comment until she came to the end.

"That is quite sad," he remarked.

"In a way but, because she performed good deeds, she earned her soul, and her place in heaven."

He rolled onto his back. "I cannot see me entering the pearly gates."

"Why not? Are you such a bad person?" As soon as the words had left her mouth, she regretted it. She did not want to know anything about him.

"Let us not talk about me." She sensed him facing her again. "I want to know about you."

"But I have told you nearly everything already, about my sisters and brother."

"What did you say your brother's name was?"

"Frederick."

"Frederick Fisher? Ah."

"Do you know him? I am sure he does not know you. He has never mentioned you."

"Has he not?"

When he did not elucidate, she tried to rack her brain for any instances of Frederick referring to a Luke Lancaster, but could not think of any occasion he might have done so.

"No, and anyway," she closed her eyes and curled into a ball, her usual position for sleeping, "I am tired. Pray, allow me to sleep without interruption."

"Mmm, I as well. Good night, fair maiden."

"Good night…" *No, do not fall into his trap,* "…sir."

"Sweet dreams."

"Shush."

"I am only being polite and saying things polite people say at bedtime."

Her coat-cover slipped off as she tried to find a comfortable position, and his arm reached out and pulled it on. "Thank you, but you may remove your hand, now," she hissed when he left it on her shoulder.

"Just making sure you are warm, my dear, nothing else."

"I am perfectly warm, thank you. Now, may we go to sleep?"

"I am not stopping you. It is you who keeps talking."

Too conscious of his closeness, she felt more awake than she had done during daylight hours, and try as she may, sleep eluded her.

Her eyes opened wide when he whispered, "Just relax, my darling. You will never drop off otherwise."

Moving further away from him, she retorted, "I was perfectly relaxed, thank you, until you woke me."

"Oh, yes? Then, pray tell me why you were tossing and turning like a dervish?" His breath felt hot on her face as he spoke.

"And stop teasing me with your endearments. I am not your darling."

She gave up and sat upright, "And am never likely to be, so just stop."

He sat as well, mumbling, "More's the pity."

"I expect you have a wife and a horde of children at home, so why are you lingering around in this forest with me?"

"Ah, my dear, that is where you are wrong."

"Just one or two children, then?"

"Not one."

"Just a wife, then?"

"No, not even one of those."

"What about a fiancée to whom you have pledged your troth, and whom you have vowed to love for ever and a day? I do not believe you have reached such an advanced age without being betrothed."

He laughed, a deep, sensuous laugh which ran a thrill through her body. "And what age do you suspect I have reached, young lady?"

Finger on chin, she considered for a moment. "Well, at least thirty, if not more. You do not have any grey hairs, but that does not signify anything. My mama told me she started going grey before her thirtieth birthday. You are not bald, but again, that need not tell your age, for Papa has been so, or rather was..." Her voice tailed off. What was she doing lying here with this man when her Mama needed her?

She turned over and yanked the coat and dress that were her covers and snuggled under them. "Now, please leave me alone and let me sleep."

In the morning, no matter how ill Sybil appeared, she would leave at first light. Her mother could not be forced out of her house. Money was needed to keep the roof over the family's head, and she would provide that money by marrying Lord Hairy Head.

Sleep came eventually, in fits and starts, having been disturbed by her itchy legs more than once.

When she awoke at the first rays of sunshine, Luke had disappeared. "Good," she mumbled, "I shall not have to tell him my plans." She shook her maid. "Sybil, are you awake? How do you feel this morning?"

The maid sat up. "Hungry."

"Oh, thank God. You must have come through the fever. But I am sorry, for we have no food left. We only had some beech nuts and blackberries." Stretching her back, she looked around, then bent down and whispered, "I am determined to leave today. Do you think you are strong enough to accompany me? I could go and fetch you some berries while you decide."

The maid stood up but wobbled and clung onto Florence's shoulder. "Oh, ma'am, I am not sure. How long have we been here?"

"This is the third day."

"Oh, my goodness. Your mama must be going out of her mind with worry. Have you not been able to send word to her or your aunt?"

She shook her head. "If only. Perhaps I should have caught one of those pigeons up there in the trees and tied a message to its leg and told it where to go." Regretting her facetiousness, she bit her lip. There was no need to take her frustrations out on the poorly maid.

"I am desperate for a…" she lowered her voice, "…a... Do you think you could help me to the bushes?"

"Of course. His lordship seems to have vanished, so we do not need to hide too well."

"But, he might come back. I could not bear it if he saw me."

As she helped Sybil, she glanced all around. Where had he gone? Had he deserted them? Left them to rot in the forest, while he went home to his fiancée?

He had not denied having one. But why had he kissed her, if he had? Her mama had warned her that men could be fickle creatures, and would not stay faithful, if an occasion arose. Had her papa been unfaithful? Surely not? She could not believe he would have cheated on her mama. She could have had any man she wanted, but chose him. He had been very handsome in his youth, in fact as he had grown older, as well. Her friends had often envied her, because he had been so good-looking, especially when he had grown that handlebar moustache that he used to grease. "I am keeping up with those in vogue," she remembered him telling her once, when she had asked him why he had grown it. "Do you not like it?"

"Well, Papa, if you like it, and you want to keep up with the fashion, who am I to say otherwise?"

Actually, he had been a vain man, always checking his face in a mirror as he passed one. But what harm was there in that? 'If you have it, flaunt it', she had once heard someone remark.

Their toiletries finished, she asked Sybil once again, "Do you want to come with me, or wait here until either his majesty returns or I send someone to you? That is, providing I can find my way to civilisation, of course."

"I think I will come with you, ma'am. I do not fancy staying here on my own. What if 'his majesty', as you call him, does not return, and you cannot give precise instructions as to where I am. I could die here, all alone, starving to death."

"Very well, then." She wrapped a coat around Sybil's shoulders and put on her own, for the air had a decided chill, and they set off in the opposite direction to the one she had taken the day before. It made for a very slow journey, with Sybil having to stop every few minutes to take a breath.

Chapter 5

Florence awoke, her back wet with sweat. Heavy breathing came from close by, and relief flooded through her when she realised it came from her sister's bed. She lay back, remembering being rescued by a yokel in a horse and cart. She and Sybil had stumbled onto a farm track, and the man had come along as they had been deciding which way to go, and taken them to his house. There he had given them a hot drink with bread and cheese, apologizing profusely that he had not had anything more substantial to offer them. Sybil had only nibbled at the crust like a squirrel, but Florence had wolfed it down, regretting it later when she had been doubled over with indigestion.

Poor, wretched Sybil. Mama had called for the doctor straightaway and she had been put to bed. He had wanted to examine Florence as well, but she had told him he had no need. Then her mother had noticed the bites on her leg. He had advised poultices, so she lay with her leg bound, having been warned to keep the bandages on for at least two days, and confined to her bed for at least that length of time.

But she needed to be out and about, to tell Lord Head she would accept his proposal, if he still wanted to marry her.

Sybil had been warned, on pain of dismissal, not to tell anyone about Luke Lancaster, to say they had been on their own in the forest. If word leaked out that she had been in the company of a man, her suitor would not entertain the idea of marrying her.

Those enigmatic blue eyes, though, and those full lips would stay in her memory for ever. She wondered if he had returned to the glade, and if so, what his reaction would have been.

"Forget him," she muttered, making Eliza stir.

"Are you well, my darling sister?" Eliza sat up. Florence could just make out her silhouette in the first light of dawn peeping through a chink in the brocade curtains. "Would you like anything? A drink, or something to eat?" She pushed back her covers and climbed into Florence's bed.

Moving over to make space for her, she replied, "No, I do not need anything, now I have you."

They hugged for a long time, silently, and then Eliza pulled away. "Was it truly awful, out there with the savage beasts, with just Sybil for company?"

Smiling, she replied, "No, we did not see any savage beasts." *Except Luke Lancaster.*

"But what did you do all day? You said you only had berries and chestnuts to eat. And how come you were not soaked to the skin when it rained yesterday?"

"Sweetheart, I do not wish to talk about it. It is too raw in my memory."

And I shall only give myself away and tell her about him. But I must not. She cannot keep a secret, so I must be strong. "Tell me what has happened here. Have I missed any gossip?" Not really interested in the affairs of her friends and neighbours, too absorbed in her own thoughts, she just wanted to change the subject, and gossip was her sister's favourite subject.

"Well, Agatha Brownley ran off to Gretna Green, so they say, eloped to marry some penniless pauper. Her father hared after them when he found out, but arrived too late."

"Agatha Brownley, who's she?" Florence yawned, not really concentrating on the shenanigans of some woman she could not remember. "Do I know her?"

"Of course you do, she is the step sister of the brother of…"

Florence stopped listening. She could not care less who the woman was related to.

"Do you not remember now?"

"I am sorry, dearest, but would you mind awfully if I went to sleep?" She yawned again. "I am so tired."

"Of course, my beloved." Eliza jumped out and returned to her own bed.

"Thank you, I shall speak to you later."

Turning to the wall, she closed her eyes, but a certain gentleman's face kept appearing. *Go away.*

She thought she had voiced her thoughts silently, but her sister replied in a sulky voice, "Would you like me to leave the room?"

"No, no, I did not mean you." She could not tell her to whom she had been shouting. Why could she not eradicate his face from her mind? He had abducted her and Sybil, committed one of the most heinous crimes in the land. If they caught him—which, of course they would not do because she would never tell anybody—but if they did, he would probably hang. She stuffed her fist into her mouth to muffle any sound.

"Are you sure you do not want anything, Flo? You keep moaning."

Pulling her covers over her head, she replied, "Please, just go back to sleep."

If only she could do so. If only she could forget, once and for all, the memory of his kisses, how alive she had felt at his touch. Nothing would ever compare to that, she knew for certain, but she had to continue with her life and marry Lord Hairy Head. Taking in a deep breath, she resolved to make him a good wife and forget all about Luke Lancaster. Or, maybe when Lord Hairy kissed her, she could imagine it to be him. Would her husband know she lusted after another? A wife should not have feelings for another man. But what if those feelings never went away? What if they stayed with her for the rest of her life, no matter how hard she tried?

Fists clenched, she curled into a ball, as she had done beside him the night before. *You will go away, you will.* With one hand she beat her breast, and with the other, she touched the area over her heart. How fast it beat. She would have to find some way of getting it to beat as hard as that whenever Lord Head came near. She had no idea how. The man still repulsed her, but she would have to, if her mother were to be saved from ruin.

She pushed back the covers, knowing she would not drop to sleep. Eliza had clearly done so, though. Little snoring sounds erupted from her mouth, rather like those made by the horse she had left behind in the forest. *Oh, dear. I hope Luke went back and took it to safety. I should hate to be the perpetrator of its demise.*

She gripped the bandages to prevent them from falling, crept over to the other side of the room and pulled on her dressing gown. The maids should be up, so she would go downstairs and have a cup of tea.

The look of surprise on Lilian's face, when she answered the bell in the drawing room, brought a faint smile to her own. She evidently had not been sacked, but could she be 'up the duff', as Eliza had speculated? "Tea, please," she ordered, sitting in one of the armchairs, pulling her dressing gown around her.

"But, ma'am, I thought you were confined to your bed. Pray, return and I shall bring you a tray."

"I am here now, so I may as well stay. It is rather chilly, though. Do you think the fire could be lit? Oh, and a blanket would be lovely."

114

"Yes, certainly, ma'am." The maid began to withdraw, but Florence called her back.

"Please could you draw the curtains before you go?"

Having done that, she bowed out, making clucking noises with her tongue, clearly put out of her usual early morning routine.

Head back against the chair, Florence surveyed the familiar room, with the faded blue-striped curtains and dingy wallpaper of blue and gold-patterned intertwined leaves. It had not been so drab before, had it? She tried to remember when it had last been decorated. Not in her memory, at any rate. And it would definitely not be done so now, not until she could marry and bring in some money.

A shudder ran through her. What had seemed like a perfect solution in the depths of the woods, now, in the clear light of day, gave her a sick feeling in the depths of her stomach. "But you must, for Mama," she uttered.

Lilian returned with a tray. "Please forgive me for taking so long, ma'am. The kettle had not even boiled, it is so early." She set it down on a side table. "Would you like me to pour it for you?"

"No, no, thank you. My arms are working perfectly well. So are my legs, for that matter. I do not know why they want me to loiter in my bed. I see no point in it whatsoever."

"Well, ma'am, these things can creep up on you without you realising it. If the doctor advises rest, then you should heed him." She stood twiddling her apron. "My aunt, she suffered a similar fate, and seemed fine when she returned home, and three days later, they found her dead in her bed. You really should take notice, ma'am."

"Your aunt was...?" She had been about to say, 'kidnapped', but closed her mouth in time. Blowing out her breath, she continued. "Well, I feel absolutely fine, so they will not find me dead, I assure you. Pray do not let me keep you from your chores."

"Yes, ma'am. Sorry if my words disturbed you. I did not mean them to do so."

"Yes, yes, yes." She waved her away. "Do not give it another thought. I am not at all disturbed, as you can see."

She held out her arms, as if that might put the maid's mind at rest. She left, clucking once more.

Florence poured out her tea, the chink of the tea strainer against the china cup calming her nerves. Maybe it was the normality of the action, after the turmoil of the last three days. Saying she was not disturbed had been a whopping big lie. She had never felt so troubled in her whole life. But she had to manage it, deal with it, cope.

Should she tell Eliza? They had always shared their innermost thoughts and feelings.

A confidante would be so helpful. Her sister might find a solution that she had not thought of, a different way out that would not involve Lord Hairy... *Stop calling him that. You have to look him in the eye. How will you do that without thinking of the silly name?*

But there were no other suitors banging on the door, asking for her hand. Well, except Harry Edwards. He had wanted to marry her the previous year but, although he was very sweet, he had no money. Her father had absolutely forbidden it. Too young, anyway.

He would have been better matched with Eliza, but she had had no interest in him. She did not go for 'sweet' young men. Her favours were more likely to be bestowed on blaggards and ruffians. Rather like Luke Lancaster, in fact. Ha! What an irony. Would her sister have given in to the kidnapper's advances? *Well, you almost did. If he had not pulled away, anything could have happened.*

The parlour maid came in and lit the fire, apologising for not having done so earlier, and removed the tea tray. The effect of the fire soon reached her, but she wrapped the blanket around her legs and sat back once again, eyes closed, trying to shut out his image.

Awaking with a start, frightened that the pouncing lion in her dream was a reality, she heard her mother's voice in the hall. Should she call out? She would rather stay in the quiet. Her mother could disturb a crowd of chattering starlings with her voice, but she might as well face her. "I am in here, Mama."

The door opened with a bang. "Oh, my darling girl, what are you doing up at this unearthly hour? I crept into your bedroom to check you were all right and your bed was empty. I thought for a moment you had vanished again."

"Oh, Mama." She reached her face up for a kiss. "I am so sorry. It did not occur to me that you would do so. I am fine, as you see."

"But the doctor said…"

"Beggar the doctor."

"Florence! He knows what is best for his patients. You should listen to him."

Her arms in the air, she retorted, "Why does everybody have to lecture me? Surely I know what is best for me?" At her mother's downcast face, she relented. "But take no notice. I am in sore dudgeon. It's just that… Oh, I do not know. If it will please you, I shall return to my bed after I have eaten. Breakfast would be nice."

"Of course, my dear, I shall have a tray brought in."

About to protest that she would rather go to the breakfast room, she thought better of it. It would be best to humour her mother, in case she did not pluck up enough courage to accept Lord Head.

Her mother pulled the bell and gave the maid the order.

"Would you like me to partake of mine in here with you? I would not mind," she suggested after the maid had gone out. "I could call her back and ask for two servings."

"No, Mama, I know you like to do things in the proper way. I shall be fine, honestly. You go and sit comfortably at the table."

"Very well, my dear, if you are certain."

She reached out and gave her a hug. "Very certain."

A moment later, Eliza popped her head around the door. "Mama told me you wanted to eat alone. Is that true?"

"Well, I did not want to upset her order of etiquette, that was all. You know how she dislikes being disrupted."

"So, would you like me to join you?"

"No, my dear, you go and join Mama. I am sure she will want to regale you with my foolhardiness at leaving my bed."

Her sister raised her eyes to the ceiling. "I am sure she will. I shall put in a good word for you, if you like. That is, if I do not agree with her." She quickly closed the door when Florence picked up a cushion and aimed it at her.

The delicious smell of bacon wafted towards her as the maid brought it in. "You must be ravenous, ma'am," she said, putting it beside her.

"I am. I have not eaten properly for three days. I was too tired last night, and too mythered. I shall enjoy this. Thank you."

"Well, do not scoff it down, ma'am. It is not good when you have had an empty stomach for so long."

119

"Thank you, Lilian. I shall make sure I do not 'scoff' it, whatever that means. I thought it meant to make a mockery."

"I'm sorry, ma'am, it's an expression my pa used to use to us children when we ate too quickly. Would you like me to cut the bacon?"

"No!" she shouted. "I am not an invalid."

The maid's face fell and she backed out, bowing, without saying anything further.

I should not have bawled at her like that, she rued as she chewed the tasty food. She intended to savour every bite but, after a few mouthfuls, she put down her knife and fork, unable to eat any more, however appetising the sausages and mushrooms looked. "I hope she does not hand in her notice," she muttered, more wretched than ever. "She will never have been spoken to so severely." The Fisher household was renowned for its affability. Everyone spoke of it, how the servants were the happiest and therefore, the most loyal. People queued up to be employed there. Well, if she did not marry Lord Head, they would all have to be dismissed. Her mother could not afford to keep them.

She dabbed her mouth with her napkin. *Just get on with it. If it has to be done, it has to be done. Maybe I should go and see him forthwith, before I drop my bottle, or whatever the saying is that Frederick uses.*

The blanket fell off so, instead of yanking it back, she stood, but her head spun. She plonked down.

"Oo, what happened there?" Maybe the events of the past few days had affected her more than she had realised.

Unused to being ill, she stood up again. The same thing happened. *This is not like you, Flossie,* she could hear her grandfather say. But the nickname brought back the memories she had been insistent she should forget. "Forget him, for goodness sake," she screamed, bringing her sister running in.

"What is it, Flo? Are you in pain?"

"Not physically, no, apart from an ache in my foot."

Eliza knelt down and took her hands. "This affair has bothered you more than you are making out, has it not? Did something happen that you have not told me?"

Should she confide in her? It would make her situation so much easier but, as she knew, Eliza had never been one to keep a secret. But before she knew what she was doing, the whole story cam out.

Eliza stood up and ran over to close the door. "You cannot let Mama know about this. Your reputation will be in tatters."

"I know that, sister, dear. Why do you think I have been reluctant to say anything?"

"And you actually spent the night lying beside him? Oo, how did it feel? Do tell me. Did he…?"

"Of course, he did not. I am still intact, but…"

"But you wanted him to? Is that what you are saying? Oo, my prim and proper sister. Not so, after all. What a turn up for the books."

"Look, Lizzie, if you are going to be like this, I shall wish I had never said anything."

"Shh, I hear Mama outside." Standing with her hands in front of her, like a child being chastised, Eliza turned towards the door.

It opened and their mother entered. She looked at the tray that still held the now-congealed food. "You did not eat very much. Let me remove it."

"No, Mama, call the maid. You should not be doing such a thing." Eliza pulled the cord.

"Florence was…" Florence flashed her eyes at her, warning her not to divulge what she had just learned. "She should be in bed, should she not, Mama? I shall help her upstairs."

She let herself be led out of the room, her mother fussing around her like a hen. "Yes, she should. You are quite right. Go with your sister, my dear. I shall come up in a little while and see if you need anything after I have sorted out tonight's menu with the cook. I had thought to invite Lord Head and several others to dinner, but if you would prefer it, perhaps it would be better to have just the three of us. Frederick is away for a few days, visiting his friend in the country."

Her resolve vanished. "That would be splendid, Mama, thank you. I do not feel up to visitors just yet." Especially him, she might have added.

"Good, good that is settled then. Oh, by the way, I received a reply from your aunt this morning. She is so relieved you are safe and sound. My poor sister must have been at her wit's end. She says you may visit another time."

"Yes, that would be lovely. Tell her when you write back, that I am so sorry to have put her to so much worry." She kissed her and made her way towards the stairs, feeling very groggy indeed. Perhaps the beech nuts had been poisonous. Her whole system felt wrong. Oh, well, if she died, it would take away the problem of whether to marry or not. She would not have to worry about anything ever again.

Eliza helped her into bed, and sat beside her on the easy chair, her face eager for more information, but Florence did not feel in the mood. "Pray, leave me now, sister. I feel so weary. I think I will have a nap."

"If you wish." Eliza stood up, disappointed. "But I want to hear more when you have rested. You cannot leave me in suspense."

"Just make sure you do not tell anyone, and I mean, anyone at all. Do you promise? I must have your word, if I am to rest properly."

Eliza put her hand on her breast. "Cross my heart and hope to die. I promise I will not divulge your secret to anyone."

"I have warned Sybil as well. Would you find out how she is, please? I meant to ask Lilian earlier, but it slipped my memory."

"I will. I think I shall go and visit my good friend, Elizabeth, first, but I shall enquire when I return."

"She is also called Lizzie, isn't she? It can become quite confusing at times."

Eliza laughed. "Yes, it can." She bent and gave Florence a peck on her forehead. "Anyway, farewell. Sweet dreams."

"Do not forget your promise."

"I will not."

After rummaging in her wardrobe for her favourite shawl, Eliza went out with a wave, leaving Florence trying to sleep, but her mind would not switch off. 'Sweet dreams.' That was what he had said to her. Would she be forever thinking of him when someone spoke a word he had used?

Chapter 6

Eliza took off her bonnet and threw it on a chair. "Lizzie has invited us to her soirée tomorrow evening. Do you feel up to going, Flo?"

Florence had been sitting at the window of the drawing room, trying to concentrate on her book, but watching the white clouds outside instead, making the shapes into objects. A dragon, here, a peacock there, and a deer. "Well, I suppose it has been four days since my return. I had better make a start somewhere."

"And her soirées are so discreet. There will only be about a dozen people there." Eliza pulled the bell. "Have you had tea yet?"

"No, I do not think I have."

"You do not think?" mocked her sister "You really are not much better, are you?"

The maid came in.

"Tea, please, Lilian, and cake." After the maid had bowed out, Eliza asked, "Where is Mama? I suppose she will want to come?"

"Um…she said she was…um…I really do not remember. She wore her best hat, the one with the pink roses, and the dress she had last year, even though she deemed it to be old-fashioned, and seemed in a tizzy."

"Maybe her friend, that French lady, Madame Orgé, summoned her. She has become very intimate with her just lately. I do not like it."

Florence laughed. "*You* do not like it. You are sounding more like her every day. Do you recall that time she forbade you going for a drive with that fellow, Monsieur Arti-something or other? He was French, was he not?"

"That is not the reason I do not like her seeing so much of Madame. It has nothing to do with her nationality. I just distrust the woman."

"Well, it is pleasant to see her smiling for a change, and if Madame Orgé can put a smile on her face, then I am all for it."

The tea was brought in, stopping the conversation. Eliza bit into the cake. "Oh, I thought it was going to be coconut, but it is not, it is plain sponge."

"You should have specified which you wanted, dear sister, then you would have no cause for complaint." She took a nibble. It tasted like cardboard, so she put it down.

"See, you do not like it, either. You tried not to pull a face, but I was watching. Shall I ask for something else?"

Florence pushed her plate away. "No, I did not really want anything in the first place."

Eliza sat on the arm of her chair, stroking her hair. "You are still out of sorts, are you not? That Luke

Lancaster has really knocked the wind out of your sails."

"But I must not let him." Florence patted her sister's hand, and stretched her arms above her head. "Lizzie's soirée is just what I need to have me back on my feet. A nice little get-together with just a few intimate friends. Have you any idea who else will be there?"

"Well, there is one piece of news you might be interested in."

"Go on, tell me."

"Do you remember that handsome man I fancied with the tiny mysterious scar on his chin—that friend of Lord Hairy's?"

"Um…yes. What about him?"

"I have just seen him driving through the park."

"So?"

Eliza's bottom lip jutted out. "He had a very pretty lady with him. Much older than him, though."

"Maybe it was his mother?"

Eliza clapped her hands. "Ha-ha, I had not thought of that."

"And, anyway, he is not going to stay celibate, just in case you are introduced to him, is he?"

"He does not even know I exist. How can I make myself known to him?"

"Be careful, Lizzie. He could be the wildest rake in the country. You do not know anything about his character."

"And never will, if left to you. Oh, I almost forgot. Your Lord has gone to the country for a few days, so you can relax until he returns."

"Lizzie!" She jumped up and poked her sister in the chest. "How could you have forgotten such an important piece of news? You cannot care for me a jot, if you cannot remember to tell me that as soon as you come in."

"I am sorry." Eliza picked up her bonnet and walked towards the door. "I had intended doing so, but I had still been thinking about Mister Scarface."

She looked so downcast, Florence ran across to her and gave her a hug. "No, my dearest, I am the one to be sorry. I should not have shouted at you. Pray, forgive me?" She lifted Eliza's chin and waited for her to smile.

"Of course, I do. How could I stay cross with you, my dearest, darling sister? The best big sister in the whole world."

"Do not overdo the praise." The door opened and her youngest sister came in. "Ah, here is Felicity. Are you not having your lessons, my dear?"

The girl plonked down on one of the beige sofas. "No, they've finished for today."

She sprawled most unladylike, arms held out and legs spread apart.

Florence looked at the clock on the mantelpiece. "Good gracious, is it that time? I have done nothing at all, and it is four o'clock already. Where does time go?

And please sit more demurely, my darling. You look most undignified."

"Tempus fugit." Felicity sat up and puffed out her chest, the pink material of her dress stretched and tight. "I learnt that this week."

"Ah," Eliza stroked her chin, "how well I recollect learning Latin. I hated it. All that conjugating. And what good is it to me, now? I can hardly go around spouting 'tempus this and tempus that' to my suitors, can I?"

"It might impress them that you have attempted to learn it, though," suggested Florence.

"Maybe I should attend your next lesson with you, Fliss, and brush up on it." She ruffled the child's hair.

Felicity knocked away her hand and jumped up. "Lizzie Locket. If you call me Fliss, I shall call you Lizzie Locket."

She stuck out her tongue, dancing around the room, singing, "Lizzie Locket, Lizzie Locket."

Eliza stalked towards the door. "I care not what you name me. In fact, I quite like it, so there." She wrinkled her nose at her little sister.

Florence put her hand to her temple. "Children, children, must you bicker so? My head is spinning with your squabbles."

"Sorry, Florence," they both said together.

"Would you like us to leave?" asked Eliza, looking at her solicitously.

"No, ignore me. You were only having a little banter."

She took a deep breath. "Tomorrow is Saturday, so no lessons. Shall we all take a ride in the park? Oh, we do not have a carriage any more, do we? And I have never enquired after Henry. I have been so wrapped up in my own petty concerns, I have not looked into how he fared. Did he return home safely?"

"Eventually, yes, so I am told," replied Eliza. "And Mama has borrowed a carriage from a friend of a friend. We could not manage without one, so she asked around."

Florence pulled a face. "Poor Mama. The trouble I have put her to. She hates asking for favours. Papa was always the one to do any negotiating, was he not? I hope it comes with horses. One of them ran off, but the other, I fear, is still in the middle of the forest."

"No, it isn't," piped up Felicity. "A man brought it back. Did nobody tell you?"

Florence jumped up. "What sort of a man?"

Felicity puffed out her cheeks, "Er..."

"Who told you? When was this?" Florence put her hands behind her back to prevent her from shaking the child.

"Days ago. I heard the servants talking about it. He was rather scruffy, so they say, with wild hair sticking up all over the place and his trousers covered in dirt."

With wide eyes, Florence looked at Eliza and then turned to her younger sister. "Um, do you not have a book to read, dearest child, or a game to play?"

"No. Why are you trying to be rid of me?"

"I would not do that. I just thought you would rather do something child-like, that is all."

Hands on hips, Felicity glared at her. "I'm not a baby, Florence."

Florence patted her head, smoothing down some of her ringlets that had come astray. "No, no I am not insinuating that you are."

Eliza took her hand. "Come, my darling, Fliss." She raised her eyebrows to see if the girl would react, but she did not. "You have not started that scrap book yet, have you? Where did those magazines go? I could cut out some pictures for you to stick in it."

Brows drawn together, Felicity looked with suspicion from one to the other. "Do you know that man, then?"

"Which man?" they both asked in unison.

"Well, you seem to have gone all peculiar since I mentioned the man who brought back the horse."

"No, you are imagining things." Eliza shooed her out of the door. "Come on, let's make this scrap book to show Mama on her return."

Left alone, Florence slumped onto the sofa. How did he know where she lived? Why had he not tried to contact her? Of course, she would not admit him, but that was not the point. What if he told all his friends about the escapade? Would he be laughing at her behind her back, sniggering behind his hand, and uttering indecent suggestions?

But maybe, he did not reside in or near Ambleside. Maybe he lived miles away, and so his friends would not have heard of her, and would be in no way likely to come across her. She racked her brain to try to recollect what he had actually told her about himself. Not a lot, she concluded. He had always changed the subject whenever she had asked about him.

The following evening, determined to forget about Luke Lancaster, she attended the soirée with Eliza, wearing her best paisley dress, and her favourite emerald and diamond necklace and long, dangly earrings.

Her sister, similarly attired, but the paisley in a darker shade, and her jewellery consisting of an amber necklet and stud earrings, looked magnificent. She wished she could look as confident.

They entered the room, occupied by at least twenty people, and she pulled her sister's sleeve. "I thought you said there would not be many here. The room is packed."

Eliza stood on tiptoe, looking around as if searching for someone in particular. "It does not matter, Florence. I do not see him."

"Who? Surely you are not looking for…"

132

"Who, dear sister? You cannot think I mean your beau from the forest?"

"Do not call him that. He is no more a beau than Rip Van Winkle. And please, I beg you, do not refer to him again."

Eliza slumped. "No, he is not here. I did not think he would be, but I had hoped."

"Do you refer to Mister Scarface? Is that not him over there, talking with that beauty in the pink flouncy frock that might have been the height of fashion ten years ago, but is definitely old hat now?"

"Florence Fisher, it is not like you to denigrate a fellow female. I do not think I have ever heard you do so before. You are usually so mild-mannered. It is I who has the acid tongue." Eliza walked further into the room, towards the man in question. "Come, shall we introduce ourselves?"

Florence pulled her back. "No, we shall not. If Mama had come, we could have asked her to do so, but without a chaperone, we must stay low. Please, do not make a show of yourself by being indiscreet."

"Very well, if you must, spoilsport. Look, there is Elizabeth, let us go and talk to her. That should be safe, should it not?"

Her eyes raised indulgently at her sister, she followed, stepping sideways as they made their way through the crush of people.

Many of the guests were unknown to her, but she caught her breath when she spotted the broad back of a tall man with fair hair. Oh, no! She turned back towards the Lizzies, but they were prattling on, heedless of her. Her whole body shaking from head to foot, she made her way to the balcony before he might notice her. Then the man turned. It was not him. In fact, from the front he did not resemble him at all. His long, wide nose and bushy eyebrows were not at all like the classic roman god of her dreams. Her breath let out in puffs, she continued towards the balcony in search of air, eager to escape from the noise and laughter of the party.

The light from behind her lit her steps to the lawn. Why had she come? Why could she not hide herself away from the world? She had known the damned man for three days. How could such a short acquaintance have affected her so? *Pull yourself together, woman. Just forget him. Surely that's possible?*

If only they could return home. But they had only just arrived. She could not spoil her sister's enjoyment by leaving so early.

Keeping to the path, she stopped at the sound of clandestine voices. Better not disturb the lovers, whoever they were—probably an illicit relationship, if they were canoodling in the cold.

With a shiver, she turned and went inside. Rubbing her cold arms, she looked for her sister. Surrounded by her friends, she seemed to be having a good night, laughing and joking, with not a care in the world. She, herself, had been just the same, only the week before.

134

How could things have changed so suddenly? Her feelings needed controlling. She would never see him again, and as soon as Lord Head returned from the country, she would marry him, and live a—maybe not as happy a life as she might want—but a respectable one, with lots of children running around, pulling at her apron strings, and giggling in the way happy children did. As she made for the group around Eliza, she pictured the children with eyes of cobalt blue, and with little dimples in their chins.

"Does Lord Head have a dimple?" she asked the closest lady, one of Eliza's special friends, who looked at her in astonishment.

"I beg your pardon?" asked the lady.

"Nothing, I am sorry. I do not know why I asked that." Of course she would not know. Nobody would. His beard covered his cheeks.

"Ah, Florence," called one of the others. "Do tell us about your escapade. How did you manage with just your maid? And her injured, with a fever, too, so I hear?"

Florence glanced at Eliza, but she had struck up a conversation with someone else. Clearly, she had not told them the truth, thank goodness.

"I do not recall much about the 'escapade'. It all seems like a blur," she fibbed, hoping her red cheeks did not betray her, for she was unused to lying. She could not enlighten them, though.

"What a pity."

The young lady had so much rouge on her cheeks she looked like one of Felicity's dolls. Florence could not take her eyes from it. Her fingers itched to wipe it off.

"Yes, I agree," chimed one of the others. "I only came tonight because I heard you were attending, and I so wanted to hear all about it."

"Then, ladies, I fear you will all be disappointed. It is all too raw. I have never been so afraid in my life. I can tell you that."

"Did you have to beat off wild animals?" asked another lady, joining them.

"She will not divulge anything," the first lady told her. "I think there must have been a man somewhere in the equation. Do you not think so? Is that why she will say nothing?"

Florence held her breath, for fear they would hear her gasp. "I need some fresh air," she managed to splutter a moment later. "I do not feel well. In fact, I feel very unwell."

"Probably the effects of being in the outdoors for so long," she heard someone say.

"It cannot be good for you, all that fresh air. It must have been a shock to her system," said another.

Not the kind of shock you mean. She raced to the door, pushing past ladies in their crinoline dresses, and men smoking cigars, careless that she might be the perpetrator of ash cascading onto the ladies' naked bosoms.

Outside, she wondered if Eliza had inadvertently hinted something. Should she ask her sister outright? But that would seem as if she did not trust her. Well, if the truth were to be known she did not. She would not come right out and say anything, but her nature was such that she loved to tittle-tattle. She might not have even realised she had inferred anything.

After staying outside as long as would not seem improper, she returned to the fray.

"Stop moping about," hissed Eliza, an hour later. "Someone will be suspicious, for it is most unlike you to be so quiet." She pulled her hand. "Come on, there is a game of cards in the side room. I love cards, and so do you, do you not?"

"Usually, but I do not feel like playing tonight. I would only lose, from not paying sufficient attention to my partner."

"Oh, bumblebees. Give it a try. You never know, with your luck, you will win, anyway."

They played for an hour or so, and then she yawned, trying vainly to hide it behind her fan. "I am so sorry."

"Do not apologise, my dear," replied the dealer. "You must still be very weak after your mishap." Florence gaped at her. Did everybody know? She must have been the main source of gossip for the last few days if even this lady, a visitor, had heard about her.

"Yes, I am. Thank you for recognising." She looked around for a clock. Could she escape without appearing rude?

Eliza turned to her with a pleading shake of her head. "Not yet," she mouthed. "Just another half an hour, sister, please," she said aloud. "I am on a winning streak. I do not have them very often."

"Very well. I think I might manage half an hour. It is too smoky in here, though. I shall take another walk outside."

Eliza's shriek of joy echoed around the room, proving she had won once more.

Florence made her getaway, collecting her shawl from the cloakroom, before stepping outside once more.

A full moon greeted her, and the sound of an owl, hooting in the trees at the bottom of the garden, eerie in the still night. An answering cry came from above her head. She looked up, rewarded as a white barn owl flew by her, not ten yards away, illuminated by the light streaming from the windows of the house.

Her peace was shattered when a rough hand grabbed her around the waist and pulled her behind some bushes where he gripped her head and kissed her passionately.

She tried to kick, not knowing who her assailant could be, but she could not move, for his arms held her in a vice-like grip. A certain scent gave her an inclination, though. Eventually, she managed to break free by twisting her head.

Her mouth opened to scream for help, but he covered it with his hand. "Do not make a sound."

She could not have done so, if she had wanted. Bereft of breath, she slumped into Luke Lancaster's arms.

Above his hand she could make out his eyes, wide and threatening. But she did not feel scared. Not in the least. She felt alive.

"You left without saying farewell," he whispered in her ear.

Recovering from the initial shock, she pulled free. "How did you find me?"

He refused to let her go, though, and yanked her back into his embrace. "Easy. Once I knew your brother's identity, I knew who you were."

"What has my brother to do with anything? He is not even here."

"I know. Just you and your sister came."

She stepped back, and this time he allowed her to do so. "Have you been watching me?"

His right eyebrow rose. "I had to make sure you were unhurt."

"Pah, a likely story. That would have been obvious as soon as you saw me."

"Anyway, you had better return to your hosts, before they come searching for you." He blew her a kiss, jumped over a low wall, and disappeared into the darkness, leaving her more bewildered than before.

Eliza's voice carried across the lawn. "Florence, are you out there?"

"Yes, dear, I am coming." She ran towards her.

"You look rather dishevelled, sister dear. Have you had an assignation with a gentleman out there?"

She could not tell her. "I…um, I did not see a bush until I walked into it." *Or, rather, was pulled behind it.* "Are you ready to go now?"

Eliza pulled up her kid gloves. "Yes. You must have put the kibosh on my luck, for I lost every game once you had gone."

"Do you have to use such slang words?"

"Yes, but I just need to say goodbye to Lizzie." Eliza stalked off.

Florence followed, gave one last look around to make sure he had well and truly left, and went inside.

Would everyone know she had been kissed so well? Her sister must have noticed something, even outside, in the dim light. She put her finger to her lips. Did they look swollen? It had not been a tender kiss. Quite the opposite. She could taste blood on the inside of her bottom lip, and licked it away quickly. The flickering candles in the huge chandeliers gave plenty of light for people to notice.

Head down, she pushed her way to the opposite door, out into the hall without anyone accosting her, or asking her how she fared.

In the carriage, on their journey home, Eliza sat back. "I am so disappointed, Flo. I really thought I would win lots of money to help Mama out. Did you win anything?"

"I do not remember. I was not paying attention." She opened her bag and counted out the few coins in her purse. "No, it does not look like it."

Eliza reached forward and grabbed the coins. "If I had known you had this much money left, I would have borrowed it. You are so selfish, sister. I might have won a fortune with this amount."

She took them back. "But you might have lost it for me, which is more likely, if, as you say, your winning streak had come to an end."

"But it might have come back."

"We will never know, now, will we? So put your bottom lip away." Even in the faint light, Florence could see the lip stuck out even further. "Mardy breeches," she mocked.

"Lily-white angel."

Not in the mood for a slanging match with her sister, she did not retaliate further, and they continued the remainder of the journey in a sullen silence. Florence wondered if she had imagined the episode in the bushes. From the taste of her lip, she knew she had not. Why had he come? To check she had come to no harm, as he had told her? But he must have known she had not. In fact, he must have been watching her at her house, to have known she would be at the soirée. How else could he have been aware of it?

The next few days went by uneventfully, and Florence assumed life had returned to normal.

They attended more parties, and no stranger intervened, or came dashing out of the bushes. Luke Lancaster could be laid to rest. He had ensured she had come out of the escapade unscathed, and had returned to his home, wherever that may have been.

She made discreet enquiries to see if anybody knew anything about him. Not wanting to attract too much attention, she dare not give away many details, so could find out nothing about him.

Hearing that Lord Head had returned from his visit she determined to give him his answer. "No more dilly-dallying," she told Eliza as she rustled through her wardrobe in a bid to find the most appropriate dress.

"The blue one suits you best, but it may be too…might give him the wrong impression," her sister replied, holding it out in front of her.

"Yes, the neckline is rather low, but I could always insert something, but no, that would spoil the effect. I think I shall wear the green one. It fits me well, and is comfortable. I need to feel comfortable when I address him." She took a deep breath, not relishing the idea, but determined to go ahead with it.

"Oh, sis," Eliza looked into her eyes, "are you sure this is what you want?"

"I would not go that far, but it must be done. Where is that maid? Oh, I wish Sybil would recover. I cannot seem to hit it off with this one nearly as well. Lace my corset, would you, while we wait for her?"

Dressed to her satisfaction, she surveyed her appearance in the long mirror.

Eliza stood behind her. "You are rather pale. Here." She twizzled her around and pinched her cheeks.

"That's better. We do not want you going to your soon-to-be-husband looking like a ghost, now, do we?" She pinched them again. "Now, how about your hair? Would you like me to dress it for you?"

"Yes, please. This new maid, Mabel, cannot get the right effect, but are you sure? Are you not going out?"

"I can spare half an hour. Lizzie will wait. We are only going for a drive in the park." Eliza brushed Florence's curls and pinned them up in the way she liked best. "You know I would put her off, if you would like me to accompany you to Lord Hairy Head's residence."

Florence covered her mouth to prevent herself giggling. "Oh, please do not call him that. I shall have such difficulty keeping a straight face when I speak to him. But, no, I would not want you to give up your entertainment just to come with me. You have fun while you can, before you, too, have to accept

143

some…" Her mood changed and she put her face in her hands.

"Oh, Flo-Flo, surely we can manage without you having to make such a sacrifice? It does not seem fair."

"Life is not fair at times, dear sister." She blew out her breath in a hiss. "But we have to make the most of it."

"There, how do you like that?"

She stood up. "That is wonderful. You know how to work a miracle. Maybe you should take up hairdressing as a profession. Then I would not have to marry. We could all live off your earnings."

"Ha! I can just see Mama's face if I suggested that. It would be an idea, though. Not as a hairdresser, of course, but something else. It could be something to look into; better than marrying someone I do not like. What else could I do?"

"I was jesting. I did not mean you to take it seriously. Now, how do I look?"

"Beautiful, as usual." Eliza reached forward. "Another pinch should do it. There, off you go to your destiny."

Florence gave her stockings one last tweak, patted down her dress, and put on her shoes, dreading the next hour or so. "Courage, that's what is needed. Bravery, nerve, pluck and all the other words that mean the same. Enjoy your drive in the park. Maybe you will meet some handsome man with even five thousand pounds a year, and save us," she said.

"Or maybe I shall see my Mister Scarface. I am told he is well off, but do not know to what extent. Lizzie tells me she saw him with yet a different lady the other day, so there is still hope."

"It means he is a philanderer if he is seen out with a different escort every day—one you should steer clear of," Florence remarked as they made their way downstairs.

"Oh, he would have to settle down if he started courting me," replied Eliza, her head so far in the air she almost tripped. "I would not stand for any philandering. At least Mister Hairy Head has not been seen with anybody else since he asked you to marry him."

"No, I do not think I would have any trouble on that score. Anyway, would anyone else fancy him, with that mole on his cheek?"

"Ugh! Oh, sorry, it is just that it gives me the shudders each time I see it. You will have to look past it when he kisses you."

"Hopefully, I shall not have to do that too often. He has not even tried to do so yet, and does not seem the sort to be very amorous."

"Not like your Luke Lancaster, you mean?"

They had reached the front door and Florence whipped round, glaring. "Shush. Do not let anyone hear you. And, anyway, he is not *my* Luke Lancaster.

He is nothing, nothing at all. So, do not refer to him again."

"As you wish, sister dear. I shall walk with you as far as Lizzie's house." Eliza pulled her shawl around her. "It is chillier than I had thought. I hope we do not catch cold."

"Maybe you should go back for your thick coat. It is very cold indeed. We do not want you coming down with a chill."

"I do not have time. I will be fine, do not worry." They hurried on their way and Eliza gave her a hug before disappearing down her friend's front drive.

Florence's steps faltered. The street she had reached, in a busier area of the town, milled with people and traffic. An open-topped carriage approached, the occupants looking the other way. She stopped. Him, for sure, laughing at the beautiful lady beside him. But no, as they drove past, she could see his features more clearly.

I thought you told Eliza he meant nothing to you, you silly goose, so why do you keep tormenting yourself? Snap out of it. You are going to see Lord Head. What is the point in thinking of someone else?

At his mansion, she hesitated. Could she go through with it?

Shoulders back, about to open the gate, she stopped when one of her friends came up, arm in arm with her new husband.

"Good day, Florence, how lovely to see you."

She bowed courteously, as did the couple.

"I heard about your terrible time in the forest. It must have been horrific. Have you met my husband?"

"Yes, good day, sir." *Please do not hinder me, or I might change my mind.*

This particular friend, though, was renowned for her tittle-tattle. She barely drew breath between sentences.

Five minutes later, Florence still stood holding the latch of the large iron gate. She had not needed to respond. Each time she opened her mouth to say something, to escape, her friend would start on a different subject.

"But I am delaying you." The friend patted her arm. "Were you about to go in there?" She pointed to the large house at the end of the drive.

"Well, I had…"

"You know, he—Lord Head, that is—is a very dear friend of my papa's. It was such a shame about his change in fortune, was it not?"

"I am sorry. What do you mean?"

"Had you not heard? He lost almost everything."

"No, no, I had not."

She let go of the gate. "I…um…" Turning away, she tugged at her bonnet as her friend's husband bowed to her.

"We must away, darling," he said to his wife. "We shall be late, otherwise."

"Of course, dearest. Well, farewell, Florence. It was pleasant to chat with you. You must come and visit soon." She waved as her husband yanked her arm and they hurried along the street, leaving Florence in another quandary. What would be the point in accepting a man whose fortunes had changed? Did that mean he had no money anymore? Or just that he did not have as much as before?

In any case, her resolve had vanished. With a quick look at the house, she turned and continued towards the town.

Examining the lace on a pretty blue dress in a shop window, she wondered why life could be so awkward at times. Just as she made one decision, someone put a spoke in the wheel and she found herself changing her mind again. Lace like that would look well on her dress. But could she afford it? Not if she was not going to marry Lord Head.

What would be the point in looking in shop windows if she could not buy anything? She wandered around the town for a while, not wanting to return home just yet to face her mother.

But she would not want you to marry him if he has no money.

Walking the long way around, she arrived home, or rather, was blown home. The wind had increased in strength, and black clouds had gathered overhead, threatening rain, so she rejoiced that she had made it before it fell. Eliza would not be so fortunate, though.

After taking off her outdoor wear, she went in search of her mother. Better get it over with.

Chapter 7

"So I could not do it, Mama."

"But I have heard nothing about these rumours concerning Lord Head. Are you sure it was he to whom your friend referred? Maybe that girl was just trying to put you off?"

"Suzanne, it was Suzanne, Mama, and she can usually be trusted. She said her father is great friends with him."

Her mother shook her head and sat down. "I still cannot believe it."

Florence sat on the arm of her chair and took her hand. "How can we find out for definite? Who amongst your friends is most likely to know?"

"I know not, my dear. We shall just have to pack up and leave. Find a little cottage in the country and hide away."

"Maybe I can find some other suitor to propose, or Eliza might do. Do not give up hope, yet, Mama."

Her mother sniffed and picked up her teacup. "Your sister is too young and flighty. I do not have any hope for her doing so yet." She sipped her tea with such a melancholy air that Florence felt guiltier than ever. She had known it would not be easy to tell her what she had found out, but had hoped her mother would understand.

"The maids will all have to go, except my personal maid, of course. You and your sister can easily manage without one, and we shall have to rally round and serve ourselves."

Florence opened her mouth to dispute her, but found herself forestalled. Her pitiful face upturned, her mother continued, "We cannot do without a butler, but the footmen could go. That would save a few pounds. Cook would have to stay but the rest of the kitchen staff… Maybe we could cope for a little while longer?"

"Shall we go through the household books? We could see where the most savings could be made."

Her hand up to her brow, her mother nodded. "Now?"

"Yes, why not? I do not have anything pressing, do you?"

"Well, I had thought of going to see my friend Madame Orgé. She is such a tonic. She raises my spirits no end."

"You could visit her this afternoon. Come on, let us find these savings."

"But you know how useless I am at bookkeeping."

"But I am not, and I shall go through it with you."

"Very well."

Having finally persuaded her mother, she pulled her along the corridor.

Half an hour later, she yanked at her hair in despair. "They have not been kept up to date. Whose responsibility is it to do so? I thought Frederick to be in charge?"

"Well, he is, I suppose, but he has been very busy."

She picked up a piece of paper. "What is this bill?"

Her mother grabbed it from her. "My new hat. I had to have a new one. The lace on one of my others is coming adrift."

"I thought we had agreed we were having no new clothes."

"Well, a hat is not really classed as clothes, is it?"

"And this?"

Her mother put on her glasses and peered at the receipt. "That is not mine. It must be something to do with Frederick."

"That brother of mine will be the ruin of us, not my decision to decline Lord Head. I despair. Does he not realise the seriousness of out situation? Where is he?"

"He has not yet returned, but do not be cross with him, my dear. He needs things we women do not. A man in his position…"

She slammed the box shut. "He will not have any position if he continues spending money we do not have."

"Do not go yet, dear." Her mother put her arm around her. "We have not sorted out where we might make savings. That was why we came."

She opened the box again. "Well, any decision we make will have to be adhered to, Mama. There is no use saying one thing and doing the opposite."

"I know, I know. It is just so difficult, when you have been brought up having whatever you want, whenever you want it. Surely, you understand that?"

"I do, Mama. I apologise if I sounded abrupt. One saving we could make would be to send Felicity to school. She would not need a governess, then."

Her mother gasped. "How can you suggest such a thing? Send my little girl to a smelly, disease-ridden school? Not on your life."

"Mother, they are perfectly clean places. She would be fine."

"No, no, no." Her mother picked up the pile of receipts and invoices. "There must be some other way. Not that."

Two hours later, Florence had still not convinced her, and no headway had been made. Everything she suggested was pooh-poohed as being a necessity. "I shall have to sell myself on the streets, then, if we cannot find any other way," she joked, smiling at her mother's aghast face.

"I know you are jesting, my dear, but please desist. My nerves will not stand it." She took out a handkerchief and dabbed her eyes. "I think I shall go for a lie-down. I am weary after all that paperwork."

Florence helped her out of the room. "Shall I confront Lord Head, and see if the rumours are true?"

"Oh, no, my dear. You must not do that. Just think how mortified he would be if they were."

"Well, what are we to do, then?"

As they entered the hall, the front door bell rang. "I wonder who that can be," sighed her mother, as the butler opened the door.

Florence stepped back in astonishment when the very man they had been discussing came through it. "Lord Head, I had not been expecting you."

"Bang goes my nap," whispered her mother into her ear. "Good day to you, sir," she called aloud. "Pray, enter." She ushered him into the drawing room. "Shall I ring for tea, or would you prefer something stronger?"

"A brandy would be very welcome, thank you, ma'am." He seemed to be avoiding looking directly at Florence. Had he come to admit his downfall, and retract his proposal? That would save her a problem.

"Is it still raining, sir?" her mother asked, not seeming to have noticed, or trying to act normally.

"No, ma'am. It is not raining at all."

"Ah, good, good."

He shifted nervously from foot to foot.

"Pray, sit down, sir. You look most uncomfortable standing there."

He lifted his coat tails and perched on the edge of the sofa.

"Where is that maid?"

"I will do it, Mama." Florence poured out a small drink and handed it to him. He was forced to look at her as he accepted it. He put up his hand to stroke his hair. His eyes looked bloodshot. Had he been drinking already?

"Thank you, I...um..." He drank the brandy down in one gulp, and sat twizzling the glass between his fingers. "Would it be possible, ma'am," he addressed her mother, "to have a word in private with your daughter?"

Her mother cocked her head to one side. Although tempted to shake her head, Florence's curiosity had been aroused.

"Yes, of course." Her mother stood up, raising her eyebrows, as if to say, "Accept if he offers," and left, not quite closing the door behind her, more than likely listening through the crack.

"I am glad it has stopped raining," Florence remarked when he did not offer anything, but scrutinised the patterns in the carpet. "My sister, Eliza, has gone for a drive, and I should hate her to be soaked."

He nodded.

What else can I speak about? "Um, I bumped into a friend of mine this morning, Suzanne Smith. I understand you know her father?"

"Yes, yes, I do."

She waited for a moment to see if he would add anything further, then began, "She...she told me..."

"About my misfortune, I suppose?"

Should she admit it?

"It is not as bad as they make out." He looked up, then, and reached out his hands. "And I am still a wealthy man, I assure you." Her heart sinking, she stared at the mole on his cheek as he went down on his right knee. "So, Miss Fisher, my offer of marriage still stands. Please say you will do me the honour? Please."

Biting her lip, she felt so tempted to say no, but how could she send the family into ruin? "Yes, sir," she whispered, before she had time to change her mind.

He jumped up and enfolded her in his arms. Remaining rigid, she tried to find pleasure in the act but, try as she may, she could not.

Her mother rushed in, her face so full of glee, Florence could not regret her decision.

"Oh, sir, you have made me the happiest mother in the kingdom. We had heard…but never mind that." She turned to Florence. "We shall spend the next week sorting out your trousseau. Oh, I am so happy. And I can help you choose your wedding dress. I still have mine, you know, but do not think it will fit you, for you are much taller than I, and slightly more slender, although I used to be so in my youth, you know. But we could have it altered."

As if trying to show her future son-in-law that she still had the trim figure of a youngster, she paraded around the room, hands on hips, prattling on until Lord Head walked over to the door. "I really must be away, now. I shall call again, my dear, to finalise the date and whatever needs to be done. Do not worry about the finances. I shall pay for the wedding. Yes, I shall pay."

Florence had been about to decline that proposition. It would not be right, but her mother shrieked, "Oh, Lord Head, that would be a great weight off my mind. You are too, too kind."

"Mama!"

"Yes, dear. Is it not a wonderful offer? Can you imagine? White horses and a crystal carriage?"

"No, Mama. We will discuss this later. Good day, Lord Head."

He lifted her hand, kissed the back of it and, with the merest touch, stroked her right ear lobe. "You may call me Marmaduke."

Afterwards, how she kept a straight face on hearing such a name, she could not remember. She almost spat at him, trying not to laugh. How Eliza would giggle with her. It had never occurred to her to wonder what his Christian name might be.

"Florence, my wonderful, gorgeous daughter. I am so pleased for you," spouted her mother, after he had left.

"For me, Mama, or for you?"

"How could you say such a thing? Of course, it is for you. You are to be married." She clapped her hands, her face a picture of ecstasy. "You do not loathe him too much, do you?"

"I am sure I will come to have some regard for him, eventually. But do not ask me to love him. I think I shall never do that."

"Well, you never know, my dear." Her mother began waltzing around the room. "I did not love your father when we first married."

No, and I do not think you ever did, she thought, but kept her counsel, not wanting to wipe the grin off her face. Let her have her moment of pleasure.

"What finery we shall all have. I must go and tell my dear friend. I have been telling her all about you, and my hopes for your betrothal. She will be as pleased as I am, I just know it."

She flounced out of the room, singing.

Florence slumped into an armchair, her head back, eyes closed. *What have I done?*

Eliza found her still there an hour or so later. "Oh, Flo, I have had the most wonderful morning, apart from being soaked in that shower, but that was what made it so wonderful." She walked over. "What is the matter?"

"I have done it."

"What? Accepted Lord Hairy Head?"

She nodded.

"And now you are already regretting it." Eliza knelt down next to her, rubbing her hand.

Florence told her of the morning's events.

"So, I hope he is not lying, when he says he is still wealthy. You had better not be making this sacrifice for us all to be no better off."

"Me, too. You should have seen Mama's face, though, sis. I have never, ever seen her so animated."

"She will spend any money he does have. I'll bet she is down in the town already, looking through pictures of wedding outfits. What sort of dress will you wear?"

"I might just alter Mama's. I have not seen it yet. It might be full of moth holes."

Eliza laughed. "Maybe you could start a new fashion in holey wedding dresses. May I be your maid of honour?"

"Of course. You did not need to ask. And Felicity will be my bridesmaid."

"Have you arranged a date?"

"No, I have not moved from this room since he left. He said he would sort all that out. Anyway, what were you starting to tell me when you came in? I hope you do not come down with a cold again, after your soaking."

Eliza stood up, not quite concealing a grin. "That is unimportant, now, after your news. I can tell you about that another time. And I feel fine. Shall we go and rummage around in Mama's chest and see if we can find this wedding dress?"

"I don't know. Would she like us doing that?"

"Oh, pah, she need not know. I am curious to see what it looks like. She has never shown it to us, has she?"

"No, I do not recall her doing so. Oh, very well, then, let's do it."

They ran up the stairs and opened the chest containing their mother's old clothes, and those she did not want, but could not bear to part with, mostly because they no longer fitted her.

"This must be the one." Eliza held up a yellowing dress, stinking of camphor. "It must have been very pretty, with that Nottingham lace collar, but there is no way you are wearing it, dear sister. I will not allow it."

"Let me see." Florence took it from her. "Perhaps it could be washed, and the colour restored. Apart from that it is perfectly acceptable."

She held it against her. "A panel of something along the bottom would lengthen it, and extra lace on the sleeves. I rather like it."

"No, you do not, and neither do I." Eliza grabbed it. They both froze at the sound of material ripping. Eliza's look of horror mirrored her own. "That's torn it," she joked, turning it over. A gash about a foot long had opened down the front. "There is no way that can be mended."

"I am sure I could." Florence examined the dress. "I am very adroit at needlework."

"You may be adroit, sister, but you are not a miracle-worker. Here, give it to me. I shall fold it and put it back where it was. Mama need never know." She did so and closed the chest.

"But that is deceitful. We should at least confess."

"Nah, what's the betting she never looks in here from one year to the next."

"You and your betting. What if she does?"

"Then we shall have to own up, but until then, she can remain in blissful ignorance."

They descended the stairs. "I shall have to find something else. Maybe I could put an advertisement in the newspaper, asking if anyone

has one they no longer require—a jilted bride, or someone like that."

"Florence Fisher, do not be so silly. You are having a new dress, if I have to make it myself."

"Now, that would be a sight I would love to see—you, sewing."

"I am willing to try, for your sake. It would be unlucky for you to make it, so that leaves me and Mabel."

"Oh, Lizzie, how good you are to me, but I would not put you to so much trouble. I will have no option but to call the seamstress. She will think we have fallen out with her, we have not had any new dresses for so long, apart from my violet one."

"Good, I had been hoping you would come to that conclusion." They reached the drawing room. "Do you fancy a game of cards?"

Florence moved her head from side to side? "Do I? Not really. I need to finish sewing that petticoat I started days ago." She kissed her sister's cheek. "I can use it as part of my trousseau, together with that nightdress I began but never finished. If I am to be married, I shall need new clothes, so I had better make a move." She shuffled off towards the sewing room, not feeing any enthusiasm for the needle, but if needs must... She could not let her husband see her old, tatty underwear. Shuddering at the thought, she put a spring in her step.

Three days later, she, her mother and Eliza stood at the front door, ready for a walk into Ambleside. The sun came out from behind a cloud, and the autumn air felt mild after the rain had left the stone walls of the houses brown instead of their usual cream.

"I still need my thick coat," protested her mother, when Eliza told her she would be warm enough with her shawl, for she had already been out and found it pleasant. "You know how I suffer with my chilblains in the winter."

"Mama, it is not winter. It is barely autumn. Look, the leaves are only now turning bronze. Many have not fallen off the trees yet."

"That does not signify anything. I would rather be too hot than too cold. There are some suspicious-looking clouds over there."

"Where, all I can see is blue sky ahead of us."

"Then you are not looking in the right direction. Where's Felicity? Is she coming with us or not?"

"She ran back for her doll," replied Florence. "She wants to show her to the sheep, if we go that far."

"Do you not think her rather old for playing with dolls? You two stopped doing so well before the age of ten or eleven."

"Mama, she is only nine."

"Is she? I had thought her to be much older than that."

Florence exchanged glances with Eliza. Could their mother be going senile? At fifty years old, she should not be.

Twitching her beaky nose, her mother stepped outside. "It smells fresh."

"Mm, it smells very pleasant," added Florence, tying her hat tighter.

Felicity ran out. "Please may we take the puppies?"

"Oh, no, dear. They would only run round our feet and trip us up," replied their mother, although Florence had been about to say yes, but closed her mouth.

"You cannot beat the sun on your face, the wind in your hair, and delightful company," she said instead, linking arms with Felicity as they walked along King Street. "What do you say, little sister?"

"I like being called 'delightful'."

"Well, so you are. Where would you like to go?"

"May we go past that curious little house on Rattle Gill that spans the Stock Gyll? It's the smallest house I've ever seen."

"Certainly," replied Florence. "It's over two hundred years old, and was built as a summer house, so they say." She turned to her mother. "Maybe we could sell our house and buy that. It would just about fit the five of us."

"Do not be ridiculous. Where would the servants sleep, and how would I fit all my clothes?"

Florence laughed as Felicity continued, "Then we could go down to the lake to see the swans. I love it when they hiss at you."

Felicity unlinked her arm and skipped ahead, humming.

"What a funny child," remarked Florence, walking beside her mother as Eliza sprinted to catch up with their youngest sister. "I would have thought the swans would have scared her, but, oh, no, not our Felicity, eh, Mama?"

"You used to be terrified of them. I recall one time when you almost fell in the lake when one came up and stuck out its long neck at you."

"Well, I was much more introverted, was I not?"

Her mother tucked her arm into hers. "You were the only shy one amongst all of us. But you have come out of your shell in the past few years, especially since your coming-out. I think you will make a wonderful partner for his lordship." She looked at her and smiled. "It will be all right, you know."

Florence tried to smile in return, but it came out more as a grimace, not that her mother noticed. "I hope so. But let us not talk about that. Let us enjoy the fresh air and Mother Nature." She called to Felicity, "Do not go too far ahead, my dear."

Eliza shouted back, "I shall keep my eye on her. Do not fret."

"Did I tell you I saw a charming outfit in a shop yesterday?" asked her mother.

"Yes, Mama, you have told me three times already."

"But do you think Lord Head will put up enough money to pay for one such as that? It had the new bustle, with a row of frills at the back, and a colour like ivory, and the material…I just had to go inside and feel it. Shot silk, it was."

"I don't know, Mama. I can hardly march up to him and say, 'How much can we have? My mama wants the most expensive dress in the land,' now, can I?"

Her mother pouted. "Do not mock me, my dear. What do you think is the usual protocol in this instance?"

"I have no idea. I have never been betrothed before."

"I suppose I shall have to settle for second-best."

"You will still have a beautiful costume. I shall make sure of that. The seamstress is coming tomorrow. She will have plenty of ideas to make you the best-dressed mother-of-the-bride in the land. Now, pray do not be gloomy on such a lovely day. Rejoice in the blessings God gives us. Do not wallow in the self-pity of the ones we think we are missing out on. Is that not what the parson told us on Sunday in his sermon?"

"You are right, my child. I must do as you say." Her mother threw her arms up, yelling, "Rejoice, alleluia," attracting the attention of several people walking past.

"Perhaps not quite so loudly, dear Mama. We do not want the whole world and his dog goggling at us." As she said that, a cocker spaniel ran up to them. "See, Mama, I am right." She bent down to stroke its head, and gasped when she looked up at its owner. Cobalt-blue eyes grinned at her from beneath a tall black hat. He raised the hat and gave a slight bow, before walking on, accompanied by the most beautiful lady Florence had ever seen. Unable to breathe, she stood stock still.

Having continued walking, her mother turned back. "Florence, what is the matter, my dear? You look as if you have seen a ghost."

Had she? Seen a ghost? Surely, if he lived in the neighbourhood, she would know him, or, at least have heard of him? But visitors poured into the area to take in the sights, so that might have been his reason for

165

being there. And he could not have known she would be taking the air at that very moment. *Well, maybe, Miss Flossie Knickers, he is not here to see you. In fact, by the way he smiled at his companion as he walked away, he did not give you a second thought, so do not go reading anything into the encounter.*

"Florence," called Felicity as they continued down Lake Road and reached the lake itself. "That waterfall over there, what did you say they are called?"

"A floss," she replied absentmindedly.

"Ah, yes, like me and you, Flossie, Fliss and floss."

They all laughed until the child ran ahead. "Ah, look at this duck. The poor thing, its leg's mangled. It can hardly waddle."

Breaking out of her trance, she gave a cursory glance back at the couple who had gone a way off, and caught him glancing back at her. He winked. *What's he playing at? Why does he not introduce himself as any ordinary citizen would do? But would you want the whole world to know? Of course not. So it is solicitous that he does not do so.*

Eliza gave her a peculiar look as she joined her sisters. "Who was that couple with the dog, Flo? They—at least he—seemed to know you?"

"The dog? I do not know them. I just acted in a friendly manner to the dog, so they must have found me a friendly person." She took a deep breath.

"I am not so sure." Eliza narrowed her eyes, but Felicity pulled her sleeve, distracting her, to Florence's relief.

"Here, look, it's this duck."

They all watched the bird as it tried to climb over a rock. Felicity reached out to help it.

"Oo, do not touch it, my dear," squealed her mother. "It might dirty your clothes."

While their attention was focused on the bird, Florence looked back again, but the couple had vanished, probably into one of the many tearooms for which the town was famed. Should she suggest doing the same? She decided it would be an expense they could ill afford, and, anyway, what if they entered the same one, and she came face to face with him? She would not be able to contain her feelings. Her face would go bright red, and Eliza would definitely know. The best thing would be to go home and take their refreshments in private.

Eager to avoid her all-seeing sister, she kept close to her younger one. Felicity danced and sang as they continued their walk out of the town and into the countryside, raising all their spirits. "I have learnt a new rhyme this week." She pointed her doll towards sheep in a field. "Do you know it, Florence? It's about a lamb. It goes, 'Mary had a little lamb, its fleece as white as snow.'" When Florence shook her head, she carried on. "'And everywhere that Mary went, the lamb was sure to go.' Would it not be lovely to have a pet lamb? I wish I could have one." She turned and called, "Mama, please may I have a pet lamb?"

Her mother looked up from examining a flower at the edge of the field. "A pet lamb, did you say? Whatever for? Do not be so silly."

Felicity whispered to Florence, "I knew she would say that. I just wanted to shock her."

"How naughty of you," laughed Florence. "You should not goad her."

"But it's so easy."

"That does not matter. You should behave, especially now she does not have Papa to back her up or, rather, to enforce discipline. Mama always left it to him to give us the spankings. Mind you, we older ones probably deserved them."

"I don't do anything to merit a spanking, so I should never receive one, should I?"

Florence gave her a hug. "You are fortunate you are such a good-tempered girl, but goading Mama is not a good idea. She is very fragile, and we do not want her dropping into the depressive state she used to be in, years ago. She used to have a fit of the vapours at the drop of a hat, but, funnily enough, since Papa died, it happens less and less."

"What are you two talking about so earnestly?" called their mother. Florence looked back and saw she had lagged behind, Eliza having gone on ahead, seemingly in a dream. "Nothing, Mama. Do you want us to wait for you?"

"No, no, I am quite happy, walking along here all on my own, while my daughters race ahead."

Florence rolled her eyes. "We had better wait."

Eliza pulled up as well, then turned and came back to them. "Is this not dreamy? Just look at that expanse of water."

"May we take a ride on a boat?" asked Felicity. "It's ages since we did so."

Florence thought about Luke Lancaster and his assertation that he often took sortées out onto the lake. Could that be where he had disappeared to?

She patted her little sister's head, almost knocking off her bonnet, as she looked around at the boats bobbing about on the water. Could one of them contain him? "No, my dear, not today."

"Will we be able to when you are married to that Lord Head? We will have loads of money then, won't we?"

"We shall have to see. I do not know how it will work. If he will grant you all an allowance, or… I really do not know. We have not discussed it."

"Well, my dear, I think you should do so soon," added her mother. "We need to know how much we can spend on luxuries."

"Mama, he admitted he has lost a lot of money, so there might not be luxuries. You might still have to keep your hand on the purse strings."

Eliza reached out and took her mother's hand, and steered her back the way they had come. "I think it is time we returned home, Mama. We do not want to tire you."

"Yes, thank you, dear. It is good to see one of my daughters looks after my welfare."

Florence almost choked. "That is unjust, Mama. I always…"

Eliza gave her a look as if to say, 'Do not pursue it,' and they made their way home.

Felicity looked up at her with concern in her eyes. "That was unfair of Mama. Do you think she meant that you do not care for her?"

"No, darling. She is just weary. We have come too far. We should have turned back ages ago. Do not worry yourself. I am not going to give it a second thought, so you must not, either. Sing me another rhyme."

"Do you know the one, 'Mary Mary'?"

"The one with a sheep?"

Felicity took her hand and swung it. "It's not a sheep, it's a lamb, but no, the other one."

"Oh, yes, she is quite contrary, is she not?"

They sang the song all the way home, Florence, trying hard not to be offended by her mother's words. She had her mother's best interests at heart all the time. She was marrying Mister Hairy Head, for goodness sake. She would not be doing that, if she cared not for her.

Chapter 8

The butler greeted them on their return. "A visitor is waiting for you in the drawing room, Miss Florence."

"Oh, who is it? Anyone nice?"

"It is Lord Head, ma'am."

Eliza gave her a sympathetic look and dragged Felicity up the stairs, but Missus Fisher clapped her hands. "Oo, may I come in with you, Florence? I would like a word with the gentleman."

"Mama, you will not discuss finance, will you?" When her mother's face dropped, she added, "I beg you not to. It would be too embarrassing for words." They handed the butler their coats and gloves.

"But we need to know, my dear." With a wave of a hand, her mother dismissed the servant. "Your late father, God rest his soul, never allowed me to have anything to do with money, so I am sorely lacking in that department."

"Yes, that is probably why, so it is too late to start now. Leave it with me."

"But I must say good day to him. I insist . Surely you would not deny me that pleasure?"

"Of course not, Mama." She had been about to say she never denied her anything, but forced a smile to her lips and opened the door.

Lord Head stood sideways at the mantelpiece. "Such a regal profile, do you not think?" whispered her mother as he turned to them.

"Good day, Florence, and good day Missus Fisher." He flicked the ash from his cigar into the ashtray and bowed low. "I hope I find you in good health, very good health."

"Oh, yes, sir," replied Missus Fisher. "I apologise for keeping you waiting. We have been out walking, and I had begun to tire, but the sight of you has raised my spirits no end."

He smiled, a smile that did not reach his eyes, and turned to Florence. "The fresh air seems to suit you, my dear. It has given a ruddy glow to your cheeks and your rosebud ears. It enhances your natural beauty."

"Why, thank you, sir." She smiled at the reference to her ears and had no need to reply further, for her mother intervened. "Yes, sir, is my daughter not the most beautiful girl in the town?"

She nudged her. "Mama!"

"But you are. Lord Head should be well pleased. You will make pretty babies together, what with his dark hair, and your pretty face."

"Mama!" squealed Florence, even louder. Her face grew hotter and hotter. "P…pray, excuse my mother, sir," she stuttered.

But he did not seem in the least embarrassed. He grinned as he took her hand and kissed it.

"My feelings exactly. My feelings exactly."

As his head bowed, she could only stare at the thick, black hair in front of her with disgust, hoping he would not sense her shudder. Babies? Babies, with his hair?

He looked into her eyes, and she forced the smile back to her face. "I hope we have many," he said. "Do not you, my dear? Many babies?"

She tried to pull her hand away. How could she go through with this arrangement? His very touch sent shivers down her spine, and not pleasant ones. She opened her mouth to refute him, but he turned away and pointed to a paper weight on a table. For a second she thought he would pick it up, but his inherent good manners meant he just bent and peered at it, hands behind his back. "Ah, my father used to collect these. They can be quite fascinating, can they not?"

Missus Fisher went over to him. "Oh, them, they belonged to my late husband, God rest his soul. I do not have much partiality for them, myself, but if you are fond of them, sir, then, I shall start liking them straightaway."

"Come here, Florence," he ordered. "Have you seen this exquisite piece of workmanship? How the glass blower managed to gain such an effect is beyond me, beyond me."

"Yes, Papa used to rave about them, too. He had one that contained an insect inside it. Now, that, I do find fascinating." She turned to her mother. "Do you know what happened to that, Mama? I should like to show it to Lord Head."

Missus Fisher made a moue with her lips and shook her head. "No, my dear. I am sorry. Maybe the maid will know?" She turned to the lord. "Anyway, sir, I am sorely lacking in manners. Let me ring for a drink."

He put his hand on her arm. "That will not be necessary, ma'am. No. I had one while I waited. They did not think you would be long, so I thought I may as well remain until your return."

"Had you any specific reason for calling, sir?" asked Florence. "We would not have stayed out so long if we had known you were coming."

"No, nothing in particular. I just wanted to see your pretty face and ears and assure myself I had not been dreaming when you agreed to be my wife."

He put his hands on the sides of her shoulders. "You have made me and my hair the happiest man alive, my dear, the happiest man." He smirked as if he had made a joke.

Her mother beamed behind him. "You are allowed to kiss her, sir, now you are betrothed," she gushed. "I give you my full permission."

Eyes closed as dread filled her, Florence sensed his face coming closer, and tried not to purse her lips, hoping it would be a little peck on the cheek. His lips felt warm and tender, though. Not at all as irksome as she had anticipated. He kept them there for a few seconds, and she relaxed. When she opened her eyes, she saw him grin. He did not look half as severe. In fact, she could almost say he looked half handsome when his face lit up like that. Maybe she could grow to like him a little.

He cleared his throat. "Well, my dear. I must depart." He picked up his cane and hat.

Missus Fisher tugged at Florence's sleeve. "Ask him," she mouthed. "The money."

Florence shook her head, but her mother would have none of it. "Pray, good sir," she blurted out, "would you…? How much may we spend on the wedding?"

"Mama, please do not bother Lord Head with such matters." Florence tried to pull her towards the door.

"My dear mother-in-law to be, you may have as much as you need. Nothing is too good for your daughter, nothing."

Missus Fisher rubbed her hands together, a huge beam on her face. "Oh, thank you, thank you, kind sir. I knew the first moment I set eyes on you, that you would be a generous person." She turned to Florence. "See, I told you so, my dear."

"You, sir, may have cause to regret that statement," Florence told him as he went through the door.

"No, my dearest," he replied. "I meant every word, every word. Oh, I almost forgot, I have been to see the priest, and have set the date."

"You almost forgot something as important as that?" squeaked Missus Fisher.

"Well, to be truthful, I wanted to leave it until I was going, to give a more dramatic effect."

"When is it then, the date?"

Florence held her breath. The wedding would be a reality now.

"How about four weeks on Saturday?"

Her mother's shocked face stared at him. "Four weeks? But that is nowhere near long enough to finalise all the arrangements."

"Is it not?" He grinned. "Oh, very well, then, how about next April, the week after Easter? Is that date free in your diaries? Hopefully the spring weather will be clement by then, very clement."

Missus Fisher cuffed his arm. "I can see I shall have my work cut out with you, young man, teasing me like that."

Florence shook her head at her mother's intimate stance. Before Lord Head had finished making his farewells, she rounded on her. "Mama, you should not speak to him in such a way. It is far too friendly."

"Oh, pebbles. If I cannot act in a sociable manner with my own son-in-law, then it is a sad world. He is rather pleasant, is he not? If I were twenty years younger, I might have had designs on him myself."

You would be welcome to him, thought Florence. If only that could be the solution. Once the thought had entered her head, she began to work out how she could master a plan to bring them together, to solve everybody's problems. Well worth a consideration.

She would put the idea to Eliza and sound out her feelings on the matter.

Upstairs in her room she changed out of her outdoor clothes and donned an old apron over her blue dress, intending to while away the next few hours painting. Her artistry was mediocre but she enjoyed bringing the pictures alive on the paper. Landscapes were her favourite, portraits beyond her capabilities. All the faces she painted looked alike, even if they had different coloured hair. Noses were a particular problem, so she steered clear of faces.

Eliza found her in the morning room, an hour or so later. "Here you are. I assume your suitor has gone?"

"Oh, he left ages ago." She held up a picture of a sheep against a backdrop of mountains. "What do you think of this?"

"Well, is the sheep supposed to have a silly grin on its face?"

She thought it rather a splendid attempt, and miffed at her sister's unappreciation, she retorted, "That is not a funny grin, that is just its mouth. See if you can do better."

"Oh, you know I cannot draw at all. My efforts would be laughed out of the house. I think I shall play the piano for a while. I have neglected my practice."

They carried on with their respective hobbies for a while, Florence, tapping her foot to the lovely music her sister played. "Was that Mozart or Brahms?" she called when Eliza stopped. "I am never sure."

"Actually it was Beethoven." Eliza laughed as she stood up, flexing her fingers.

"Silly me. I should have known. He is your favourite, is he not?"

"Yes. Pathetique is my real favourite. That and The Moonlight Sonata. I just swoon at that."

"Talking of swooning, sister, I think Mama has taken a fancy to Lord Hairy."

Eliza stepped back, a look of horror on her face. "Did I hear you correctly? Mama and Lord Hairy Head?"

"Yes, you should have seen her fawning over him earlier."

"I do not believe it." She closed the piano lid. "How hilarious."

Florence blew on her painting to dry it, and put it down. "I agree, but if we could somehow… No, it is too preposterous for words. But, I wish we could find some way of throwing them together, so he prefers her to me, and marries her instead."

Eliza came across and took her hand. "He would not go back on his word. He has asked you to marry him. There is no way he would change that, even if he grew fond of Mama, and there is not really time for him to do so. He would not renege, so you may put that idea to bed, once and for all."

"I knew you would say that. It is a pity, though. The wedding is to take place in April."

"Will that give you time?"

"It will have to. He has already booked the church. That is what he came to tell me."

"Oh, my. You could still change your mind, you know."

"No, I cannot. I have given my word, so I must go through with it." She tidied away her paints. "And he may not be quite the monster I had thought him to be. He kissed me."

"And?"

"And what? It was just a kiss."

"Ah, but, did it send your senses reeling like Luke Lancaster's did?"

"I have never told you anything like that."

"Maybe not, but I could tell that they pleased you. More than the lord's, eh?"

She tried to deny it, but could not. "Anyway, Luke Lancaster is well and truly forgotten. I have told you, he does not exist any more. He was a mere fragment of my imagination. So please do not refer to him again." She stalked out of the room, trying to ignore the smirk on her sister's face.

Talk of the upcoming wedding was eclipsed for a while when the girls prepared themselves for a ball to be held at Lord Skelton's house the following week.

"I do hope that friend of your lord's turns up again," gushed Eliza, as the maid combed her hair up into her favourite style, with a bun at the back, and little ringlets dangling at each side.

Florence sat patiently waiting for her turn. "Sybil should be well by the wedding. Thank goodness, I shall not have to wait in line then. But which friend do you mean?"

"Do you not remember me telling you about him? Mister Scarface?"

"Oh, yes, that one."

"But I do not call him by that name anymore, not since he…"

"Eliza? Have you seen him again?"

She grimaced. "I did not tell you straightaway, but do you remember the other day when we went for the walk with Mama?"

"Yes, go on."

"Well, that morning, Elizabeth and I were walking along the street and we bumped into him."

"So?"

"He gave me such a smile, my insides turned to mush."

"But did he speak to you?"

"Not exactly." She flinched. "Ouch, Mabel, please be more careful."

"I'm sorry, ma'am. I was wondering what 'mush' meant."

"Mush? You have never heard of 'mush'? What a sheltered life you must have led. It means…it means all gooey." She pursed her lips as she said the word. "And, well, mushy, like…" She blew out her cheeks and turned to Florence. "You tell her, Flo."

"Me? I do not know. My insides have never turned gooey or mushy." Florence sat brushing her hair, watching their reflections in the mirror.

"Not even…?"

She flared her eyes at her sister's image, to warn her not to continue. "So, he just smiled and walked on, without saying a word? And you think that signifies that he fancies you?"

Eliza shrugged. "Maybe not fancies, but he must like me, must he not, if he smiled at me?" She stood up, her hair finished, and the maid crossed to Florence. "So, if he is there at the ball, I shall try to nurture that beginning into something more."

"I wish you good luck, sister dear."

"The young lady who accompanied him might have something to say about it, but she will soon recover from her disappointment."

"Eliza! They might be betrothed, for all you know."

"I would not think so. She was not the same lady I saw him with in the park."

"The older one you mentioned, who I said could be his mother?"

"Yes, nor the one I saw him with a day later."

"I have warned you before. He must be a flirt. You are too young to have your feelings trifled with. I think you should stay away from men like that."

"We shall see," came Eliza's retort, as she pulled up her dress.

The house shone with lights beaming from the windows as they drew up. They straightened their dresses, before entering.

"I am so excited," exclaimed Eliza.

"You will behave, my dear," warned her mother, looking resplendent in her costume of dark purple shot silk. "If you wish to bag a rich husband like your sister has, then you must act with decorum."

"I always do, Mama. You slight my character, by hinting otherwise."

"Remember to watch your tongue. Once something is said, it cannot be..."

"Forgotten. Yes, I know, Mama. You may rely on my mouth being closed at all times."

The butler announced their names and, once they had said a few words to their hosts, they joined the fray of laughing merrymakers.

"Do you see him?" Eliza asked Florence, after their mother had left them to find her own friends.

"Not your Mister Scarface, but Lord Hairy Head is over there. Do you think I can avoid him for a while?"

"It seems not, sister dear, for he is already making his way over."

He bowed. "Good day, Florence, Miss Eliza."

"Good day, sir. My mother is over there." She pointed across the room, where her mother sat chatting.

He looked that way, but then turned back to her with a puzzled expression. "I hope she is in good health?"

"Oh, very good health. She is the healthiest person in our house. I am sure she would love you to go over and say hello."

Eliza nudged her, and she felt a fit of the giggles coming on. "Pray excuse us," Eliza said in a wobbly voice.

"I shall, I shall," he replied. "But may I mark your card for the first dance?"

"Oh, yes, of course." Trying to suppress the titters that she could feel bubbling over, Florence handed him her card.

"I do not usually dance, but I feel I should not deprive you, my dear, of at least the first one."

His insinuation sobered her up. "Do you mean you wish me to remain seated for the whole evening, just because you do not dance? I assure you, sir, I intend to dance every single one."

"But we are betrothed, betrothed."

"So I am not allowed to enjoy myself? No, sir, it is not official yet so I am not about to 'deprive' myself of the pleasure of a reel or a waltz. It may be your choice, but it is not mine."

The band tuned up. Eliza had been seized already, so she followed him onto the dance floor, her body rigid and unbending, seething inside at his remark, but she soon unbent and swung agilely to the music.

At the end, he showed her to a seat, and Eliza ran over. "I have four dances marked already, Flo. Did I understand correctly? Does he…" she indicated to the retreating back of the lord, "…not want you to dance all evening?"

She nodded. "But he can go to blazes. I have not come to sit talking to old ladies. I am not yet married to him. I shall do as I please."

"You tell him, sis. Ah, there is Elizabeth. I must go and speak to her. Your friend, Tabitha, is over there. Oh, I do like her dress. What a delightful shade of…puce, would you call it?"

"I would say more brownish-purple, myself. But, yes, I must go and say hello. I have not seen her for a few weeks. She has been away." They went their separate ways, each to their own friends, and even though she was not claimed for every dance, she had a few names on her card by the time she decided to try the refreshments.

Lord Head pushed his way towards her as she wondered which titbits she fancied. "I see you are determined to defy me, my dear."

"It is not a question of defying, sir. Our engagement has not been announced yet, so it would seem peculiar if I did not dance. Do you not think so?" She fluttered her fan at him, trying not to appear too coquettish,

"Well, I suppose so. I had not thought of it like that. I am just so eager for us to be married, I feel that the whole world should know about it. The whole world."

"Pray contain yourself. People may overhear." As she leaned forward to help herself to the salmon, he took the spoon and dished some onto her plate.

"Thank you," she muttered, aware that the action could cause raised eyebrows, "but it would be better if I served myself."

Eliza joined them. "What a fabulous spread. Are you trying that mouldy cheese, sir?"

He looked taken aback, swiping his hand across his hair. "No, Miss Fisher. I do not eat cheese after four o'clock in the afternoon. It gives me nightmares. Terrible nightmares."

"Oh, how awful for you." She placed a large wedge of it onto her own plate. "We could not live without cheese, could we, Florence?"

Florence looked at the huge piece. There was no way in the world her sister would be able to eat that much. Digging her fork into some pie, she declined to answer, giving Eliza a warning look from under her brows.

An innocent face smiled at her, her head cocked to one side.

"I'll speak to you later," she mouthed.

"I love cheese, too," piped up Elizabeth, clearly unaware of the situation. "But I prefer cake."

The lord having put her in a bad mood yet again, Florence tried not to look at the girl's portly figure, thinking, uncharitably, that it showed. Her appetite waning, she wandered away from the table, but once she had tasted the delicious salmon, she went back for more. Someone nudged her arm, knocking her plate from her hand, and she looked up into cobalt-blue eyes.

Transfixed, she watched him bend down to pick up pieces of the plate as the footmen rushed over and urged him to leave them.

"What are you doing here?" she hissed.

"The same as you, apparently, ma'am, enjoying sociable company and good food."

Moving away, so the damage could be rectified, she saw people around her staring. "I must apologise to Lord and Lady Skelton for breaking their crockery. Pray, excuse me." She hurried off, her heart beating at twice its normal rate.

Her mother stopped her. "Are you well, my dear? You look rather flushed. And was that you creating that disturbance just now?"

"Yes and yes. I am fine, thank you, Mama, just a trifle embarrassed. I do not know what came over me. The plate slipped from my hand." She did not look behind her in case he had followed.

"Never mind, dear. These accidents happen." She took her arm and tried to steer her over to her seat. "Come and sit down."

"But I need to give my apologies to Lady Skelton. They will think me a vandal if I do not."

Eliza nudged her way through the crowd of people who had gathered to see the damage. "Florence Fisher, the smasher of crockery."

"Do not make me feel any worse than I do already."
She hid her face in her hands and allowed her mother
to sit her down. "I shall never live this down, shall I?"

Spotting Lady Skelton coming towards her, she
jumped up and grabbed the lady's arm. "I am so sorry,
milady. I should have been more careful."

"Pray, do not worry about it, my dear. It is only a
plate. It can be replaced. The main issue is, do not let
it mar your enjoyment of the evening." She urged her
back towards the food, the broken pieces having been
cleared away. "Come and finish your meal."

"No, no, thank you, milady." *I cannot risk seeing him
again.* "I had already eaten sufficient, thank you. The
salmon was the most delicious I have ever tasted. You
must give Mama the recipe."

"Well, if you are sure you do not want any more?"

She nodded, still keeping her gaze from the faces
regarding her with such interest.

"Very well, and I repeat, do not give the matter any
further consideration."

I cannot say I would be able to do that. "Thank you. You
are too kind."

As soon as the dancing started again, no longer the
centre of attention, she made her way to the powder
room to escape further notice. She closed the door,
stood with her back to it, and took several deep
breaths. What could he be doing there? Had he been
alone? She had not noticed anybody with him, but he
could have left them on the other side of the room

while he fetched their food, so that did not signify anything.

Someone banged on the door so she went out, found her mother, and sat beside her, making a bridge with her fingers, pressing them together, staring at them.

"Eliza seems happy," her mother remarked. "Do we know that gentleman with whom she is dancing?"

Without even glancing at him, she shook her head, thinking, *Probably Mister Scarface, if she is lucky.*

A young man, whom she had met once before, asked for the next dance and she obliged, although her inclination had evaporated. Unable to make meaningful conversation, he probably thought her to be stuck-up or shy. Whichever, he handed her back to her mother with a bow, and walked off.

"I see your fiancé does not dance very much," remarked her mother, fanning her red face.

"No, he dislikes to do so. A sore point."

"That is a pity. One of the main pleasures in life is being held by an attractive man, gliding gracefully around the floor. Your father was very adept at it. One of the few things we had in common, our love of the dance." She tapped her foot to the music, watching the myriad of different-coloured dresses whirling around.

Keeping her head down, Florence saw a pair of polished black shoes coming towards her. Someone else wanting a dance?

She really did not feel up to any more dancing, and wished they could leave, but knowing they could not. Sighing, she resigned herself to accepting.

Her breath left her body when she looked up to see who he might be. "No." The word forced its way out of her mouth as she shook her head.

Her mother looked sternly at her. "Florence, what is the matter?"

The man stood in front of her, patiently waiting, his left brow arched.

"Mama, I do not feel well."

"Nonsense, my dear." She turned to him. "I assume you wish to dance with my daughter, sir?"

"I do, indeed, ma'am." He bowed.

"But…"

"But nothing, my dear." She yanked her up.

"What do you think you are doing?" she hissed in her ear. "You are making a scene, again. Pull yourself together. I cannot imagine what has come over you tonight."

She had not option but to accept. With a flourish, Luke Lancaster led her onto the dance floor. Her lips tightly sealed, she tried not to gaze at his handsome face as he swirled her around with abandon.

"Desist, sir, everybody is watching," she murmured when they came close.

She needed to make him slow down, for people were giving them curious glances.

"But this dance needs energy for it to be truly appreciated." He continued with the steps. Gradually one by one, the other dancers stepped back to watch, many with disapproving faces, until they were the only ones still dancing. "Stop, now," she hissed. The music finally stopped, and everyone applauded. "Now, look what you have done, sir. You have made me a spectacle."

He escorted her off. "I apologise if I have done so, but you were magnificent." He bowed low as Lord Head came puffing over to her.

"My dear, how could you do such a thing?"

"I beg your pardon, sir," intervened Luke. "What business is it of yours what this lady does?" He looked pointedly at Florence's third finger and seemed relieved to see no ring there.

"She is my…" Lord Head stopped, clearly realising that, as the engagement had not been announced, he could not declare it. "My very good friend, and you, sir, have shown her up, shown her up."

"The lady does not seem worried about it," Luke declared. "And, anyway, why should a lady who is so proficient not be allowed to show off her prowess?"

"Because it is not the done thing."

"Excuse me, gentlemen, I am here," protested Florence. "You have no need to talk about me as if I were not."

"Of course, my dear." Lord Head looked pointedly at Luke. "If you are leaving, sir, that door over there is the closest. That door over there."

Luke gave her a wink behind Lord Head's back and bowed. "Good day, *milady*." He pronounced the last word with extra emphasis, then turned on his heel and left.

"Well," declared the lord. "I trust you came to no harm, my dear?"

"No, sir, I have not suffered at all." *Except my senses.* "I need air. Shall we adjourn to the balcony?"

"If you wish, but I must not stay out there too long without my greatcoat. I am afflicted with a weak chest from time to time, so do not want to exacerbate the condition."

"Pray, do not bother then. I shall wander out on my own."

"Are you sure?"

"Of course. You sit by the fire over there with your friends and keep warm. We would not want you catching a chill, would we?" *Even though I would have thought your full head of hair would keep you warm.*

Relieved, she went outside. The cold air took away her breath. Snow! They would have to leave straightaway. The journey home took half an hour, and the road could become impassable in that time.

She went closer to the rail. How come nobody had said anything about the garden being covered?

As she turned to go back inside, to let her mother and sister know, a body blocked her way. "It is rather early in the year for snow, is it not?"

"Um…yes." She tried to push past him, but he stepped forward.

"Maybe we will become snowed in, and have to stay the night?"

"I certainly hope not. Lord Skelton will not have enough beds for us all." Trying once more to pass him, she kept her gaze down, her breath coming out in gasps as she avoided eye contact.

"Maybe we could share again." That remark could not go unacknowledged. Her head shot up, and her eyes swept the balcony to make sure nobody could have heard. "I think not, sir. How could you suggest such a thing?"

"Well, we did it once, so why not again?"

He seemed to be enjoying taunting her. That had to be his aim. He could not possibly be implying anything else.

"We did not share a bed. It was nothing like a bed."

"Ah, but it might just as well have been. We did sleep there, after all. By the way, has your maid recovered?"

"Just about. And please stop touching me." His hand caressing her arm was sending such thrills through her whole body her legs had turned to jelly. "Someone will see."

"Is that the only reason?"

"Maybe I do not like it?"

"Ah, but your eyes tell me differently."

Desperate to move, but unable to lift her feet, she looked away so he could not see into her soul. "It must be the poor light out here."

A low laugh erupted from his throat as he lifted her chin. His face came closer and she held her breath, waiting for the kiss she wanted so much, but a voice behind her made her jump away.

"Is this man accosting you, my dear?"

"No, no." She jumped back. "He was just…"

"The lady had something in her eye, sir," announced Luke, producing a white starched handkerchief. "I was about to remove it."

"You were standing very close. Very close indeed. Closer than you should have been." Lord Head stormed over and grabbed her. "I shall remove the offending article, so please leave."

"And what right do you have, sir, to order her about?"

"She and I are…" he began, but Florence shook her head at him. "I am a very good friend of the family, so I have the right to defend her from unwanted attention."

Luke raised his arms and swept them in a circle. "I see no 'unwanted attention', sir." By this time several people had come out to see what the altercation could be. "But you are causing a rumpus and embarrassing the young lady, so I ask you to step aside, so she may enter the house. I am sure she is frozen, standing out here, while you create a scene."

Luke pushed the lord aside, and escorted Florence inside, making a path through the watching guests with a flourish of his hand.

Lord Head followed, grunting in her ear.

Her mother hurried over. "Florence, what is going on?"

"Nothing to worry about," Lord Head butted in before she could reply. "I have the matter in hand, in hand."

Luke bowed to her mother. She could see him eying her up and down.

"Who is this gentleman?" her mother asked in a softer tone, clearly taken aback at his handsome features.

"Luke Lancaster at your service, ma'am."

Florence heard a gasp behind her and turned to see Eliza's animated face. She tried to tell her by facial gestures and a slight shake of her head not to say anything, but her sister pushed her way in front of him. "May I be introduced to the gentleman?" she squealed.

"No, you may not," retorted her mother. "We know nothing about him. Who are you, sir? And how do you know my daughter?" Florence sagged. *Please do not tell them,* she begged silently.

Before he could reply, she intervened. "He does not know me, Mama, he… I just met him outside."

"And what were you doing out there on your own?"

"Just taking the air, Mama, that is all. Now, please may we continue with the dancing?"

Lady Skelton came across. "Is everything well, my dear. It is not your evening, is it? First, the plate, and now this."

She looked up at Luke, and her face changed to a huge grin. "Luke Lancaster! I did not hear the butler announce you. Thank you for coming all this way. How are you? Where have you been?" She steered him away, plying him with questions.

Missus Fisher looked up at Lord Head. "I think a drink would be beneficial, do you not, sir?"

"Of course, ma'am." He turned to Florence. "Come and take a seat while I find you a drink. That awful man must have upset you. I am so sorry, so sorry. I shall not let it happen again."

She ushered him away. "I am fine, thank you, but a drink would be very welcome."

Eliza tried to catch her attention. She dared not look at her, for her face would give her away. Luckily, someone whisked her sister onto the dance floor, sparing her the indignity of explaining. The time would come, though.

"It has begun to snow, Mama," she pointed to the window. "What will happen if we cannot make our way home?"

Her mother peered out. "I am sure it will not be serious. If you would prefer, we could leave as soon as you are refreshed. Poor Eliza will be most disappointed. She seems to be having a good night, but, to tell you the truth, I am ready to depart, anyway."

Chapter 9

"Oh, Flo," gasped Eliza later that night as they prepared for bed. "I wish we had not had to leave so early. The snow had almost disappeared. We would have been fine, staying until the end."

"Yes, I am sorry to have cut your evening short."

"But I did manage to have two dances with Mister Handsome Face." A dreamy look came over her as she hugged herself. "Do you not think he is the most good-looking man on this earth?"

"He is not Mister Scarface any more, then?" She took the pins out of her hair, allowing it to fall loose.

"Oh, no, his scar is scarcely noticeable any more. Anyway, his name is Peter Iredell."

"You were introduced to him, then?"

Eliza sank into her bed, pulling the covers up under her chin. "Well, no. I asked Elizabeth to find out for me. Anyway, what about you and Luke Lancaster?"

"Nothing." Florence blew out the candle and snuggled down into her own blankets. "Good night, sweet dreams." As soon as she had said that, she regretted it, the memory of his hands on her sending shivers of pleasure tingling down her spine.

"Oh, no, sister dear, you are not getting away with it that easily."

Florence felt Eliza shifting. "Come on, tell me what happened. How did Luke Lancaster come to be at the ball? Did you know he would be there?"

"Of course, I did not. Now, please, go to sleep." She yawned loudly to give emphasis to her words. "I am very tired."

"Well, I am not. I am wide awake. I have never felt so awake. And I want to hear more about…"

"Please, Lizzie. We do not want bags under our eyes in the morning. What if you saw your Mister Iredell while we were out walking? He would not be very impressed, would he, if you did not look your best?"

Eliza yawned also. "I suppose not. But I do not think I shall sleep for hours."

"Well, I beg you to try."

Five minutes later, soft snorting noises betrayed the fact that her sister had indeed fallen into the land of nod, whereas her own brain would not switch off, no matter how hard she pummelled the pillow to make it softer. She lost count of the sheep jumping over the gate after she had reached a hundred, and starting again did not help. Luke Lancaster's face would not leave her. Even some of the sheep turned towards her, looking suspiciously like him.

Who was he? And why did he keep cropping up? Missus Skelton clearly knew him. Maybe she could send a visiting card to that lady and drop his name into the conversation while they sipped their tea. Her mother would probably press her for answers in the morning. What would she tell her?

However, the subject of Luke Lancaster did not arise when they went down to breakfast the following morning. Her mother's usual aplomb had left her. She marched up and down the breakfast room, her hands in the air, ranting and raving about Frederick. Florence could not make head or tail of what she was saying. "Calm down, Mama, I beg you, and explain the dilemma in words of one syllable."

"He has ruined us, for sure. As if our situation were not bad enough, he has finished us. We will end up in the debtors' prison. I know it."

"Mama," Eliza tried in vain to make her sit down, "it cannot be as bad as you imagine. Why do you not take a whiff of your smelling salts and then tell us what has happened?"

"Smelling salts? They will not help us now. We are doomed." Her head in her hands, she burst into tears.

Florence looked at Eliza as they steered her onto the sofa and sat her down. "What on earth can have happened?" she whispered.

"I have no idea."

"He has gambled away everything we own, that is what has happened," sobbed their mother.

"Gambled?" exclaimed both girls at the same time. "When?"

"But how do you know about it?"

Missus Fisher wiped her tears and took a letter out of the pocket in her pinafore, waving it in the air. "This is how I know. This portent of doom."

Eliza snatched it from her and they both pored over it, trying to read the scrawly writing. Penmanship had never been Frederick's forte. "What is that word?" she asked.

"It looks like 'cards'. Yes, it is," replied Florence, screwing up her eyes to better see the squiggles. "He has lost at cards? Is that all? Surely, that does not mean disaster? He has done so many a time before, has he not?"

"But this time it is different. I just know it in my bones." She began to sob once more.

Florence took the letter from her sister and went over to the window. "I cannot see anything catastrophic in the letter, Mama," she called. "Pray, do not upset yourself so."

Eliza followed her. "What does it actually say?" she asked in an undertone.

"Well, he says he will not be returning home for a few weeks. I suppose that has made Mama suspicious. He does not usually stay away that long, does he?"

Her lip caught between her teeth, Eliza shook her head. "No, I agree," she replied at length. "Where is he staying?"

"It does not give that, just 'with friends'.

"Mama is wretched, indeed. How may we cheer her up?"

Before Florence could reply the butler appeared. "Lord Head to see you, ma'am."

"Oh, no," she gasped. "That is all I need."

"He is probably here to castigate you for last night," offered her sister, not putting her mind at rest at all.

"More than likely. I had better speak to him." She went over to her mother, who still sat on the sofa, dabbing at her eyes.

"Yes, go, child. Eliza can keep me company. You go and cavort with your fiancé."

She backed out. "Mama, you know I would stay and sort this out, but I must not keep him waiting."

"Of course not, manners mean more than an ailing parent."

"Mama?"

Her mother waved her away. "Go."

How annoying her mother could be at times. Surely she did not mean what she had implied? She had just been feeling sorry for herself. As usual.

She entered the morning room, where she found Lord Head pacing up and down. Trying to gauge his feelings, she hesitated before going up to him.

He turned, his face giving nothing away, and held out his hand. "My dear."

"Good morning, Marmaduke. I…"

"You do not have to apologise."

She had not been intending to do so.

"I understand that fellow had been haranguing you. It was not your fault. Not your fault at all."

Halfway across the room, she stopped. How pompous. Through gritted teeth, she replied, "That is too kind of you, sir." Best not to let him know she would have willingly gone with Lancaster, anywhere at all.

"We will put the episode behind us. I intend taking a ride through the park today. Would you like to accompany me? Perhaps your sister also?"

"I am sure if she does not have other plans, she would be delighted. Thank you. I shall go and ask her now, so you will know how many there will be." He followed her out to the drawing room, where her mother and sister sat on the sofa.

Felicity ran in before them.

"Would my younger sister be allowed to come as well, sir?" asked Florence.

"Where, Florence?" Felicity grabbed her skirt. "Where might I be allowed to go?"

"For a ride in the park. Would you like to, that is if Lord Head deems it fit?"

The man coughed. "I… I do not see why not, my dear. Bring the whole family. I have carriages galore. Yes, carriages galore."

"Oh, yes, please. Shall I go and fetch my best coat?" The little girl beamed. "I can finish my lessons when I return."

"Mama, would you like to come? It would take your mind off Frederick's antics."

Her mother put up her hand and wiped her brow. "I do not feel up to it, not today. I think I may have a lie down."

Florence looked questioningly at her sister, but she just shrugged. "What are your plans, today, sister? Would a drive suit you?"

"Um, yes, thank you. That would be lovely."

Lord Head coughed again.

"Oh, my dear," Florence put her hand on his arm. "I hope you are not coming down with influenza. Do you think it wise to be taking the air today?"

"It is nothing. Do not concern yourself. I shall leave you now, and return in say, an hour? An hour? Would that be time enough for you *all* to prepare yourselves?"

"Yes, sir." Florence suppressed a smile. How long did he think she needed to don a coat and hat?

He bowed and left.

She turned to her younger sister, "Felicity, run and tell your governess you are coming out with us, while I escort Mama upstairs. By the way, what brought you down here in the first place?"

"Um… I think I wanted to ask Mama something. I can't remember what, though." She ran towards the door. "I can tell the governess I am going out for a nature lesson."

"No, that would not be truthful," she called after her, but she had gone.

"Oh, you and your pernicketyness," moaned her mother. "Surely, anything outside could be classed as a nature lesson? Help me upstairs. I feel so weary."

"I am worried about you, Mama." Eliza took one arm and Florence the other. "Perhaps I should stay with you, after all."

"No, no, I shall be well once I have had forty winks. You enjoy yourself. I shall be fine here, on my own."

"But you will not be alone, Mama. There are the servants."

"Yes, yes, I know."

Florence rolled her eyes at Eliza. Their mother could turn on the sympathetic air so well, making them all feel guilty.

Felicity had not reappeared by the time the butler announced the re-arrival of Lord Head. "I shall find her," called Eliza, running up the stairs, as Florence looked out the door to see a large carriage with four beautiful white horses at the front. *He has gone to town,* she thought, *to ensure we all fit in. It is lovely, though.*

"Are you all ready?" he asked, looking behind her.

"The other two are on their way."

She went up to the horses, and stroked the front one. "Aren't these magnificent? Do they all belong to you?"

"Of course, my dear, of course. You would not expect me to use somebody else's, would you?"

"No, it is just that my father never owned such as these."

"Well, my dear, you will be moving up in society, once we are married."

She had never considered herself beneath him, not while her father had been alive, anyway. Did he think himself superior to her and her family? Evidently. Then why had he asked her to marry him? Why not keep within his own class barriers?

Eliza and Felicity came out, and she thought she heard him murmur under his breath, "About time."

"Hurry up, hurry up," she called. "We do not want to keep Lord Head waiting."

"Good day, sir. I am sorry we…" began Eliza.

"Never mind," he interrupted. "You are here, now. Let us not keep the horses standing any longer than necessary."

They all climbed in, Felicity raising her eyebrows at her and grimacing. "Sorry," she whispered, then said aloud, "What a beautiful day, sir, to be taking a ride."

Florence could not suppress a grin at her young sister's pronouncement, but his lordship's face did not change. He merely kept his gaze on the sky, evidently miffed, as he had not repeated a single word.

"Indeed it is, Felicity," she answered for him. "How observant of you to notice. Not a cloud in the sky. A beautiful day, indeed."

She could see Eliza, sitting next to Felicity, opposite her and the lord, trying to keep from grinning, and had to look the other way. "Do you not agree, sir?"

This time he looked down and stared at Florence's ears. "Yes, of course. I had been trying to concentrate on the effectiveness of breathing in fresh air, but if you would rather strike up a conversation, that is fine by me."

Widening her eyes as a warning to Eliza, who snorted, she pulled her bonnet forward and stated, "No, my dear, if you do not want us to talk, then we can be as quiet as mice, can we not, sisters?"

Another grunt from Eliza had her kicking her sister's leg to stop her. Felicity opened her mouth to speak but Florence shook her head, her own lips tightly shut to show her what she meant, so the child looked around her with an exaggerated gesture, her hand over her mouth.

This is going to be an unusual morning, she thought. *How can he expect us to sit silently?*

They managed it, however for the five minutes or so that it took them to reach the park.

Lord Head took off his tall hat, smoothed his hair, replaced the hat and broke the silence. "I hear your brother is in difficulty."

The older two girls gasped.

"How do you know that, sir?" asked Florence.

"My dear, it is all over town, all over."

Felicity reached forward and pulled her arm. "I didn't know. What does he mean?"

Florence patted her hand. "Nothing for you to concern yourself with, dearest." She turned to the man beside her. "What exactly are they saying?"

He turned his head slowly and looked her in the eye. "Only that he has lost everything, and brought ruin to your whole family, your *whole* family."

"In that case, why are you bothering to take us out for people to stare at us? I suppose you are worried about my dowry." Had everybody been jeering at them? She had not noticed anyone doing so. In fact, she could see someone coming towards them in a carriage, waving. "I think you had better turn the horses around, sir, and take us home. We would not want to tarnish your reputation by being seen with you."

"I can stand it, my dear. I shall face them with impunity. You are not to blame for your brother's misfortune." He gave a slow wave to the passing carriage, as if to prove his point.

Eliza kicked her foot, indicating with her head to look at the occupants of the other carriage. The man inside lifted his hat. Accompanying, Lady Skelton, Luke Lancaster looked as eye-catching as ever. "Good day to you all," he called.

Lord Head had clearly not recognised him. "Who was that?"

"Um… Was he one of the guests from the ball?"

"He looked vaguely familiar, but I cannot put a name to the face."

"He is very handsome, is he not?" piped up Felicity, swivelling her head to take another look.

"Is he? I did…um…not notice," she stuttered, as a blush rose up her neck.

Her other sister poked her again with her foot, under cover of their long dresses, and pointed in the other direction. "There is somebody we know. It's Elizabeth." She waved madly, but then withdrew her hand. "But who is she with? My goodness, I swear it is my…I mean Mister Iredell. How can she be with him? Oh, Florence, I knew we should not have left the ball early. She must have entrapped him after we left." She threw her arms up. "Oh, it is so unfair."

Watching Lord Head's reaction out of the corner of her eye, Florence tried to calm her. "Eliza, dear, pray do not vent your emotions in public."

"Well, my chance has evaporated. I had been so hopeful."

"Your chance of what, Lizzie?" Felicity asked innocently.

Lord Head banged his cane on the carriage side. "Do we have to endure this fit of histrionics? Maybe, we should turn back, after all." He called to the driver to take them home.

Florence admitted she would not be averse to doing so. In fact, she relished the idea. The sooner they were out of that damned carriage the better.

Once home, after leaving her lord, clearly in the foulest of moods, they hurried inside.

Eliza's eyes filled with tears. "I cannot believe she would do such a thing to me. She knew I wanted him. She must have been plotting all along."

"It might be entirely innocent, my dear sister."

"But he has not invited me out yet. She has beaten me. He would not have asked her if I had been there. It is all your fault. If we had not left, just because you were worked up into a state over Luke Lancaster, I would now be the one riding with him, waving to all and sundry. I hate you." She ran up the stairs before Florence could stop her.

Felicity took off her bonnet. "Florence, did she mean that? Does she really hate you?"

"No, no, dearest." She watched Eliza's fleeing back, her feet not seeming to touch the stair as flew up it. "I am sure she did not. She is just vexed."

"Who is Mister Lancaster? And why did you have to leave the ball early? Please, tell me. I am old enough now to know about these things. I shall be twelve very soon."

She knelt down beside her, unfastening her coat buttons. "Not now, my darling. You had better find your governess."

"But she won't be expecting me yet. We have only been out for about half an hour."

"Then find a book to read, or something, there's a good girl."

"Very well. Will you tell me about the man later?"

"Yes, yes. Off you go."

Dragging her legs up the stairs, Felicity did as she had been bid.

Florence took off her outer clothes, wondering if, thinking them to be completely destitute, Lord Head would change his mind about their marriage. Would he be within his rights to do so? She would not be able to sue him for breach of promise, under such circumstances. And she would not blame him if he did. In fact, she would welcome it. The more she knew of him, the less she liked him. She could not think of one redeeming feature, except his money.

The following week, having not heard from her lord, she assumed her hopes had been realised. Barely speaking a word to her since the outing, Eliza moped around the house, her face sullen and dour. Her mother had kept to her bed for the past few days, saying she had a bad cold, if not, the influenza, so life seemed very dull in the Fisher household.

As she descended the stairs, wondering how to occupy the morning, the front door opened and Frederick wafted in.

She did not know whether to greet him or send him packing, but he ran to her and enfolded her in his long arms. "Ah, sis, how pleased I am to be home. You will never guess what a week I have had."

Pushing him away, she retorted, "You are not the only one. News of your behaviour has reached the whole county."

"Ah, sis, do not be cross with me. It has all been settled, now."

"Settled? What do you mean?"

"An influential benefactor has paid all my debts. I am a free man again. Is that not fortuitous?"

"Well. If it is true, then, it is very fortuitous. But who is this benevolent guarantor, and why has he done it?"

"That I do not know. My solicitor just informed me that it had all been paid."

"I wonder if it is Lord Head. He was very…how can I put it? Very scathing, the last time I saw him. Perhaps he thought it would solve the problem."

"Anyway, whoever it was, I am very grateful. I can now continue with my life."

"Well, not as before, I hope."

"No, no. I am a reformed character. No more gambling for me."

She made a sound like a snort. "When have I heard that before, brother dear? I will believe it when I see it."

He took her hands in his, his face serious. "I mean it, sis. I would not bring down wrath on my family again. I had a moment's aberration. I swear it will not happen again."

She took a deep breath. "Well, just remember that next time you are tempted."

He turned to go. "Where's Mother?"

"She took to her bed. The news knocked her backwards, I am afraid to say."

"I will go and apologise straightaway." Halfway up the stairs, he twisted round. "By the way, do you know a man called Luke Lancaster?"

"What?"

"He appeared out of the blue. Apparently he knows you."

"He…um…he…I met him at Lady Skelton's ball." Why did her heart flutter so, just at the mention of his name? "Why, what did he say?"

"He said your eyes reminded him of cornflowers on a summer's day. He must have danced very close to you to observe such a thing. I cannot say I ever take notice of my partner's eye colour, or even her hairstyle, or anything like that, when I am dancing. You must have left quite an impression." He continued upwards, oblivious to her racing emotions.

She entered the morning room on shaky legs, and sank into a large armchair. Why had he re-emerged? Just as she had been learning to forget about him. And why had he made such a remark to her brother?

She would have to have words with him, if she ever saw him again.

"A lady to see you, ma'am," announced the butler as Florence sat unpicking her embroidery.

"To see me, Crakeplace? Who is it?" He gave her the calling card, and she read, 'Lady Janet Head'.

"Lady Head? But Lord Head is not married."

"I think it is his mother, ma'am."

"His mother? Oh, my goodness, have I missed something? Has she made an appointment, and I have forgotten about it? Is he not with her?"

The merest of grins crossed his mouth as he replied, "No, ma'am, he is not and you have not." He turned to leave as she ran to the mirror to check no hair had fallen out of place, and that she did not have cabbage in her teeth. Wiping her clammy hands down her skirt, she raised her head high, trying to recall if she had met the woman before. Lord Head had told her his mother had moved to a cottage in the depths of the countryside, miles from Ambleside, and that she had turned into a recluse after his father had died. Why on earth had she come all this way to see her?

"Show her in, Crakeplace."

Lady Head did not look at all as she had imagined. A dainty black hat sat on her black hair, and her black clothes showed she still grieved for her dead husband, even though he had died four years before. Her sharp brown eyes seemed to bore into Florence as she came forward.

Florence bowed. "Good day, ma'am."

The lady's nose twitched as she looked around the room without extending any greeting and, with no preamble, she announced, "I understand my son has asked for your hand in marriage?" She did not wait for a reply, but continued, "I have told him it is a most unsuitable match. I hear you are practically destitute.

There is no point in denying the fact. All my sources report the same. How much is your dowry?"

Florence opened her mouth to speak, but Lady Head carried on. "It is of no matter. It will not be enough, no matter what your answer might be." She walked over to a picture on the wall. "Humph, not an original, I see."

"Ma'am, I…"

"Pray do not interrupt. I have not finished."

Florence closed her mouth as Lady Head continued to insult the hangings on the walls and the wallpaper, which she had to admit, had seen better days. Even the ornaments on the mantelpiece came under review.

She could stay silent no longer. "That one belonged to my grandmother, ma'am. I will not allow you to disparage it." She picked up the miniature depicting two small boys on a swing, and hugged it to her bosom. "And if you are intending to belittle everything in my house, then I shall ask you to leave."

"My dear," Lady Head turned towards her, "I have no wish to remain a moment longer. I cannot see whatever possessed my son to offer for you. You are a plain, mousy, impertinent gal, with not an ounce of breeding or decorum. Good day." She flounced towards the door which opened as if by magic, and Crakeplace appeared with her cane, and escorted her out.

Florence flopped onto the sofa, still clutching the miniature, feeling as if she had run around Lake Windermere and back.

What an abominable woman! Her son was a pussy cat compared with her. How could she accept him now? More to the point, what would her life be like if she did so? Picking up her embroidery, she jammed in the needle, and pulled it out the other side, jamming it back through as if she were sticking it in the lady's eyes.

"Whoa," she muttered, throwing it across the room. "You cannot let someone rile you to that extent. Calm down." She took deep breaths and stood up. The miniature fell to the floor. She had forgotten she had dropped it into her lap. "Please do not be broken," she cried. "That dragon will have won, then." Luckily it remained unscathed, so she replaced it on the mantelpiece, making sure it stood proudly, and picked up her needlework. Still seething, she did not take care. The needle pricked her finger, and blood mingled with the red and yellow flowers growing around the cottage door of the picture she had been so painstakingly stitching. "Oh, oh, oh," she groaned, thinking, but not saying aloud, a few most unladylike words her mother would be appalled that she knew, let alone thought.

Two hours later, Crakeplace announced another visitor for her. *Now, who can it be?* she thought. *I hope it is one of my friends. I am in sore need of cheering up.*

But she was to be disappointed. "Lord Head."

He rushed in, without taking off his hat. The butler stood in front of him, indicating that he should do so.

"Oh, my dearest girl, I am so sorry. I understand my mother has been to see you."

She nodded.

"You must understand… I hope she did not upset you. Did she upset you?"

"Well, upset could be one word I might use."

"Oh, she did, didn't she?" He took her in his arms and squeezed her, knocking off his hat and messing his hair.

Wondering if she should reciprocate, she saw the butler, on his way out after picking up the hat, raising his eyebrows at such behaviour. Her arms by her side, she remained rigid. It was not his fault his mother was such a dragon. But she still blamed him, somehow.

He eased away. "She can be rather scathing, at times, but you must not take offence."

"Huh! Take offence? I have never been spoken to in such a manner in my whole life, Marmaduke. She found fault with everything and everyone."

He caressed her ear. "She became very depressed when my father died, very depressed."

She swivelled her head to knock away his hand and hissed through gritted teeth, "That is no excuse for rude behaviour."

"I know, I know." He went across to lean on the mantelpiece, staring into the fire in the grate. "I can only apologise again." His head jerked up, as if a sudden thought had occurred to him. "It does not mean...? You are still going to marry me, aren't you?" He hurried back, taking her hands in his. "Please do not say she has won, that you have changed your mind, I beg of you."

She had been about to say that very thing, for how could she marry him after that? But the look on his face tugged at her heartstrings and she could not do so.

"I love you," he said in a quiet voice. "There, I have said it. I know it is not right to do so, not until we are formally engaged, but it is the truth. I know you do not harbour the same feelings for me, but I am sure I can make you happy, very happy indeed."

Staring at the mole on his cheek, his protruding ears and black hair, she remained silent, still unsure how to reply.

"I realise you have had a shock, and I do not expect you to answer straightaway, my dear, so I shall leave you now, and return tomorrow. Yes, tomorrow. Good day to you."

"Good day, sir."

For a second, she thought he would kiss her, but she stepped back involuntarily, and he walked away, his shoulders drooped, his whole demeanour that of a broken man. She almost ran after him, but what could she say? She did not even know herself.

Her mother came in. "Was that your fiancé just leaving?"

"Yes." *But maybe not my fiancé much longer,* she thought, as she helped her mother onto the chaise longue. "How are you, Mama?"

"I might have been better if he had stayed to speak to me."

"But I did not know you were coming down, else I might have detained him." Not that she would have done, of course. "Would you like me to ring for tea before I go out?"

"You are going out? Where to? I thought you might stay and keep me company for a while."

Pondering if she could bear to remain in the house a moment longer, she bit her lip as she rang the bell. "Could not Eliza entertain you, Mama? I do not think she has any plans today? Not that she would tell me. She is still in high dudgeon from the other day."

"But I want *you*, dearest. You have much more interesting parlance." She lay back, her eyes closed.

Florence sat down as the maid brought in a tray of tea and biscuits. "What would you like to talk about, Mama? The weather? The state of the parliament? Our good queen, Victoria?"

"Do not be facetious, dear. It does not become you. Maybe not conversation, then, just play me something on the piano. One of my favourites."

"But Mama, you know Eliza is much better than I at playing. Shall I find her?" She made for the door.

"I see you are determined to fob me off. Do as you please. I care not."

Sighing, Florence lifted the piano lid. "I am doing nothing of the sort, Mama. You are perfectly aware that the piano is not my strong point, but if you do not mind me playing wrong notes, then I shall play for as long as you wish."

She thumped on the keys, the strident noise hurting her ears. Her mother moaned, but she carried on, releasing her frustrations. After a few minutes, she relented and played one of her sister's favourites, Beethoven's Moonlight Sonata. This calmed her, the soothing notes banishing the previous discord.

"That was beautiful, my dear," swooned her mother when she finished. "I did not hear one single incorrect note. I do not know why you denigrate yourself so much. It was perfect. Come here." She beckoned her to sit beside her. "I know why you are in such a bad mood all the time nowadays. You do not love Lord Head, but he seems a very nice man."

"Yes, Mama, he is, and I have to go through with this engagement, for all our sakes. It's just that, I… Oh, I do not know what to think." She stood up.

"Off you go for your walk, now. Clear the cobwebs from your mind. I find a stroll in a strong breeze can do that. You will feel much better afterwards."

"Yes. Are you sure you do not need anything?"

"Well, another hot drink would help. Ring the bell."

Chapter 10

Missus Fisher prepared for a dinner party to celebrate the engagement, and formalise it. "Just a small one, mind you. We must not overspend," she declared, much to Florence's amusement. However, they could not invite one set of friends without asking another, and the list grew longer by the day.

"The whole of Ambleside and Bowness as well, will be here at this rate," complained Florence, who had readily agreed to a small affair, for she did not relish being the centre of attention. "Why not request the pleasure of all the inhabitants of Windermere as well, for that matter?"

"Now, you are being silly, my dear." Her mother put down the list. "I think that will have to do. But, what about…?" Picking up the wad of paper once more, she waved it in front of her, but at Florence's glare, she placed it back on the table. "Very well, but you know Edwina Thrush had twice as many as this at her daughter's betrothal do."

"That is because she has twice as much family. They must be the largest in the area, cousins and second cousins, aunts and uncles, babies and toddlers crawling all over the place, in every nook and cranny."

"Florence, please do not be so vulgar."

"It is true, though, Mama," piped up Eliza.

The day before, she had made up with Florence, after discovering that her Mister Scarface had eloped with one of the daughters of a rich widow. Apparently, he had no money and needed to marry well. Florence had wanted to say, 'I told you so', but had kept her counsel, just thrilled to have her sister back in her confidence. "You have included Elizabeth and her parents, haven't you?"

"Of course," replied her mother. "I would not leave them out. I am sure, though, that I have forgotten somebody important."

Florence picked up the papers and locked them in a drawer. "Well, it is too late now, Mama. They, whoever they are, will have to remain uninvited. I am not adding one more name to the list."

"But, what if I remember, and it would be too terrible if they did not come?"

"Mama! Enough, if you please. Now, have you decided on your costume?"

"Well, seeing as your fiancé has agreed to pay for that as well as the wedding, I thought I would have a bright pink…"

Florence threw up her arms in disgust. "Mama, you will not."

"Ha, ha, caught you. You two girls are not the only ones who can play tricks."

"Thank goodness for that," grinned Eliza. "I had visions of this bright pink blancmange, drifting amongst the guests, shocking all and sundry with its brilliance, making them shield their eyes."

"Oh, please do not jest. It would be too awful for words." Florence smiled. "But what have you decided on?"

"Oh, something simple, with, perhaps, just a hint of elegance."

"That sounds ideal, Mama. Now, I had better start writing the invitation cards, or we shall have no guests at all."

"I would help, Flo," volunteered Eliza, "but you know my writing is too scrawly." She picked up her gloves from a side table. "I am off to see Elizabeth, to sympathise with her over our fate. She fancied her chances with him as well, you know." She looked at Florence. "And do not dare say, 'I told you so'. I can tell you have been dying to do so, ever since I informed you of that blaggard, Scarface's, wicked actions."

"Me? Say something like that? As if I would." She laughed. "You know me too well, dear sister. I have been biting my tongue. But at least, none of our close friends has been tarnished by him, so be thankful for that."

Eliza kissed her. "You always know best. What would I do without you?" She bit her lip. "You will still be there for me after you have married and departed, won't you, when I need you?"

"Of course I will. We are a twosome, are we not? No husband can come between such a force."

Her mother hugged them both. "You two have always been close. It broke my heart to see you at loggerheads. But we can put that behind us, and move forward, as they say."

They both grinned, saying in unison, "Yes, Mama," and Eliza left the room.

"I need to find cook," her mother declared, following her, "to have a word with her, to discuss the food for the party. Do you have any preference, Florence?"

"For food? No, whatever you think best, Mama. I leave it in your capable hands."

An hour later, flexing her aching hand, she counted the number of cards she had written. Not nearly enough. At that rate she would be there all day. She picked up the quill once more. The next name on the list did not register in her brain. She did not recognise it, so put the card to one side, to ask her mother about it later, and carried on with the rest.

"Oh, it is a new lady whose acquaintance I made a few weeks ago," replied her mother, when she tackled her about it.

"But, Mama, I thought we agreed we were not inviting just anybody, only close friends."

"But she is a close friend. In fact, I must admit, she is my dearest friend, so I insist."

"What about Madame Orgé? I thought her to be your dearest friend."

"Oh, she is, as well. But she is very French and having an English confidante suits me better."

"Very well. What difference will one more make?"

"Precisely. And who is paying for this affair? It matters not to you what it will cost."

"It is not the outlay, Mama, that bothers me."

"Then what? You are perfectly at home in crowds, so I cannot see what your problem is."

"Neither can I. Do not take any notice of me. I am being a worrypot."

Her mother put an arm around her shoulder. "It will be fine, I know it. Trust your dear mama."

Florence looked back at Eliza as they descended the stairs. "What a wonderful sight, Lizzie. Does it not look magnificent? They have done us proud."

"It certainly is, sis, and all for you. It is fortunate that Lord Hairy Head has put up the cash to pay for it, for we could never afford all those decorations."

"I do not deserve all this fuss. I would much rather have had a low-key affair, with just two or three friends. And please do not call him that. It is so hard to refrain from grinning at his hair."

"I am sorry. I really must stop it, for I too, have to hold back, and I fear that one day I shall say it aloud to his face. How embarrassing would that be!"

They both laughed as they continued to the drawing room, where several of the guests had assembled. "Some eager beavers are here already," whispered Eliza.

"Yes, keen to see me despatched, I expect. Oh, there is my fiancé. I suppose I had better go over and greet him."

"Do not sound so enthusiastic, sis. Folk will think you are not ready for this match."

"I am as ready as I will ever be."

Before she could make her way to him, Lord Head rushed to her. "Oh, my dearest, you cannot believe how elated you are making me this night. So elated."

I wish I felt as thrilled, she thought, putting on a brave face and smiling. One of the other guests had her back to them and she heard her ask her companion, "Do you think an engagement will be announced tonight?" The companion nudged her, smiling at them, and the lady turned around. "Oh, Lord Head, good day to you, sir. I did not see you there. How are you? I mean…"

"Good day, madam. I am well, thank you, very well. And your fine self?"

She nodded her head up and down.

"Oh, yes, I am very well too. What a lovely day it has been, today, has it not?"

Florence grinned. If at a loss as to what to talk about, use the weather.

More guests arrived, and Florence worried they would not all fit around the table. Surely she had not sent out that many invitations? Excusing herself from the lord, she went in search of her mother. She found her deep in conversation with a lady she could not recall seeing before. Waiting until their conversation came to a lull, which seemed to be some considerable time, for the lady scarce drew breath in between sentences, she tugged at her sleeve. "Mama, please may I have a word."

Her mother gave her apologies to the lady and followed her. "Mama, I surely did not send cards to all these people. Where are we going to sit them all?"

"Well, my dear, I do have to admit I invited one or two others. You do not mind, do you?"

"I do not even know that lady you were speaking to just now." Florence felt her eyes filling with tears. "How could you do this to me?"

"Calm down, my dear." Her mother steered her towards the outside door which a footman opened. "It will be fine. I have sorted everything with Crakeplace. He assures me they will all fit. It might be a squeeze, admittedly, but do not worry. It will mar your features. And we so want you to look your best tonight, now. don't we?"

Wishing she had a handkerchief, she sniffed. "Yes, Mama, of course. I hope you are right."

"Of course I am. Mothers are always right. Now, come back in when you are recovered. I must return to our guests."

Standing looking over the dark gardens, still sniffing, but trying to compose herself, she sensed someone joining her, and a white handkerchief appeared from behind. "Thank you," she muttered, assuming it to be her fiancé. "I am just somewhat emotional." She turned and her breath left her body. "You? What are you doing here?"

He cleared his throat. "I accompanied my aunt."

"Your aunt?" She blew her nose, holding the hanky close to her face, trying to stop her hand from shaking.

"Yes, Lady Kendall. Apparently, she has become great friends with your mama."

She offered him the hanky, but he shook his head, so she kept it in her clenched fist. "L…Lady Kendall? But that is not your name."

Several other people filtered out so she stepped away from him. He stood back as well. "She is my mother's sister."

"I must go in. My guests await." She pushed past him, her senses reeling as he brushed her hand with his finger. Just the lightest of touches, but enough to send her raw emotions spiralling. How could she face her guests?

Eliza approached as she entered the room. "Flo, what is it? Are you unwell?" No reply would leave her dry lips. "Come outside and take some fresh air." Eliza tried to pull her towards the door.

"No!" she shouted, arousing several people nearby. "No, I am fine. Not out there."

Her sister looked surprised at her outburst. "Why, what is out there? Or rather, who?"

When she did not enlighten her, Eliza looked from her to the door, a puzzled expression on her face. "Stay here. I shall investigate."

Florence pulled her back. "No, please, I beg of you. It is nothing. I am fully recovered now. Let us mingle with the guests."

"If you are sure."

She dragged her sister in the opposite direction and tried to make meaningful conversation with her guests.

With a shaking hand, Luke Lancaster lit a cigarette and took a deep drag. *I knew I should not have come. How can I watch her become betrothed to another? For I am sure that is what this dinner party is all about.*

Since the incident in the forest, he had thought about no other female than Florence Fisher. Admittedly, he had tried to, by taking out young ladies for rides in his barouche, or escorting them to balls and to the opera, in a bid to rid himself of her image, but it had not worked. He had fallen head over heels in love with her. When he had returned that morning, and found her gone, he had been desolate. Her tell-tale reactions told him he affected her. She could not love that pompous lord, so why become engaged to him? Rumours abounded that the family had fallen on hard times, that the brother was a wastrel. That had been the reason for him putting up the money to rescue him when he had come to grief with his gambling. He had sworn Frederick to secrecy, not wanting Florence to know what he had done. Why had he not shown his hand earlier? There had been plenty of opportunities. But he could not. He had obligations and, anyway, she had seemed so eager to escape from him in the forest.

He stubbed out the cigarette and left.

During the meal, Florence spoke animatedly to the lady beside her, Madame Orgé. Luke Lancaster had been placed at the other end, on the opposite side, which meant that every time she glanced in that direction, the soft candlelight would show him gazing at her, so she had to cast her eyes down to the new tablecloth that her mother had assured her to be of the finest quality. One time Lord Head, sitting opposite her, noticed, for he leaned forward and looked pointedly past the lady on his right, to see up the table. A look of displeasure crossed his face when his gaze alighted on Luke, who tipped his hand to his forelock with a grin.

What did he think he was playing at? And why had he come to torment her? Surely he knew it was her engagement party, even though it had not been announced? That would come later. Did he not realise the effect he had on her? Maybe he did, and that was his reason. To trifle with her emotions.

The food must have been delicious, for everyone seemed to be eating it with relish, but it all tasted like sawdust in her mouth, even the dressed crab, which usually suited her palate.

She abstained from the first dish. Oysters. They had never been a favourite of hers, and she felt she would have been sick if she had tried them. She nibbled at a thin slice of bread, occasionally placing it back on her napkin, trying to appear to be eating heartily, in case anybody noticed her lack of appetite. Hopefully her soon-to-be-officially fiancé would put it down to nerves, if he did so.

"'Ave you been to zee teatre, Florence?" asked Madame Orgé. "I love eet, all zose actors and actresses."

"Not lately," she replied, forcing a piece of stuffed chicken into her mouth.

"I used to be an actress, you know."

"Yes, Mama told me."

She went on to regale her with stories of her life treading the boards, not expecting replies, and not receiving any.

Finally Lord Head stood up and lifted his glass in the air. "May I propose a toast? Please raise your glasses to our delightful hosts."

Everyone followed suit.

Florence held her breath, thinking that this would be the announcement time, but he invited the rest of the men to adjourn to the drawing room.

She plonked back down onto her chair, letting out her breath in relief.

After the men had drunk their port and smoked their cigarettes, they joined the ladies in the parlour.

"My daughter, Eliza, will now entertain you on the pianoforte," announced her mother, shoving a reluctant Eliza towards the instrument. "She is a very consummate player, you know."

"Do I have to?" hissed Eliza. "This is supposed to be Florence's evening. Should she not be the one to play?"

"You are more accomplished. Florence can turn the music for you, if you like."

"Please, Lizzie," Florence begged in an undertone. "Just do as Mama says."

Once her sister started, everyone sat listening, enraptured looks on their faces. Florence peeped upwards from the music sheet, and caught Luke's eye. His lips not quite smiling, just turned up slightly at the sides, he stared at her. Mesmerised, she could not take her eyes from him, until Eliza played a wrong note, and she realised she should have turned the page.

"Keep up, please," whispered Eliza. "I shall make a hash of it, otherwise."

"I am sorry. I shall concentrate from now on."

"I suppose you were ogling your Luke Lancaster. I saw you earlier."

"Shush. Do not let Marmaduke hear you."

Another wrong note, as Eliza giggled, made their mother jump up, clapping her hands. "Was that not delightful?" Everyone applauded as she rushed over to the piano. "What do you think you are doing, you pair?"

"Sorry, mama," they replied in unison.

She turned to the gathering. "Would anybody else like to play?"

Luke stood up. "I would sing if Miss Fisher would accompany me on the piano."

A hushed whisper spread around the room, as everybody looked to see who could be so bold.

"Or even a duet, if Miss Eliza would like to remain where she is and play for us."

"But I cannot sing," began Florence, appalled at such a notion.

"Of course you can, my dear," contradicted her mother. "You have a beautiful voice. Everyone says so."

"So be it, then." Luke strutted up to the piano. "What would you like to sing first?"

"First?" Florence almost choked.

"How about 'Love's Old Sweet Song? Do you know that?"

"Does it start, 'Just a song at twilight?'" asked Eliza. "I don't think I have the music."

"Then we shall sing it without."

Aghast, Florence stared up at him as he began to sing. She waited until the chorus, and then joined in. Once into her stride, she sang with confidence, enjoying the moment, swaying to the rhyme, in perfect attune to the man beside her. When he came to the line, 'Love will be found the sweetest song of all' he stared into her eyes, and she knew.

She broke off, and ran out of the room. How could she marry an ugly, pompous man like Lord Head, when Luke Lancaster looked at her with such love in his eyes? She had seen it. Her imagination could not be deceiving her.

The library door slammed behind her, and she leaned against it. Ignoring a loud hammering, and a voice calling her name, she hid behind a chair. A squeak betrayed the opening of the door. Curled up, she dared not look to see who had followed her.

"Florence? I know you are in here."

Memories of playing hide and seek with her father flooded her brain, and she burst into tears. Tender arms reached around the chair and engulfed her. Cigarette smoke caught in her nostrils, and she knew straightaway who it must be.

"Oh, my darling," he murmured in her ear.

Too overcome to speak, she nestled in his arms, the place where she belonged, not with Mister Hairy Head.

Footsteps outside made her pull away, but he resisted her efforts, and kept a tight hold on her.

"Someone is coming," she muttered.

"I know."

"They must not see us like this."

He released her as her mother sailed in, her face like thunder. "What on earth was that display for?"

"I am sorry, Mama."

Luke stepped up to her. "I must apologise, Ma'am. It is my fault. I should not have asked your daughter to sing with me."

"But what was the harm in that? She did not need to go haring off in a tantrum." Her mother grabbed her arm. "Come, I think Lord Head is about to make the announcement."

"Mama, I...?" Florence looked up at Luke.

His features hardened. "So..." he began, "it is your betrothal he will be declaring? I wondered as much." He turned away.

She could not bear to see the anguish in his eyes and turned to her mother, waiting to take her to her doom. "I am sorry, Mama..."

Her mother tried to pull her to the door. "You are going through with it, my girl. You cannot back out now."

"No, I cannot do it. I...I..."

She pulled free and stood in front of Luke. "What did you call me just now?"

Without a word, he stared at her with hopeless eyes.

"It matters not what this man said to you, girl," declared her mother. "I do not know what is going on here, and do not want to. You have your duty to perform. Come along."

"Luke?"

Surely, he would not desert her now. Why did he remain silent?

He reached out and touched her hand. "You must go."

"No. One word from you and I shall not."

"Florence, come this minute!"

With drooping shoulders, he walked over to the fireplace.

She followed her mother down the corridor.

With a heavy heart, Luke Lancaster watched her walk out. He should have stopped her. He should. But he could not. He had no right. It would not have been the first time he had taken a young lady from her family. Some years before, he had thought himself in love with a certain Margaret Bowe. He had thought her to be as much in love with him, but had found out she had merely been trifling with him, to make another man jealous. Fortunately her father had caught up with them before they arrived at Gretna Green, and no harm had come to her, and her reputation had not been sullied. The family had managed to keep the affair quiet, and she had married the man she had wanted soon after.

That had been one of the reasons he had snubbed Florence. His greatest wish would have been to grab her there and then, and make passionate love to her. But he did not know her true feelings towards him. Just because she had clung to him did not mean she harboured any deep affection. She had just been emotional. Her eyes had told him one thing, but he had not known her long enough to fathom what she really thought.

After all, she could not leave the forest quickly enough. Admittedly, that had been different circumstances, but, all the same, she had made her position clear. She despised him. Not that he could blame her.

He stared at his haggard face in the mirror above the fireplace. His hair stuck up, and no amount of smoothing it down would flatten it, even spitting on his finger like his mother had done when he had been a young boy.

Maybe he should pay his mother a visit. She lived quite a journey away, near Cockermouth.

She would be pleased to see him. He had not seen her for a few months, not since he had lured Florence into the forest. Guilty that he had not been for so long, he straightened his jacket and waistcoat and determined he would go on the morrow.

"Is there any point in returning to the party?" he murmured into the mirror, picking a stray hair from his shoulder. He went into the hall, thinking to find the butler and ask for his greatcoat and cane.

A girl sat peeping through the banisters on the landing halfway up the stairs.

"Hello," he whispered, "Who are you?"

"Felicity," she whispered back. "Mama said I couldn't come to the party. I'm too young. But I will soon be twelve. That isn't young, is it?"

"Well, Miss Felicity, it is compared to me."

"Why, how old are you? Oo, I'm sorry. I shouldn't ask strangers that, should I? In fact I should not speak to unknown visitors at all, so Mama says, not without an introduction. But now we have already spoken, I suppose we aren't strangers any more, are we?"

He climbed the single flight of stairs and squatted beside her. "No, Miss Felicity." He held out his hand and she shook it. "I am pleased to meet you. May I introduce myself? I am Luke Lancaster. There now, we have been formally introduced."

She beamed at him, and then cocked her head to one side. "Haven't I heard my sister, Florence, speak about you?"

"Oh, have you? In what context? I hope it was nothing defamatory."

"Um, I don't think so. That means saying nasty things, doesn't it?"

"You are right, it does."

237

"Well…" She seemed to ponder for a moment, but before she could reply, a door downstairs opened and Florence ran out, slamming the door behind her.

"I'd better hide." Felicity ran up to the next floor.

Luke watched his beloved swizzle around, her hands on her head as if agitated. But he could not go to her. He had made his decision.

She disappeared again, and the door through which she had come opened and the other guests poured out, speaking in furtive whispers. He crept down the stairs and mingled with them, found the butler and took his leave.

Waiting in his carriage for his aunt, he hoped his hostess would not have noticed his bad manners in not saying goodbye, but thought she would be too excited about her daughter's betrothal to have realised. One of the other guest's remarks kept coming back to him, though. It did not make sense.

"Oo, my head. I should not have drunk so much of that punch." Eliza turned over in bed, covering her eyes.

Florence sat propped up by pillows, reading. "It is your own fault. I have no sympathy."

"Oh, pray do not lecture me, sister dear. I am not the one who has brought ruin upon our heads." She brushed her hair from her face. "I know not how you can sit there so calmly, after what you have done."

"I am not at all calm. I have barely read the first page, and I have been awake this past two hours or more." She put down the book. "Do you think he will sue me for breach of promise?"

"I would not think so. It is not the same as when the man calls off the engagement." Eliza sat up, squinting. "Anyway, he would achieve nothing. We have no money. I could not blame you, though, for not marrying Lord Hairy, but Mama will not see your actions in the same light. She will only harp on about your social reputation being ruined, and how you will have trouble finding a good husband now. I think you had better keep out of her way this morning."

"Yes, I shall try. Oh, Lizzie, I tried so hard to accept his proposal, but seeing Luke Lancaster and feeling his arms around me, I just could not do it, even though the blaggard rejected me." She flung the book across the room, and it landed on the armchair. "Why would he trifle with me like that? Why enfold me in his arms and call me his darling, to then want nothing to do with me as soon as mother mentioned the betrothal? Surely that should have spurred him on to more action, before it was too late, if he felt anything for me? Do you not agree?"

"I know not of the ways of men, sister dear. They are a breed apart." Eliza climbed out of bed and used the chamber pot. "Why don't you ask Mama if you can visit Aunt Enid for a while until the brouhaha has died down? You never did return."

"What a splendid idea. Would you not want to come as well, to keep me company?"

"Um...well, normally I would jump at the chance, but do you remember that young man who danced with you at Lord and Lady March's ball, the one with the twinkling eyes, whose name we never did find out?"

"Ah, yes, Mister A N Other, the military man. I remember. What about him. He disappeared. We never saw him again."

Eliza sat at the mirror, brushing her hair.

"Well, Elizabeth told me last night that she thought she saw him in town yesterday, so I might stay around and try to gain his acquaintance, seeing as you are no longer interested in him."

"Very well, if you would rather go out cavorting than accompany me, I shall not be offended...much."

"Oh, Flo, it is not that."

Florence threw aside the bedcovers. "I am jesting, darling sister. What I need is peace and quiet, in the countryside, away from the family. Not that I will have peace, with all those children, but you know what I mean."

"Away from Lord Head, you mean, and the ignominy of your rejection of him."

"Yes, and Luke Lancaster, of course. I never want to see his face ever again. I practically offered myself to him and he rejected me."

"It was his loss, sister. He does not know what he has missed, such a wonderful, good, generous..."

"That's enough." Florence tossed her pillow at her sister. "I am beginning to wonder if you are about to make a request. You do not usually praise me so."

Eliza caught the pillow, took it back and hugged her. "No, but I should. I shall miss you while you are away. How long do you think you will stay?"

She blew out her cheeks and unwrapped herself from her sister's embrace. "As long as it takes for the hullabaloo to fade away, maybe a few months."

A gasp escaped Eliza's lips. "As long as that? I had meant a week or two. You don't mean to leave me to Mama's moanings and groanings for that long? How will I bear it?" She twisted Florence around to face her. "Please reconsider. It will be even worse, now, knowing we shall have to pull in the purse strings even harder, until one of us marries, that is."

"Well, I shall be one less for the purse to feed, so that might help. I shall write to you every day and describe the scenery, and the antics of little Eddie and the other children, and the colour of the sky. Well, maybe not every day, but as often as I feel the urge to take up a pen. I might even write a novel, like Jane Austen or Charles Dickens. What do you say to that?"

Eliza's eyebrows rose and she spluttered. "A novel? Where did that idea come from? Although, you were good at writing stories in the schoolroom, weren't you? Why not? I think it a splendid idea. You could become famous and rich, and save our bacon that way. Yes, splendid." She danced round the small room, her arms in the air. "My sister, the author."

Florence joined in, and they tumbled onto the bed, laughing and giggling like small children, until a knock on the door sobered them up.

Hair still in rags, dressing gown open, eyes red from crying, their mother stormed in. "How can you two be so merry on this disastrous morning?"

Florence ran to her. "I am so sorry, Mama. I do not know what to say."

She pushed her away. "There is nothing you can say that will ever make me forgive you, girl."

"But, Mama…"

"Eliza, please tell your sister I will never speak to her again. If she wishes to communicate with me, she may do so through you."

Her sister looked at her with anguish and turned to her mother. "Mama, please do not say that. It is not the end of the world."

"It is for me."

Florence ran in front of her. "If it will help, Mama, I shall go and stay with Aunt Enid and Uncle Eric."

Her mother flounced out, muttering, "Eliza, pray tell your sister she may do as she pleases, as long as she does not involve me."

Florence slumped onto the bed. "I knew she would be cross, but I did not think she would be like that."

Eliza put her arm around her. "She will come around, you see. She would never cut you off completely. You are her favourite daughter, after all."

"Not any more." Florence could see no point in refuting the statement, as she usually did. "At least, now, you will be, for the foreseeable future."

"I think not. She will probably turn her affections to Felicity. I think that, even if I were the only daughter, she would still not love me as she does you or her."

"Oh, Lizzie, of course she loves you. She just does not show it. She will be relying on you, now, for Freddie is off again, to stay with his friend." She stood up and lifted her nightdress over her head. "I sometimes wonder if he prefers men to women."

Eliza's shocked face stared at her as she popped her head out of the cotton material. "You do not mean...?"

"Well, has he ever actually courted a girl?"

"And he does seem more at home with men. Oh, my goodness, the thought had never occurred to me before. For goodness sake, do not let Mama have an inkling. She would hit the ceiling."

"She would, but we may be doing our brother an injustice. We might be completely on the wrong track, so let us not pursue this line of conversation any longer. What dress shall I wear today? If I am to be travelling I had better wear something warm. The purple one, I think, with the high neck."

"I am still wondering about Freddie. I am sure I saw him with a girl the other day, so you must be wrong. It would be inconceivable, wouldn't it?"

"Forget it, Lizzie. I wish I had never voiced my thoughts. I should not have done so. It was very unfair of me. Now, would you like to help me pack or shall I ask the maid?"

"No, I will help you. I want to spend as much time with you as possible, seeing as I shall be losing you for so long."

"Very well, let us go down to breakfast, and then we shall make a start."

The maid came in and they dressed and hurried down to the breakfast room.

"Now we are here, I do not really fancy anything." Eliza put her hand to her head. "The smell of the food is making me feel rather queasy, in fact."

She rushed out, leaving Florence to complete her repast alone.

Her appetite not very forthcoming either, she toyed with a sausage and a rasher of bacon, knowing that she needed to fill up for the long journey ahead. Forcing a slice of toast, she washed it down with lukewarm tea, as the maid came in with a fresh pot.

"Oh, lovely, just what I need."

As the maid turned to go out, she asked her, "How is Sybil? I intended…I mean I feel very guilty I have not been to see her this week."

"She is almost recovered, Miss Florence. She should be back with you in a couple of days."

"Oh. I am going away today. Should I see if she wants to come? Would she be well enough to travel?"

"You had better ask her, ma'am. I cannot speak for her."

"No, no, of course not. Thank you. Oh, by the way, where will I find her?"

"In the servants' quarters, ma'am."

Sipping a hot cup of tea, she made up her mind to find her maid. She would need her for she could not travel all that way on her own.

Eventually, she found her in the kitchen, talking to the cook. "Ah, Sybil, there you are. How do you feel? Are you completely recovered?"

"Almost, ma'am. I should be back on duty tomorrow."

"Ah, good, good. I intend visiting my aunt again. As you very well know, I did not make it last time. How do you feel about accompanying me?"

Fear filled the maid's eyes. "Oh, Miss Florence."

Florence looked at the cook who carried on beating something in a bowl, with a very disapproving look. "I have to leave for a while. I expect you all know what happened last evening?"

Sybil nodded, but the cook did not look up, merely beat even faster.

Florence shifted from one foot to the other. How dare the woman judge her, not knowing the circumstances? Anyway, it was not her place. But then, if her livelihood were to be affected, if her rejection of the lord meant the servants would all be laid off, she could understand why she seemed so condemning. She wondered if she should try to explain, but could not find the words.

Sitting on the coach some hours later, after finally persuading Sybil to accompany her by telling her that if she did not she would have to leave, because there would not be a job for her, she watched the mountains pass by—hints of snow on top of them—and wrapped her cloak around her.

One of the other passengers tried to start up a conversation with a lady across from her. The lady did not seem receptive, so the man turned to her. "I love this time of year, don't you? Just look at the different hues and colours on the trees, burnt amber and gold."

Sybil had been leaning back against the padded cushions, but at the poetic statement, she leaned forward and glanced out of the window. "So they are. I had not noticed. Just look, Miss Florence."

Her animated face cheered Florence up no end, having had to endure her sullen demeanour for the past hour. "Are you a poet, sir?" she asked.

"I wish I were, ma'am. My father holds that title, not me. He has written many a poem. You may have heard of them, especially the one about the host of daffodils."

"Oh, yes, I have indeed, if it is William Wordsworth. My governess taught it to me." When the man nodded, she added, "William Wordsworth is your father? Oh, my goodness. Wait until I tell my sister I have met his son. She will be so impressed, although, I have to admit, she prefers Coleridge and his 'Rime of the Ancient Mariner'. Not me, though. I much prefer your father's work. It has more to do with nature."

The man grinned. "Would it be impertinent of me to ask your name?"

Florence looked at Sybil, who had sat back with her eyes closed. She should not tell him—she saw an elderly lady in the far corner look disapprovingly at her—but if he were the true son

of her favourite poet, what harm could there be in doing so? "I am Miss Florence Fisher, sir."

He cocked his hat. "William Wordsworth, ma'am, but they call me Willy, so as not to confuse me with my father."

What a stroke of fortune. "And where are you travelling to, today, sir?"

"All the way to Cockermouth. And you?"

"Yes, we are too. I am visiting my aunt. She lives just outside, in a village called Dovenby."

"How fortunate. I shall be staying nearby, in Tallentire."

"And your father is still alive, sir?"

"Oh, yes, he has moved back from London where he has been living, and now lives at Rydal, near Ambleside."

"To think I live just a short distance from him, and have never met him."

"When you return home, I shall find some way to introduce you to him. My fiancée is an avid fan of my father's also. I think you would find each other's company very pleasing."

"Thank you. I look forward to that."

The coach pulled up at an inn and the door opened for them to alight.

As they partook of their refreshments, Florence could not stop talking about the happy incident, so much so, she could see Sybil becoming bored with the subject.

"But have you never read any of his poems?" she asked, incredulous that anyone could not have done so.

"Ma'am, I can barely read at all, let alone waste my time on poetry."

"But I thought you looked interested when he started speaking." Florence took another bite of the egg sandwich.

"Interested in the scenery, not the words." Sybil took a drink of her tea and began to choke. Florence looked around her, wondering what to do, as Mister Wordsworth rushed over and patted the maid on the back, stopping the coughing.

"Oh, thank you, sir. You are a saviour."

"Pleased to be of service, ma'am." He touched his forelock and returned to his seat.

"How fortunate he was handy," she told the maid, who had taken out her handkerchief to wipe her streaming eyes.

Florence had been about to look back at her new friend, but something on the handkerchief caught her eye. A monogram. "Is that...? Is that the one Luke Lancaster lent you?"

"I beg your pardon, ma'am." The maid looked surprised at the question.

"That handkerchief? Is it the one he lent you in the forest?"

Sybil looked at it. "Oh, yes, it must be. I had forgotten."

Tempted to snatch it from her, she resisted by sitting on her hands. What would she want with it, anyway? He had made his feelings very clear. He did not want anything to do with her, so what would be the point in hanging onto something of his? None at all.

"Do you think I should give it back?"

"What? Oh, no, I am sure he would not relish it now, not after it has been used. You may as well keep it."

Nodding, the maid stuffed it down the front of her dress. "Yes, I have made use of it several times this past few weeks, when I have been laid up. I hear the man in question turned up at our house. What did you think of that?"

Surprised at the maid's unusual question, she had been about to reply scornfully, but closed her mouth. The thought of Luke Lancaster spurning her brought a sickness to her stomach, and she put down the food and wiped her mouth. "I do not wish to ever see that man's face again, or hear his name, so I respectfully request that you never speak of him."

"Yes, ma'am, of course, if that is what you really want."

Florence looked at the maid. Did she realise she did not mean a single word of it, that she would willingly run to him if he walked into the inn at that very moment and held out his arms?

But he would not be doing anything of the kind, so why had she even let the thought enter her head?

The door opened and a fair-haired man walked in. She almost fainted. For a split second, she had imagined her dream to have come true. But it turned out not to be him, of course.

She let out her breath and stood up. "We must return to the coach, or it will leave without us."

Sybil finished chewing. "But, ma'am, everybody else is still here. Look, even your poet."

"Well, I have had enough. I shall see you outside."

Out in the fresh air, she shivered, looking up at the dull grey sky. "Please God, don't let it snow. We still have half the journey left," she prayed.

Sybil came running out, pulling on her hat. "I am sorry, ma'am. I should not have left you."

"It is of no consequence, Sybil, and anyway, I left you, not the other way around."

"It looks like snow."

"That's what I thought. I do hope not. I just want to arrive safely in one piece, and settle down in front of my aunt's roaring fire. We might have to stay overnight at an inn, and that would mean extra expense we can little afford."

The other passengers filtered out and they soon started on their way after the coachman had also expressed his worries about the threatening sky.

The talk from everyone aboard centred on the weather, some hoping it would snow, others in like mind to Florence, wishing heartily that it would not.

"I do love to watch it falling, though," remarked the elderly lady in the corner. "It is so silent and pretty."

Most people agreed.

"And making the first foot prints in the smooth surface, that is my favourite," added Mister Wordsworth."

"Did your father ever write a poem about snow?" asked Florence, trying to turn her anxiety about having to spend unnecessary money into something more pleasant.

"Oh, yes, many a one." He went on to recite one or two, being joined by several of the other people at intervals, including Florence, who had been reminded of one she had forgotten, about a girl called Lucy Grey.

"Such a sad story. I believe it was based on an actual incident related to him by my Aunt Dorothy."

"I cannot wait to meet your father. He must have so many such stories to tell. Is he in good health?"

Willy laughed. "If you mean, will he still be around when you return, then I certainly hope so, for yes, he enjoys very good health for his age."

She laughed also. "No, I did not mean that, but I am pleased to know he will be. Around, I mean, for I can scarcely contain my excitement."

They continued their journey and arrived at their destination while the snow fell, but not heavily enough to detain them.

"I shall see thee anon." Willy Wordsworth helped first Florence, then the elderly lady, and finally Sybil, down from the coach. "May I offer my carriage? It should be waiting for me."

"No, thank you, sir. My uncle should be here to meet us." She looked along the line of gigs waiting for the emerging passengers, and saw her Uncle Eric waving. She waved back. "Yes, he is there. Good day to you. I shall send my calling card when I return to Ambleside, to come to meet your father."

"Yes, certainly, and my fiancée. She would be very pleased to meet you, I know she would."

Chapter 11

Florence awoke to the sound of grunting pigs, lowing cattle and honking geese. How she loved the countryside.

Her aunt's voice rose up from the farmyard. She stretched and yawned, wondering who she could be talking to, and padded over to the window, a blanket wrapped around her, for in her haste, she—or rather Sybil— had forgotten to pack her dressing gown. Not seeing anybody else, she assumed her aunt had taken to conversing with the animals. Not that she blamed her. At least, she would not receive an unfavourable reply. Or maybe one of the children had been out of sight, helping her before they went to school. Her aunt and uncle could not afford a governess, so the older children walked the three miles to the schoolhouse most mornings. She did not think they would be going that day, though, for snow had fallen heavily and the ground was covered in a blanket of white. A beautiful sight. She had an urge to write a poem about it, but had no paper or ink at hand, and, anyway, how would she ever compare to her favourite poet, Mister Wordsworth? She felt too humble to even attempt it.

Two of her young cousins lay asleep, entwined in the single bed on the other side of the room. She had purloined the other bed, supposedly sharing with the third, but this child was nowhere in sight. Maybe she had arisen earlier and that had been to whom her aunt had been speaking.

So as not to awake the sleeping pair, she found her slippers and quietly opened the door, closing it behind her, as she went downstairs.

"Good day, my dear. I trust you slept well." Her aunt came through the back door, stamping her feet.

Florence sat on a chair and yawned again. "Yes, thank you, Aunt, very well indeed."

"Breakfast won't be long." Aunt Enid went to the range and threw on some logs.

"Where's Violet? I assume she is not going to school today."

"She's feeding the chickens, and no, none of them will. How do you fancy bacon and eggs?"

Florence stood up. "That would be lovely, thank you, but let me do it. You must have a thousand and one other chores to complete."

"Very well, for I do indeed. This unusually early snow will put our schedule right out of kilter, I can tell you." She bustled about, taking down the washing from the overhead racks, and folding them into neat piles, in-between feeding Baby Eddie, in his highchair, with pieces of bread to keep him quiet. "I regret it will put a spoke in the wheels of any social life you might have been anticipating during your stay."

"Oh, do not worry about that, Aunt. It will be lovely to have some time away, just to relax. Not that I do not intend to pull my weight here. I shall do whatever I can."

"Giving the children a few lessons would be a great help, with them not being able to attend the schoolhouse."

"That is a brilliant idea. I shall look forward to that."

Violet came in, rubbing her hands, her nose and cheeks ruddy from the cold.

"You'd like that, wouldn't you Violet?" Aunt Enid asked her. "For your cousin to help you with your writing?"

The girl looked away, shame-faced.

"How old are you now?" asked Florence.

"Ten, nearly eleven," she replied in a soft voice.

"Then it is settled. We shall start as soon as we have finished breakfast. Will any of the others want to join in?"

The two girls who had shared her bedroom came downstairs, hand in hand. "We want to, whatever it is," said one of them. Florence could not tell if it was Margaret or Mary, the twins being identical. They gave Florence a hug as Aunt Enid placed plates of steaming porridge on the table. "Eat this, then you can do some writing as well, that is, if your cousin doesn't mind."

She turned to Florence who stood cooking the bacon. "It was actually the older children I meant, but if you wouldn't mind these two?"

"Of course not. Where are the boys?"

"Thomas has gone out to help his pa take some hay to the sheep, and Robert…actually I'm not sure where he is."

Violet looked up. "I saw him over near the horses."

"That sounds about right. He'd put the animals before himself any time." The door opened, blowing in a cold draught, and he walked in, stamping the snow from his boots. "Ah, the very person," exclaimed his mother, helping him off with his coat. "Come and have something to eat."

"Stop fussing, Ma, I ain't a baby." He gave Florence an apologetic look, as if embarrassed at being treated like one.

"No, son, but I still worry about you. You have never been robust, ever since you were a tot. Did you see your brother and pa? Are they coming in?"

"No, Ma, I didn't." He sat down and tucked into his food. Florence wondered why his mother considered him to be frail, for he seemed sturdy enough to her.

"Well, I hope they aren't long," said his mother.

They had almost finished by the time Uncle Eric and the oldest boy returned.

"Good day," they both addressed Florence.

She stood up to allow them space to sit.

Her aunt shooed the younger children out, indicating to her to sit down.

"It's raw out there," her uncle continued.

"May we go out and build a snowman, Ma?" asked one of the twins.

"Later, perhaps," replied their mother.

"I could help," volunteered Florence, guessing, from the look her aunt gave her, that that had been her hope. "I would love that." She would, too. The idea appealed to her, as long as she could borrow some warm gloves. She didn't want to spoil her kid ones.

Eddie banged his spoon on his tray, as if asking if he could as well. His mother smiled. "No, my pet, you're too young. You can barely walk yet. The snow would come up to the top of your legs." He banged again, a huge grin covering his face.

"He's a happy little soul, isn't he?" remarked Florence. "May I lift him out?"

"Well, I should leave him where he is, if I were you. He pongs a bit. I shall change his nappy in a moment."

She backed away as Violet laughed. "Don't you want to change it, Cousin Florence?"

She shook her head. "No, thank you very much. I need to work out a plan of action for this morning's lessons."

Once the table had been cleared, she set to, with plenty of paper.

Violet showed her a new pencil. "My other cousin bought me this for my birthday. She told me it had been made in the factory in Keswick. Don't you think it's magnificent?"

"It certainly is. Does it help you write better?"

"Yes, look, I can write really big words now. I couldn't do that before."

She laughed. The innocence of children never ceased to amaze her. After giving the children a session on history, trying to remember the dates of as many kings and queens as she could, she followed it with sums.

After a light lunch, they changed into their warmest clothes and, clad in scarves, hats and gloves, traipsed outside, Sybil included, to build their snowman. The snow had stopped, and the temperature seemed to have lifted, so an enjoyable time was soon followed by mugs of hot, steaming cocoa around the kitchen table.

"It looks as if it's thawing, and might be gone by the morning," Aunt Enid declared, in between sips of her drink. "You might go visiting, after all, Florence."

"Yes, I may meet up with Mister Wordsworth's niece. He is here to pick her up from his sister or his cousin, I don't remember which. I could take one of the children with me. Not Eddie, though, much as I would love to show him off, for he is such a beautiful baby." She tried to think of a plausible excuse for not taking the baby, not being in the habit of dealing with their little problems, like dirty nappies and such.

Her aunt came to her rescue. "I would not expect you to, my dear. And it depends when you go. If it is in the afternoon, you might consider taking the twins. They are no bother, are you girls?"

The twins shook their heads in unison. Florence thought it strange that everything the dark-haired girls did was as one action, even the hand movements, and facial expressions, and they stood so closely together, they seemed to be joined at the hip. Their blue eyes reminded her of Felicity's, whereas Violet's were more a green.

"That is settled, then. If the snow has disappeared tomorrow, we shall walk into town."

The girls' faces beamed, but Violet looked downcast, clearly feeling left out.

"I shall take you the following day, Violet, if your mama does not mind. We might…what should we do?" She tried to think of something special to treat the youngster.

"I still have half a farthing I've been saving." Violet turned to her mother. "You said I might spend it, or some of it, didn't you, Ma, when an occasion arose."

Her mother nodded as she changed the baby's nappy on her knee.

"Very well, we shall look round the shops and see what we can find," said Florence. "I shall look forward to that. I may even see something to buy." She hoped not, for she had brought very little money, but it would be exciting to browse, and Christmas would be upon them before very long, so she needed to think what presents she could buy for everyone.

The following day, the snow had indeed almost gone, only a few pockets of it left in crevices. In a way, disappointment smothered the feeling of relief, for she did love to see it, but she wanted to be out and about in the town. Much as she loved her little cousins, the noise in the house, compared with the quietness at home, sometimes overwhelmed her.

They looked in shop windows, the array of pretty dresses catching the twins' eyes, and causing many an "Oo" and an "Ah" as they pictured themselves wearing them.

"Do you like fancy frocks, Florence?" asked one of them. She still could not tell them apart.

Florence didn't know whether to feel affronted. Did the child consider her clothes to be frumpy?

But, admittedly, her winter clothes were of a darker and more practical material then her finer summer dresses, and could not by any stretch of the imagination be called fancy. "Yes, I do, cousin." She could not call her by her name. They would realise she did not know to which one she was speaking.

"I shall have one like that when I'm older, shan't we, Mary?" She pointed to a particularly fine example of an emerald green one with long sleeves, lace at the cuffs and collar, and pretty buttons down the front. It looked like silk.

Aha! "Well, then Margaret, you'd better start saving up, for this shop looks very expensive. That's an attractive parasol, is it not?"

The girl looked down at her own faded green dress, showing beneath a brown coat that looked a size too small, and smiled. "That's probably all I'll have enough money to buy."

Florence put her arm around her. "Maybe you will marry a rich man, with five thousand pounds a year. Then you will afford lots of dresses." *Not like me, end up as an impoverished old maid, too stubborn to accept a perfectly fine example of a man because I hanker after another.*

They wandered around the town. Florence wished she could treat the little girls to a bun in the tearooms, but did not know how long her small stash of money would have to last.

As they were about to start the walk home, Willy Wordsworth came towards them with a young girl. He stopped and bowed. "Miss Fisher, how delighted I am to meet you again. I have been telling Jane, here, all about you. She is my niece, the daughter of my oldest brother, John." He nudged the girl forward. "Say good day to the lady, Jane."

She seemed very shy, but did as bid.

"Good day to you, sir. These are two of my cousins. Miss Mary and Miss Margaret Fisher." The girls tried to hide behind her, but she could not allow bad manners and pulled them forward.

Mister Wordsworth did not seem to notice, though, as he looked around. "We were about to take some refreshment. Would you do me the honour of accompanying me to those tearooms over there?"

"Oh, no, sir. I could not impose on you." She would, however, welcome a warm drink, for the chilly air was freezing her fingertips, but he had not offered to pay. What if he did not?

"It would not be an imposition, dear lady. It would be an honour, would it not, Jane?"

"Yes, Uncle," she replied.

She had no option but to comply. The tearooms looked rather full, but they found a table at the back and sat down.

"Tea, and cake?" he asked, as the waitress came to take their order.

"Just a drink, thank you."

"We're having cake, eh, Jane? She loves their speciality." He shook out a serviette and asked the waitress for tea and Eccles cakes all round.

Jane seemed to lose her coyness as she sat next to the twins. "I made a snowman yesterday," she declared.

"So did we." Margaret grinned. "It was fun."

Florence had worked out how to identify them. Margaret did all the talking, and had a little scar, probably from chicken pox, next to her left eye.

As the children continued to talk about their exploits in the snow, Mister Wordsworth turned to Florence. "I shall be returning home tomorrow. Jane is staying here after all, with her aunt, so perhaps your cousins would like to visit, now they have become acquainted."

The twins nodded in unison as the waitress brought the order, and they looked at the huge cakes in front of them and then up at Florence.

Mister Wordsworth bit into his, followed by his niece. "Go on, eat up," he told them.

They picked them up and took a nibble. They had probably never had a cake each before, not one as huge, anyway. She copied, unsure if she would like the fruit she could see inside Jane's as she put it down to chew, a look of ecstasy on her face. However, the tangy flavour suited her enormously. "Mm, it's lovely," she exclaimed.

The twins did not seem to share her delight. They valiantly ate a mouthful of theirs, and then put them down, sheepishly looking up at her from beneath their eyelashes. They clearly did not like them. Too rich, probably.

Mister Wordsworth, too mannerly to make a remark, continued making conversation, Florence still hoping she would not have to pay. Her head shot up when she heard him say a particular name. "We—that is, my sister and I—have been invited to a soirée this evening at Lady Lancaster's. I shall hardly know anybody. I was wondering if you would be going?"

"Me? I do not know Lady Lancaster. Why would she invite me?"

He shrugged. "It was just a thought. You do not know her son, then?"

It could not be the same, surely? "No, no, I am not acquainted with many people in this area. My aunt and uncle may, but they do not mix in such high society. They are ordinary folk, and vary rarely go to parties and such." Her hands shaking, she put down the morsel she had not eaten.

"But her son lives near you, just outside Ambleside, so I understand."

"So… so, what is he doing here?"

"Visiting his mother. I am told, to escape from some lady. That is the talk going the rounds, anyway."

"And what may his name be?" She held her breath. It might not be the same person at all.

"Why, the Viscount, of course."

"Viscount?" She almost choked, and put her serviette to her mouth.

"Yes, he took the title when his father died."

Wiping her mouth, she tried to calm her racing heart. It could still be a different person. Her Luke had never said he had a title. "Do you know his Christian name?"

"Lawrence or Luke or something like that. I only know him as Lancaster."

With trembling fingers, she pinched her lips together. She had thought to be escaping from him. Had she inadvertently moved closer? But what did it matter? He had made his feelings perfectly clear, as she so often told herself. She stood. "I think we should be on our way now, girls."

They looked down at their uneaten cakes.

Mister Wordsworth came to their rescue, whispering to them behind his hand, "Do not worry, my dears. Jane can take one home. You may take the other to your mama. I am sure she will enjoy it."

Grinning widely, Mary obeyed, secreting it in her muff. Florence said her farewells and ran out of the tearoom.

Only once they had started on their way towards Dovenby did she remember her previous worries about paying.

Oh well, too late now, she thought, hoping she would not bump into the poet's son again in the near future.

Luke Lancaster sat with his mother in the great lounge, reading the morning paper, occasionally interjecting with, "Yes, Mother" or, "No, Mother."

"You are not listening to me, are you?" she uttered after a while.

He put down the paper. "I am sorry, Mother, you were saying?"

"This soirée this evening—do you think we have invited enough people? You have not had any input into the guest list."

"Mother, I came to escape people, not to entertain."

"Pah, stuff and nonsense. What you need is to mingle, not hide yourself away. This girl, whoever she is, needs banishing from your mind, and the only way to achieve that is to meet other good-looking lasses."

"Mother, I do not want to banish her from my mind." He stood up, running his fingers through his thick hair, and leant against the mantelpiece, staring at the red coals in the fire below, seeing her face as in the forest.

"That poet's son, Mister Wordsworth, has returned his card, saying he is coming. He seems a very nice man, and his sister will be coming, too, so we will have an odd number." His mother peered at her embroidery, as if she had made a mistake. "Oh, damnation. I should have done that area in blue, not pink. Now, where did I put that pattern?"

"Does it really matter, Mother?"

"I suppose not. Anyway, where was I?"

"You were saying we would have an odd number, but I shall be on my own as well, so that makes two odd ones."

"Oh, no, I have invited that pretty girl, Miss Smith, to even up. You know her mama, and actually know her, but will not recognise her, for she has grown since the last time you saw her."

"You mean that girl with the buck teeth, whose plaits I used to pull? Mother! She is a baby. I am not on the market as a cradle-snatcher." He checked his reflection in the mirror. "Anyway, I am going for a walk. Would you like to come?"

"Luke, she is no longer a child. I am sure you will fall head over heels in love with her the moment you clap eyes on her. But, no thank you. I want to finish this.

Have you seen where I put The Lady newspaper? It gives so much useful information about patterns and the like?"

He picked up a paper from the small table behind the couch. "Do you mean this one?"

"Ah, yes, that's it. Now, make sure you wrap up warmly, won't you? It is bitter out there."

He shook his head at her fussing. "Yes, Mother, I will."

A few minutes brought him into the town centre, bustling with people. Swinging his cane, he gave the appearance of nonchalance, to belie his true inner turmoil. If only he had grabbed Florence and taken away the pain he had seen on her face when he had spurned her. But how could he have done? His situation did not lend itself to an engagement, and he felt sure she would never agree to being his mistress, no matter how dire her own circumstances.

As he passed a tearoom, a girl came out, followed by a tall man, buttoning his coat, and he recognised the poet's son whom his mother had invited to that evening's soirée. Should he ignore him? But his conscience took over, and he lifted his hat and bowed. "Good day, sir."

The man appeared to be miles away, searching up the street. "Ah, Lancaster, good day to you. I trust you are well? I returned my acceptance card for this evening. It was good of your mother to invite us." He seemed to spot someone up the street and, grabbing the girl's hand, made his farewells, and hurried off.

Luke had been about to continue at a more leisurely pace, but noticed Mister Wordsworth chasing after a lady and two young girls. *Why is he running after that woman?* She seemed vaguely familiar from the back, and he thought angrily. *Why does every lady I see remind me of her? She is miles away, in Ambleside, settling down to marrying that ugly moley dark-haired…* The lady turned and he gasped. *It is her. But do not be so stupid, you insane buffoon. How can it be?*

He turned to walk off in the opposite direction, almost stepping under a carriage. *Just rid your mind of her, for goodness sake.* A noisy inn across the way looked inviting, so he marched in, ordered a tankard of ale and sat in a corner to drink it.

A black-haired barmaid came over to him. "Another, sir?"

He finished it in one gulp and handed her the tankard. "Why not? And why don't you have one with me?" Anything to free his mind of Florence.

Her eyes lit up. "Why, thank you kind sir, I don't mind if I do." She scuttled off and returned moments later, squeezing in close to him on the bench. Her breath reeked of whatever she had eaten the night before, but her face looked pleasant enough. He could while away an hour or so with her.

Florence thought she could hear someone calling her name. Still reeling from the knowledge that Luke Lancaster could be in the area, she hurried faster, trying to ignore it.

One of the twins moaned, "You're walking too fast, cousin. My legs are aching."

She slowed down. "I am sorry, girls."

"Isn't that the man who gave us the cake?"

Oh, my goodness, I hope he is not coming to ask for the money for the bill.

"And he has my gloves."

Florence turned. "Your gloves? Why would he have them?"

"I must have left them in the tearoom."

"So, why did you not say anything?"

The girl looked down at the ground sheepishly. "I didn't like to, for you seemed out of sorts."

Taking a deep breath, she watched the man coming towards them, waving the gloves in the air.

"Thank goodness," he puffed, "I thought I would never catch up with you. Your cousin left these behind."

"She's always leaving things," muttered the other twin, who Florence had worked out must be the quiet one, Mary. "Mama's always chiding her."

"No, I'm not. It's only the second time," argued Margaret.

"Never mind that, now. Say thank you to the kind gentleman for returning them," Florence told her, eager to be away, in case the man brought up the subject of the bill.

"There was one other thing I wanted to mention," he began. She closed her eyes, squeezing Margaret's hand until she heard the child squeak. "Would you care to accompany me this evening to the soirée I told you about?"

Her breath let out in relief, she had another problem. How to refuse politely? "I…um…I have not had a formal invitation," she gabbled. "It would be importune of me to turn up without one."

"Ah, do not allow that insignificant issue as a reason to refuse. I am a poet's son, and everyone knows poets are wild creatures, who make their own rules, and, anyway, my sister is going."

Florence could hear the children laughing at something behind her back, and twisted to see what it might be. As they had left the street and were on the rutted lane, she must have stepped too close to a tree, for a large twig had fastened itself to the back of her coat, giving the impression that she had a tail. She yanked it off, glaring at the girls, intending to give them a lecture once their pursuers had departed. She turned back to Mister Wordsworth. "I must decline, sir. I have to take these naughty girls home."

The man gently cuffed his little niece. "She is probably as much to blame, dear lady. Probably the ringleader. More like a boy, sometimes, she likes practical jokes. I would not put it past her to have stuck the branch there herself."

"But, Uncle, I did not…"

"Enough. You have upset the lady with your pranks. Now apologise."

Her clear blue eyes looked up, full of sorrow. "I beg your forgiveness, ma'am."

"Do not give it another thought." She felt sorry for the girl, and it might have been her own cousins who had been at fault. "I have forgotten it already."

"Thank you, ma'am," replied her uncle. "Now, about this evening?"

She shook her head. "No, I repeat, I cannot go without an invitation. Thank you for your kind offer. Good day."

She took the girls' hands and walked away.

"Well, if you change your mind…" he called after her.

How could she accept? He was not even a family friend. And didn't he say he was engaged? Just because his father lived with different values did not give her the right to do the same, even if his sister would be acting as a chaperone.

Chastising the girls, she dragged them along the lane, but her good mood soon returned as they rounded a corner and saw the River Cocker in front of them. "Shall we rest a few minutes?" she asked. "Or are you in a hurry to return home?"

Both girls ran down the riverbank. "Let's see if there are any fish," called Margaret.

"Be careful," she called.

She sat on the grass, watching the girls, giggling and squealing, as they poked sticks into the water in an attempt at tickling the fish. Would that she were as carefree. Luke Lancaster had come into her life and completely disrupted it. She would be engaged to a good man, with the family's troubles a thing of the past, if he had not abducted her. And, anyway, she still had not received a proper explanation for why he had done so. He owed her that.

Maybe she would accept Mister Wordsworth's invitation, after all. If only to have it out with him, to put her devils behind her.

"Cousin, Mary's fallen into the water," she heard Margaret shout.

She jumped up, expecting to see the little girl drowning at the very least. Relief flooded her when she saw her pull out a sodden foot. She ran down and helped her.

"Mama will scold me," the child cried. "I have only had these shoes a few weeks. My old ones didn't fit me."

"Well, hopefully, it will not be too spoiled. But what should you do now? You cannot walk the rest of the way in bare feet."

"The bottom of my frock is soaked, too," Mary whimpered.

"Can't you give her a piggy back?" asked Margaret.

"I suppose I could try." She bent down and Mary climbed onto her back. The hoops of her crinoline made it easier for the girl to stay on but, after a while she became too heavy, and she put her down.

"I'll have a go," pronounced Margaret, bending down.

"No, you'll hurt yourself."

Her own dress wet where her cousin had dripped water, fortunately, the ream of petticoats stopped it chaffing her back. "Put your arm around my waist, Mary, and hop."

They tried this procedure for a while, but the girl's leg soon ached and that idea had to be scrapped also. "You will just have to squelch your way home, I am afraid to say. You should not have gone so close to the water's edge. I did warn you."

By the time they eventually made it to her aunt's house, daylight had almost departed, and they would have needed candles or lanterns to light their way if they had taken much longer.

"Where have you been?" asked her aunt, urging them inside. "I've been worried sick. Your uncle was about to come and find you."

"I'm sorry, Mama, it was my fault," whined Mary.

"You? But you never do anything wrong. What happened?" They explained, all talking at once. Her aunt put her hands up in the air. "Very well, all right, I understand. Let's have these wet clothes off, before you catch your deaths of cold."

"It wasn't me, for a change, Mama." With a smug smirk, Margaret took off her coat.

"Yes, that does make a change. I had felt sure you had all come to grief somewhere."

Mary took the half-eaten cake from her muff.

"It's a bit squashed," remarked Margaret.

"What's this?" asked her mother.

"A nice man bought us cakes and tea, didn't he, cousin?"

Her aunt gave her a quizzical look. Florence had been about to tell her of their meeting, but had not had the chance. "It's fine, Aunt. It was only Mister Wordsworth. We bumped into him and he…well, he bought us tea and cakes, as Margaret said."

Her aunt seemed appeased as she picked out a currant. "My favourite. It is for me, I gather?"

"Yes, Ma, me and Mary didn't like it."

Their mother put her hands on her lips, an offended look on her face. "Oh, it's your cast-offs, then, is it? I thought you'd brought me a present?"

The little girls both laughed as, smiling, Florence picked up her hat and gloves from the table. "I shall take these upstairs. I'm afraid to say my dress is rather wet, as well, but I'm sure Sybil will be able to sponge off any dirty marks."

Half-way out the door, she turned. "Mister Wordsworth invited me to a soirée this evening, but I refused. There would not be time to ready myself, anyway, and how would I find my way there?"

"That's a pity, my dear. It would be something to take your mind off your troubles," her aunt replied.

She carried on up the stairs, thinking it could cause more 'trouble' as she had put it.

Sybil fussed around her. "I thought you had been kidnapped again, ma'am. I hadn't expected you to be away so long. I have mended the little tear in your green dress, look. It is hardly noticeable, now." She cackled on like a mother hen, Florence not taking much notice of her, lost in her own thoughts, until a knock at the door below alerted her attention. She hurried over to the window to see who the visitor might me, but it was too dark.

Shrugging, she took off her dress and felt her petticoats. Damp as well, so she removed them, then ran her hands over her stays. "These will have to do," she remarked. "They take so long to fasten, I do not feel in the mood to change them. I suppose I do not need them here, but I might accept… Oh, Sybil, what should I do?" She explained her predicament.

The maid knew why she had refused Lord Head, although she declared she would never understand it. "Well, ma'am, I cannot advise you one way or the other. If you want to have it out with your *abductor*," she almost spat out the word, "you will at least know his mind. But what good will that do you?"

"I know, I know." Slumping onto the bed, she put her head in her hands. "Oh, why did he have to turn up again? I came away to rid myself of him, and he is here. How much of a coincidence is that, I ask you?"

The maid bustled about, tidying the room. "Perhaps it is fate."

"Fate? You mean…do you mean you think I should… No." *But what if it is fate, and I am meant to go to him?* "If I do not go, I shall never find out, shall I?" She ran downstairs.

Her aunt looked up in surprise at her state of undress. "My dear?"

"Aunt, I have decided to go, but how am I to let Mister Wordsworth know?"

"Do you know where he is staying? Oh, yes, you told me he is with his sister? I know where she lives. Your uncle could take a message."

"Are you sure he would not mind?"

"Papa!" her aunt shouted through the back door. Florence always thought it odd that she should call him that, when he was her husband, not her father.

"By the way, who was at the door earlier?" asked Florence, waiting impatiently.

"Only a neighbour, returning something he had borrowed."

"Oh." She had wondered if it had been anyone to do with herself, but why would it be?

Her uncle came in, carrying a handful of logs.

"Florence here would like a favour." Her aunt explained it to him. "You know where the sister lives, don't you?"

"In Tallentire," Florence added.

"Oh, yes, we were there not long back." He put down the logs and dropped one onto the fire.

"Oh, thank you." Florence hugged him but, mindful that he had averted his eyes at her near-nakedness, she quickly ran back upstairs.

"Supper will be ready in ten minutes," her aunt called after her.

"Oh, I am sorry, Aunt," she called back. "I will not have time to eat. I need to make myself beautiful."

"You are already that, my dear. But you will not be so, if you do not eat. You have hardly touched any food since you came. A little bird wouldn't be able to survive on what you have consumed this week."

She blew out her cheeks, knowing her aunt to be right. "But there will be food at this get-together."

She thought she heard her aunt mumble, "I suppose so," so continued into her room, excited now she had made her decision.

As she sat in front of the mirror for Sybil to curl her hair, doubts crept in. "What if he snubs me, completely ignores me? That would be even worse." She leaned forward to check her reflection for what appeared to be a pimple on her forehead, receiving a moan from her maid.

"Please sit still, ma'am. I should hate to ruin your hairstyle." She added an ornate comb. "Do you like this, ma'am, or would you prefer a flower?"

She thought about it for a moment, her lips stuck out in a pout. "I suppose it does not really matter. Who am I trying to fool?" She took the flower her maid had handed her and twisted it in her fingers. "Maybe I should not go, after all."

"Well, ma'am," Sybil took the flower and positioned it carefully where it would give the best effect, just above her ear, "now you are ready, you may as well go. You look magnificent. If this does not melt his hard heart, nothing will, not that I agree with what you're doing. After all, he almost killed us. How can you possibly harbour feelings for him?"

"I know not, Sybil. I am a fool unto myself. And thank you for your kind words, but I fear you are biased. He may not feel the same."

She pinched her cheeks to give some colour to her pale face. "And, anyway, I am only going to find out his reasons for kidnapping us, nothing else."

"Yes, ma'am, whatever you say."

"You do not believe me?"

The maid smiled but did not reply.

Chapter 12

The sound of a carriage on the lane made her jump up. "Oh, Mister Wordsworth is here already. I do not have my shoes on. Where is my bag, and which gloves shall I wear?"

Her maid calmly handed her the gloves and bag, still with a scornful look on her face.

"Wish me luck," she cried as she ran down the stairs and through the lounge to the front hall.

Her aunt helped her with her cloak. "This red lining is beautiful, Florence." She stroked it. "Would that I had such a one."

"It is so warm, Aunt. I only wear it on special occasions. I do not know why I brought it. I certainly had no intention to gloat." She opened the front door as Mister Wordsworth pulled the bell.

He bowed. "Ah, good evening, Miss Fisher."

"Good evening, sir. May I present my aunt, Missus Fisher. Aunt, this is William Wordsworth's son, Willy."

Her aunt curtsied, wrapping her arms around herself. "I am very pleased to meet you, sir. Florence has told me so much about you. You must pay us a visit next time you are in the neighbourhood."

He bowed again and took Florence's arm.

"I certainly will, ma'am. Miss Fisher, pray, do hurry. You will catch a chill in this cold."

Florence bade her farewells and entered the carriage, being introduced to his sister. She took to her straightaway, and they chatted amicably the whole journey, Willy throwing in a sentence now and again.

Florence felt she needed to talk, to take her mind off the evening ahead. If she thought too much about it, she would change her mind, and ask the footman to turn around and take her back.

Butterflies swam around in her stomach as she alighted from the carriage and entered the large house. Fortunately the room had already filled, and she found a quiet corner to hide in, as Willy and his sister mingled with the other guests. Wanting to see Luke, but not daring to look for him, she kept her eyes firmly cast to the floor, until someone came up to speak to her. She had to look up, of course, for propriety's sake. Over the shoulder of the person in front of her, she saw him across the room, chatting to friends. Her hands clammy, she changed her position, so he did not appear in her line of vision.

"I am sorry, you were saying?" she realised she had not answered the lady.

"It is of no consequence. Oh, there is Myrtle. I must have a word with her about her daughter." The lady hurried away.

Florence sneaked a peek back to where he had been, but he had moved.

Pretending to examine her fingernails, she glanced around the other side of the room. No sign of him.

She could relax. Until a familiar voice behind her asked, "Why are you sitting here all alone?"

She jumped up. "I…um…"

"And where is your fiancé? In fact, why are you here at all?" He sounded extremely cross.

She turned to see blue eyes burning with anger. "I…Mister…um… invited…" *Why can I not speak coherently?*

She took a deep breath, looking away, anywhere but into those eyes, and fiddled with her reticule, anything to stop her hands shaking so much. "I am sorry." She turned to walk away. "I should not have come. I knew it was a mistake. Sybil warned me." From being speechless moments before, she could not stop words gabbling out of her mouth.

Her departure halted when he caught hold of her arm, asking again, "Why? I thought you had become engaged. If so, where is the lucky man?" He looked up at the candles flickering in the chandelier, and she followed his gaze. "Ah, I suppose you have come to the town to buy your trousseau? But without your mother or sister?" His eyes darted around the room.

"I am not… I did not go through with it," she muttered, as a young man pushed past her, almost knocking her over. Luke grabbed her and she fell into his arms, but he pushed her away from him, covering his mouth with his hand.

"What do you mean?" Before she could elaborate, he continued, steering her towards a door. "We cannot speak here with all this noise. Come."

She hung back, hesitant about going anywhere with him alone. "I do not think…"

He turned to face her. "What? You do not think what?"

Before she could reply, a large middle-aged lady with grey hair in a bun came rushing over. "Luke." She stopped, looking askance at Florence. "Oh, and who is this delectable young lady? You must introduce her to me."

"Mother, this is Miss Florence Fisher. She came with Mister Wordsworth. Miss Fisher, may I introduce my mother, Lady Lancaster?"

They bowed to each other, Lady Lancaster still giving her odd looks.

"Anyway, Luke, Miss Smith arrived several minutes ago," continued his mother. "You have not spoken to her yet. Come, I insist."

With a raising of his eyebrows, he let himself be led away as Florence slumped back onto the chair, grinding her back teeth to calm her nerves.

Willy Wordsworth shuffled over to her. "I trust you are enjoying yourself, my dear, although you do not appear to be mingling."

"I am fine, thank you, sir. I do not know many people."

"Then allow me to right that matter. Come along. I shall introduce you to everyone."

A gong sounded from outside the room. "Oh, do you have a partner for the supper?" he asked.

She shook her head. "No, sir."

He looked around. "I had promised my sister, but, ah, it looks as if she has found somebody more suitable, so may I do the honours?" He held out his crooked arm for her to take, continuing, "Actually, she is not my own sister, of course. She died a few years back. No, she is my sister-in-law, married to my brother John." He helped her to her seat and they sat down.

Throughout the meal, she could feel Luke Lancaster's eyes upon her, but would not look in his direction. Had he understood her meaning? What would he do? She tried to make meaningful conversation with Willy and the man on her other side, laughing at inappropriate moments, receiving raised eyebrows from those nearby, but scarcely touching the food.

When the men retired to their port and cigars, she relaxed, and chatted with the ladies, as if she had not a care in the world.

"Do you play, Miss Fisher?" asked a lady whose name she tried desperately to remember.

"The pianoforte? Not as well as I would like."

"Me, neither," began the lady, but Lady Lancaster leaned forward. "Ah, that solves the problem, then. Would you play for us when the gentlemen return?"

"Me?"

"You did just say you could play?"

"Yes, but there must be more accomplished pianists here than I. Would not one of them prefer to play?"

Lady Lancaster sat back. "No, we have heard them all before. We like new blood."

Miss Smith, a shy, young girl, with buck teeth and mousy hair, to whom Florence had been introduced earlier, lifted her head.

"Would not Miss Smith like to have a turn, as well?" Florence sought to take the limelight from herself. "I would not mind if she went first. I could turn the pages for her, if she would like."

"Splendid, that is sorted, then," pronounced Lady Lancaster.

Hoping the girl would be in agreement to her idea, she felt guilty putting it forward without asking her first. "Would that be agreeable, Miss Smith? I hope I did not put you in a difficult position."

"Oh, no, not at all. My mama says I am a very good musician, even though I hate all the practising. I shall be delighted to play, especially if Lord Lancaster is watching. My mama says I need to do everything in my power to attract his attention. Do you not think him handsome?" A dreamy look came over her face as they entered the parlour.

Not sure if she expected a reply, Florence made no answer. The phrase 'Handsome is as handsome does' came to mind. He might be good-looking, very much so, but what about his character?

She had no time to ponder as she helped Miss Smith find a piece of music she liked. Tapping her toe to the lilting music, she looked up, after turning the page, into the eyes of the handsome one. Her gaze would not withdraw. A faint smile curved his lips as he stared at her. Remembering s similar scene a few weeks before, her legs turned to jelly, but still she could not look away. Miss Smith hissed at her to turn the page. Fumbling with the music, she turned two pages by mistake, worsening the situation.

"I am so sorry," she uttered, turning it back. She felt as if she would collapse if she stayed any longer, and, repeating, "I am sorry," ran out of the room and down the hall, the music echoing in her ears.

Footsteps behind her made her run even faster, but a window at the end of the corridor meant she had come to a dead end. She stopped to catch her breath. Rough arms pulled her backwards. Closing her eyes, she wallowed in the scent of the man of her dreams as he enfolded her. They remained silent, as one, his arms around her, tightly, and she leaned back into him, not wanting the moment to end. Of course it had to, but she would not be the one to break it. She waited, not knowing what he would say, not wanting to know, just luxuriating in his warmth.

"Did I hear you aright?" he whispered. "Are you not engaged?"

She shook her head as he slowly turned her to face him. His head came closer and his lips touched hers in the softest caress, as if testing her reaction. When she did not pull away, he deepened the kiss, his lips hot and searching, his tongue easing hers apart as he licked her inner lip.

His mother's voice carried down the corridor. "Luke, where are you?"

The area where they stood had no lighting, so they could not be seen. He tore his mouth away, covering hers with his hand, whispering, "Shush," in her ear.

"Luke?" his mother repeated.

"I had better go," he whispered. "She will not rest until she has found me. Wait here for me. I shall return." He stepped forward, calling, "I am here, Mother."

"What are you doing, skulking in the shadows? Are you with that girl?"

"Which girl, Mother?" He walked purposefully past her, and Florence could just make her out, peering into the blackness. "I thought I heard a mouse or something, but it was nothing. Let us return to our guests."

Huh, nothing, am I? Just because he set her pulse racing did not give him the right to call her nothing. She flapped her arms. *Oh, why did I come? I knew I should not. If he thinks I will wait here after calling me that, he has another think coming. I am leaving as soon as, if not before, Mister Wordsworth is ready.* If it had been summer, she would have left there and then, but walking through the darkness in the bitter cold would not be a good idea, especially as she did not know the way.

Three days later, she was feeding the chickens in the back yard when her aunt called her.

"Coming, Aunt," she called back, noticing that one of the hens was limping. She picked it up to examine it, thinking that her aunt would not have anything urgent to tell her, and carried it towards the back door. A figure appeared. She gasped, almost dropping the bird.

Her aunt peered around him. "Someone to see you, my dear."

"I…um…" She turned to walk away. "I am not in a fit state of dress to receive uninvited visitors."

Her aunt looked at him. "I told you, sir, she would not want to see you."

"Please, Florence," he said in a low voice. "I have been going crazy since the other night."

"I shall leave you to it, then," muttered her aunt, wiping her hands on her pinafore as she went back inside. "But call me if you need me."

Florence continued across the yard, still clutching the hen. "I think she has hurt her leg." She sat on an upturned pail and held the hen out to inspect it.

He crouched down beside her. "We need to talk."

"I have nothing to say to you."

"But the other night…you responded to my embrace."

"I think she may have broken it. I need to show it to my aunt." She stood up and tried to walk around him, but he straightened and blocked her path.

"Look at me."

Can I? Can I look into those gorgeous blue eyes and pretend I am not affected? She raised her head, still not looking directly at him.

He lifted her chin with a gentle finger. Just the touch was enough to make her want him to take her in his arms. But she had to remain resolute. She closed her eyes, and stood immobile, her lips tightly clenched, hoping he would receive the message. However, he teased her lips open with his finger, traced the outline of her mouth, pulling it down slightly at the side, before replacing his finger with his lips.

Her eyes still closed, she sighed into his mouth, as he ravaged hers with his tongue.

The chicken woke her from her trance by squawking. She pulled away and ran. "I have to take her to my aunt. Please leave."

She ran into the kitchen. Her aunt looked up in surprise. "Has your visitor gone, my dear?"

"I hope so." She showed her the bird's leg.

"Oh, well, I had been wondering what to have for dinner, tomorrow. This solves the problem."

"He didn't stay very… Oh." She stopped as Luke came in.

"I was wondering if you would like to take a walk?"

"I have chores to complete."

Her aunt looked from one to the other. "My dear, the chores can wait. Nothing is as important as clearing the air, that's what I say. You enjoy the sunshine. It might rain later."

"But I am not dressed." What other reason could she give for refusing?

"You look perfectly presentable to me." Luke took down an old coat from the back of the door. "This will keep you warm."

"But I could not go out in that? What if we saw someone we knew?"

Wrapping it around her, he pointed outside the door. "I can see a little path leading to those woods. Nobody will see us there."

"Then I shall need my maid as a chaperone. I cannot go alone with you."

Her aunt laughed. "My dear, this gentleman looks very trustworthy. I'm sure you'll be safe with him. And I shan't tell your mama, if that's what you're worrying about." She shooed her out the door.

Safe? If he kissed her again like he had earlier, anything could happen. 'Safe' would not come into it.

"Well, on your head be it, Aunt. If I come to any harm, I shall blame you." She heard a chuckle as her aunt closed the door behind her.

Somewhat apprehensive, she kept in time with Luke's long strides. What if he did intend to ravish her? Would she be able to resist? But he would hardly do so in the woods, in the dirt and mud. Her mind flitted from one thought to the next, wishing he would say something.

At length, he spoke. "Florence, why did you not go through with the engagement?"

"I do not have to explain myself to you."

He stopped and faced her. "If it was because of me, I am sorry."

Her eyes opened wide. The arrogance of the man. "And why would you think that, sir?"

"Oh, pray, stop pretending. I know you have feelings for me, and I…" Taking off his hat, he raked his fingers through his hair, looking around him, as if for inspiration as to what to say next. "I am not a free man."

"Oh." She had not expected him to say anything like that. "You mean you are married or betrothed?"

"Well, no, neither of those."

"Then what?" She could not think of any other reason that would stop him declaring himself.

"I have obligations." He steered her towards a large oak tree and leaned against it, pulling her towards his warm body.

Reluctant to come into such close contact, especially if he was about to give her news she did not want to hear, she resisted for a moment, but the thought of one last time changed her mind. With his arms wrapped around her shivering torso, she could feel his heart beating, possibly faster than hers. She leaned her head against his chest, uncaring of what his next words might be.

"A young nephew of mine, a foolhardy kind of chap, found himself in trouble and I agreed to help him out. His mother, my older sister, had died in tragic circumstances and his father took to drink and became no help to him at all. In fact, he has probably died by now—I have not heard hide nor hair of him for months—nor my nephew." He adjusted his position and drew her even closer. Wondering why he could be telling her all this, she made no rejoinder, merely relaxed against him. "So you see, I have to concern myself with him. He has—how may I put this in a delicate way, so as not to disturb your innocent mind? He fathered an illegitimate child. The mother, a waif from the gutter, as far as I can make out, died in childbirth, and so I am helping to raise the child—a little boy, called Michael."

She did not know what to say that would sound constructive. It was entirely his business. How should it affect her?

"So, you see, my hands are tied. I am saddled with this child for the rest of his life."

Is that it? Is that his reason for denying me?

"Please say something, Flossie."

At the mention of her nickname, she jumped back. "What are you trying to say, Luke? You come here, disrupting my life, telling me your hands are tied, and then you call me that? Are you intentionally attempting to upset me?"

"No, wait, please." At the hurt in his voice, she stopped. "I am just explaining myself."

"But, why? Why not just carry on with your life and not involve me at all?"

"Because I cannot. You see, I…" he took a deep breath, "I think… I know…I am in love with you."

"Hah! What good is that to me? You are in love with me, but cannot do anything about it. Better for me that I had never met you." She turned and ran into the woods, away from his tempting body.

Half of her wanted to be as far away as possible, to never see him again, but the other half wished him to follow, to tell her that everything would be all right, that they would be able to work things out. Hiding behind a tree, she listened for the crack of a twig or the shuffle of leaves betraying footsteps, but the only sound she could hear was the wind rustling in the trees and the call of a dove. After a few moments, she assumed he had left, and returned to her aunt's home.

Her aunt looked up from her sewing. "By the look on your face, I gather your walk did not go well."

She shook her head.

"Do you care to tell me about it?"

Head in hands, she slumped down onto a chair. "Oh, Aunt, why is life so difficult?"

"My dear, it can become a lot worse, believe me. Just wait until you have half a dozen screaming children vying for your attention, then you might find out what difficult means."

"At this rate, I shall die an old spinster."

Laughing, her aunt picked up the kettle. "You're only nineteen. Your whole life's ahead of you. There will be other men. Don't give up yet."

"But I do not want other men. I want just one, and he…well, he says he loves me, but…"

"Then what's the problem. You clearly love him."

Florence rested her fingers on the hot cup of tea in front of her, and explained her predicament.

Her aunt looked puzzled. "But why would that stop him? It isn't as if the child is his. Or do you think he's covering up, and lying?"

"No, I don't think that." The hot tea warmed her insides and cheered her. "I suppose he is too gallant to want to saddle me with an infant."

"Probably. But what do you think?"

"Aunt, I know not what to think. I shall consider my options, that is, if I still have any, while I help you. What had you in mind for today?"

Her aunt stood up. "I had intended baking the Christmas cake. I like to cook it early, to give it plenty of time to mature."

Florence rubbed her hands together and stood up. "Right then, where do we start? Show me the ingredients."

Beating eggs a while later, she pondered over the idea of bringing up someone else's child. Would it be so hard? If would depend on his character. If he were to turn out to be wilful and disobedient, she might be tempted to go too far and beat him. But then, Luke had plenty of income. They would employ a nanny. She might never have to see him. He could be ensconced in the nursery all day, and just brought to her to kiss goodnight. She pictured herself and Luke sitting by the fireside, telling each other of their hopes and dreams for the future, and planning—or rather, making, babies of their own. She blushed, hoping her aunt could not see her red face. But she might not ever see him again. She had probably put him off by her precipitant action. He must have thought her to be reviled by the idea of the child, the poor innocent child.

A knock on the front door broke her reverie. Had he returned? She ran to open it, intent on telling him she had been a stupid fool, but a messenger stood there with a letter. "Does it require an answer?" she asked, miserably.

"Yes, ma'am."

She looked at the name—her uncle's. "I shall have to see if he is in. I think he may be in the fields." She trudged through to her aunt and handed her the letter.

"This must be what your uncle has been waiting for, the good news of his inheritance." Her aunt ripped it open and her face lit up.

"I did not know he was due an inheritance."

"Oh, yes, quite a substantial one. I must find him." Her aunt grabbed the old coat Florence had replaced on the nail on the back door and ran out, waving the letter in her hand.

"What about the messenger…?" Florence began, but her aunt had gone out of sight. "I suppose I had better invite him in. I cannot leave him outside in the cold," she murmured. She ushered him inside and, as she closed the door, she thought she saw a movement, as of someone lurking on the lane leading to the village. Probably a tramp or a vagabond. She slammed the door, not wanting the person to see her.

Her uncle ran in, panting and out of breath. "Pray, wait while I write a reply," he puffed as her aunt followed him in.

"Is it what you were expecting?" Florence asked.

Her aunt beamed, her head nodding up and down. "Yes, yes. Oh, I am so excited."

The letter written, Florence insisted on showing the messenger out, wanting to check if the tramp remained. No movement could be detected. She breathed a sigh of relief. But one could not be too careful. She returned to her animated relatives, who sat at the kitchen table, rereading the letter.

"Who is this person who has left you the money?" she asked, mystified as to how she had not been told of it before.

"Well, it's a long story." Her uncle looked up. "As you know, your father and I were close as children. He made his money in investments but I yearned for the outdoor life and settled on this farm. It has never made a lot of money, not like your father."

Her aunt intervened, "Not that we begrudged him a single penny of it, you understand."

"Anyway," continued her uncle with a shake of his head, "when I first came, I befriended an elderly gentleman, although I suppose he was not so elderly at the time."

"He never had any family of his own," added her aunt.

"Do you want to tell her the story or may I?"

Her aunt made a pot of tea. "No, dear, you go ahead."

"Thank you. Now, where was I? Oh, yes, this gentleman always told me he would leave me his farm in his will."

"But they couldn't find a will."

"Enid!"

"I'm sorry."

"Thank you. No, they couldn't find his will, at first."

"He died earlier this year, you see." Her aunt grimaced at the look from her husband, explaining,

"But Florence might not have realised how recently this happened."

"Well, to cut the story short…" He opened his eyes wide and raised his eyebrows at his wife, but she did not elaborate. "They found it under a floorboard just a few weeks ago, and this letter that arrived today informs me that I am the only beneficiary. I can move into the farm whenever I want. Just imagine, owning my own property! I shall be as happy as a king."

"*We* shall happy as kings, my dear. Don't forget the rest of your family in your exuberance."

He hugged her. "Of course, how could I do that?"

Florence, at last, had an opportunity to speak. She jumped up and hugged them. "I am so pleased for you both. You deserve it. So, when do you think you will move?"

"As soon as we can, eh, Eric? Could we do it before Christmas, do you think? I can picture us, hanging up the paper decorations over that huge fireplace, and a tree, adorned with little baubles and candles. Oh, Eric, it will be so marvellous. I can't wait to tell the children when they come home from school." A cry came from above. "That's little Eddie, now. He'll be too young to understand. But he'll love playing on that lawn. And the older ones will be able to climb up to the tree house."

"Maybe we should wait until I have time to repair that, for it looks very dilapidated."

"Yes, yes, of course, dear." She hurried up the stairs as Florence resumed the baking.

Her uncle put on his cap that had been knocked off in the fun. "I had better finish my tasks in the field. I don't want to leave a shoddy farm for the next tenant."

After he had gone, Florence wondered if she should stay long enough to help them move. She had intended to be home well in time for Christmas because she had not bought any presents. She looked around at the array of utensils. Everything would have to be packed up. Her aunt would need her. Her own requirements could come second.

Mixing flour into the wet ingredients in the brown bowl, she beat it until satisfied it had the right consistency, and then turned it into a greased dish and placed it in the oven.

Her aunt came down with Eddie, cooing and telling him of all the benefits the larger farm would have for him.

"Who has been looking after it since the gentleman died?" asked Florence, giving the little boy the wooden spoon to lick.

"I'm not sure. Your uncle has been up to check on it once or twice, and the animals all look well fed. That's something else, Eddie—lambs. Maybe you can have one of your own in the spring. What will you call it?"

His head to one side, he shouted, "Lamb."

"That's as good a name as any, I suppose." His mother laughed as she sat him in his high chair, took the wooden spoon from him and wiped the cake mixture from his face and hair.

Florence washed the pots, wishing her aunt all the happiness in the world, knowing that nothing would dampen her enthusiasm that day.

"If you fancy a walk later, we could go to see it, that's if it doesn't rain." Her aunt moved the curtain to one side and peered out. "Those clouds over there are rather black. But maybe they'll pass. I can't wait. Even if it thunders and lightens, I shall still go. What do you think, Florence?"

"Well, aunt, I do not feel like walking out in a thunderstorm, but yes, I would love to see it if the clouds pass over."

"It will take your mind of your own problems."

"Yes, it will, won't it?" She realised that, for a few minutes, she had not even thought about Luke Lancaster. Drat, why had her aunt brought up the subject? She would be content if she never had to think of him ever again.

After a light lunch, the dark clouds having, indeed, blown over, they ventured outside.

"It would have been quicker if we could have walked over the fields, but the pram would become embedded in the mud," explained her aunt, as they trotted along the lane.

"I do not mind. It is a nice day."

"Thomas said he'll make sure he's in for the girls when they come home from school. We could have waited until they came out, and taken them with us, but the schoolroom is at the other end of the village. And, anyway, you'll be able to see it better without them mythering you."

"Ah, but I really do not mind them, mythering or not. They are lovely girls. A real credit to you. They all are." *And maybe the only children I shall ever know.*

Florence had not been prepared for the immensity of the farm her uncle had just inherited. At least twice the size of his current one. "My word, it's huge," she exclaimed. "How will he manage all that on his own?"

"Well, hopefully, the farm hands who already work here will be kept on."

The baby had fallen asleep, so they left him in his pram while they entered the farmhouse. All looked neat and tidy.

"Has anyone been living here since he passed away?" asked Florence, wiping her finger over the wooden dresser, adorned with blue plates and other china artefacts.

"Not to my knowledge. It looks very clean, though, doesn't it?"

A man appeared at the door, making them both jump. "Excuse me, ladies, may I help you?"

"I'm Missus Fisher. This farm now belongs to my husband."

"Oh, and who says so?"

She rummaged in the pocket of her pinafore. "I thought I'd brought the solicitor's letter, but anyway, it's all signed and sealed."

"We'll see about that." The man entered the kitchen, bending his head as he came through the doorway. Florence looked up at him, intimidated by the large man's presence. She found her voice first. "Who are you, sir?"

He took off his hat and bowed. "Joel Mudge."

"And what is your position here, Mister Mudge? What right have you to question my aunt?"

"Mister Jones was my employer. I've worked here these past twenty years."

"Oh, good," gushed her aunt. "I thought I'd seen you before. My husband is Mister Eric Fisher. You must know him. He used to look after Mister Jones."

A broad beam crossed the man's face. "Of course. A caring, lovely man is your husband." He put out his hand.

Aunt Enid shook it. "I trust you will be staying on here when we take over. I'm sure my husband would welcome your expertise."

He let out a loud sigh. "You have made me the happiest man in Cumberland, ma'am. I had been hoping and praying you would say that. So relieved, I am. You'll never know how much."

"Then that's settled."

"May I show you around, ma'am, or would you prefer to wait until your husband can accompany you?"

Aunt Enid turned to Florence with a cheeky grin. "What do you think, my dear? Shall we?"

Her aunt's enthusiasm rubbed off on her and with an excitement measuring hers, she replied, "We could maybe just take a little peek."

"Yes, just to gain a feel of the place."

They followed him out of the house, and, leaving the baby still fast asleep in his pram, went over to a fence from where they could see field upon field. "That line there," Mister Mudge pointed to a row of trees in the far distance, "that's were your boundary ends."

Aunt Enid clapped her hands. "Oh, my word, I had never imagined it to be so huge. We shall have our work cut out, shan't we? I will probably need someone to help me. Are there any young girls in the village who would be prepared to help, do you think?"

"Oh, yes, ma'am, in fact my own daughter, Susan, is almost fourteen, and she is a very reliable girl, hardworking and diligent. I could send her."

Aunt Enid clapped her hands again. "Oh, I am so looking forward to this challenge. I know it'll mean hard work, but I can manage that." She turned to Florence, her animated face red and glowing. "Is this not the best view you have seen for a person to look out onto every day? Those mountains watching over us, and the bleating of the sheep and lowing of the cows to keep you company?"

Florence thought she could hear a different cry. "Is that young Eddie?" she asked, turning around.

"Oh, my word, it is." She picked up her petticoats and ran back towards the farmhouse. "I had forgotten him in my enthusiasm. Oh, pray he hasn't fallen out of the pram. He can climb now."

As they rounded the hedge, they could see him lying on the ground, next to the pram. "Oh, dear God, please don't let him be hurt," prayed her aunt, "especially now there is so much to be done."

Florence thought that a rather insensitive remark, but in the circumstances knew it to be true.

Mister Mudge overtook them and scooped the boy into his arms.

Her aunt caught up and brushed his hair from his forehead. "Are you hurt, my darling? I should not have left you. I'm so sorry. My selfishness overruled my better judgement."

"Dinna berate yourself, ma'am," he said, handing the baby to her. "He doesn't appear to be badly injured."

She set him down on the ground, his little chubby legs wobbling at first, and then he surprised them all by running towards one of the many chickens pecking about in the dust. Florence could see a large bruise already appearing on his cheek and ran to catch him. "That looks nasty, though. He will probably have a black eye tomorrow."

Her aunt touched it. "Yes, you're right. I think he will. I hope nobody says I've hit him. People can be very judgemental sometimes."

"Then I shall tell them the truth, Aunt."

"That I left him here on his own. That's almost as bad."

She could not refute the fact, but patted her arm as Eddie leaned his head on his mama's shoulder.

"You cannot be with your children twenty-four hours a day, Aunt. I am sure they will understand. They will all have done the same thing themselves at some time or other. Do not worry."

"We'd better be making tracks," her aunt said to Mister Mudge, who stood awkwardly, clearly unsure what to do. "I'm sure you have much work to do, sir. Thank you for showing us the farm. We shall be in touch."

Florence took hold of the pram handle. "Are you putting him in, or carrying him?"

"I'll carry him a little way, just until he becomes too heavy." They bade the man farewell and hurried off. "That's put a damper on the day, hasn't it?"

"I'm sure he will be fine, Aunt. Children are always falling over, aren't they?"

"Hark at the wise one." Her aunt laughed. "You'll make a lovely mother one day, my dear. I'm sure you won't allow your children to fall out of anywhere."

"I remember cutting my knee once, when I was a little girl, jumping on shadows."

"Jumping on what?"

"We were all walking along the lane one sunny day, and I was jumping on everyone's shadows in turn. All of a sudden I fell over—I know not what tripped me—Mama wondered if it could have been a twig, but we did not see one. Well, I cut a huge gash in the top of my knee, and it took weeks to heal. Then just as it had almost done so, I was larking about, even though Mama had warned me to be careful, and I fell again, and opened it up. She was so cross with me."

"Well, my dear, I find it hard to believe that you were ever disobedient. Now your sister…"

Her aunt stopped and placed the little boy in his pram.

"How is he?"

"I'm not sure, but there's a carriage coming towards us."

Florence glanced up but immediately looked into the pram, pretending to straighten the baby's blanket.

The carriage stopped at the gate, but still she did not raise her head. Her aunt nudged her in the ribs. "It's he," she whispered in her ear.

I know. Why do you think my legs are shaking? she wanted to reply, but tucked in the blanket one more time.

"Miss Fisher?"

Decorum made her acknowledge him, but she would not meet his gaze as she walked over to them. "Lady Lancaster."

Without further ado, the lady in question held out her gloved hand. Florence gawped at a pair of smiling eyes almost a replica of her son's, deep set and vivid blue, beneath a hat of royal blue to match her cloak. They had not shone as sparkling at the soirée.

"Ma'am," she muttered, touching the hand. "This is my aunt, Missus Fisher." The older ladies bowed their heads at each other.

Her aunt took the pram handle. "I'm sorry, but I must take this little one home. I'm pleased to have met you, ma'am."

Florence hesitated. Should she go with her?

Her dilemma solved itself when Lady Lancaster spoke again. "Why do you not continue with us, my dear? I would so like to become better acquainted."

"But...do you not need me, Aunt?"

"No, dearest, you stay out and enjoy the fresh air. Don't go too far, though. It'll soon be dark."

"I shall bring her back safe and sound, ma'am," Luke called as she pushed the pram towards the farm, leaving Florence with no option but to climb into the carriage with him and his mother.

"I think I have had enough, son," his mother surprised her by stating not many minutes later. "Perhaps we could turn back?"

"Certainly, Mother."

So much for wanting to become better acquainted. She had scarcely spoken a word. "Then you may as well drop me off now, to save you the bother of coming all the way back," suggested Florence.

"No, no, you have only just come aboard. My son does not bite, you know."

Does he not? I would not be so sure.

"Not unless you want me to," he mocked quietly in her ear, making her head jerk up.

She wanted to knock the amused grin off his face, but sat entranced. Why would he tease her when she had made her feelings clear?

"How long are you staying in these parts?" Lady Lancaster asked.

"I am not sure." She stared out at the mountains in the distance, their white tops still displaying snow. "It depends how long my aunt needs me. My uncle has come into an inheritance and they will be moving. That is where we have just been, to see the new farm."

"Ah, yes, I had heard about that. Hill Farm, is it not?" asked Luke.

Puzzled as to how he could have known, she queried, "You have heard about their inheritance?"

His mother leaned forward. "My son is a solicitor. Did you not know?"

How could he be? "A solicitor, what do you mean?"

"He likes to help out in his uncle's practice when he is up here, do you not, son? Ah, here we are. Just drop me off, and you may continue together."

"But…"

"You will be quite safe, my dear. Unless you would rather come in for some refreshment?"

"No, thank you very much. It would be too dark to return if I did that."

After escorting his mother to the door, Luke returned and sat opposite her.

Twiddling with the tips of her gloves, she tried to think of something interesting to say. "It has been a nice day, has it not?" she eventually offered, shaking her head inwardly at the trite comment.

He leaned forward and took her hand. "Florence?"

She pulled it away and sat back. "I do not know why you keep seeking me out, sir. You have made your position very clear."

"But I told you I love you."

The proclamation did not help. "So? What good is that to me? Are you expecting me to be your concurbine?"

He laughed. "I think you mean 'concubine', and no, I would not be so bold. You are far too much of a lady."

"So, you have considered it?"

"No, no, I did not mean that. Ah, Flossie, what are we to do?"

She could not answer that. "Just take me back to my aunt's, Luke. There is no point raking over and over what might have been."

"Would it be too much to ask if you could maybe...?"

"What?"

"No, of course not." He sat back and leaned his head against the cushioned wall of the carriage.

"Do you mean bring up a child who is not mine, not even yours?" she asked. "I am not sure."

"What if I introduced you to him? You could get to know him and then decide."

"But decide what? I do not know what you are asking of me."

Leaning forward once more, his earnest face a few inches in front of her, he kissed the back of her hand. "Well, Miss Fisher, I suppose I am asking if you would consider marrying me."

Even though she had wondered, the proposal still took her by surprise. "Oh."

His eyes wide, he seemed to be waiting for something else. "Is that all you can say?"

Opening her mouth, her voice would not work, for nothing but little moaning noises would come out.

"Please, Flossie, you know we are good together. You do love me a little, don't you?"

She closed her mouth again and nodded. Not just a little.

"So, do you think you might meet the boy?"

"Where does he live?" she asked in a low voice, still unable to speak normally.

"With my mother at the moment. What about tomorrow? I could pick you up say, at ten o'clock in the morning?"

She nodded. Had she just agreed to marry him? She could not be sure.

"You will like him, I am sure. He has his own nanny, and is very quiet and amenable."

They arrived at her aunt's house and she stood up to alight, still unsure whether she had become betrothed or not.

He pulled her down beside him and kissed her passionately. She pulled away, giggling. "Someone will surely see us."

"Let them, I care not."

"No more do I." She leaned into him once more, opening her mouth to his advancing lips, savouring the taste of him as he plundered her mouth, his hands roughly gripping her arms.

Breathless, she stood up again. "I shall see you tomorrow."

"Would that we could stay here all night."

"It would be rather cold, do you not think?"

"I know ways to keep you warm, my darling." He reached out, but blushing at the thought, she jumped down before her resistance waned.

Her aunt looked up from her knitting as she entered the front lounge. "Light that candle for me, would you, my dear. It is almost too dark to see my stitches." As Florence obeyed, she continued, "How did your ride go with the Lancasters?"

What could she say? Should she admit all? But she had not actually accepted his proposal. "Lord

Lancaster is calling to pick me up at ten o'clock in the morning, to introduce me to the child I told you about. Will you need me? I can send word to cancel the arrangement if you do."

"No, no, child, you go. I shall manage perfectly well."

As she took off her outdoor clothes, she mused on what she had been told earlier.

"He is a solicitor, Aunt. Did you know that?"

"Who, Lord Lancaster?"

"Yes, he said he knew about Uncle Eric inheriting the farm. How could he know that unless he was involved somehow?"

"Maybe he rushed the matter through for us. Anyway, I am not going to berate him for it. I say thank you very much, sir. Thank you indeed." Her aunt put down her knitting and stood up.

"How is little Eddie?" asked Florence.

"He's in bed, asleep. You were right. He already has a black eye, poor little mite. I feel so guilty."

Before Florence could reply, a knock came on the door. Her aunt opened it. On the door mat stood a messenger.

"A message for a Miss Florence Fisher," he announced.

"For me? Who would be sending me a letter?" Surely it could not be from Luke, cancelling their arrangement for the following morning? She had only just left him. He would not even have arrived home.

She turned it over. "It's Eliza's handwriting. Why would she be writing to me so urgently?"

"Open it and see." Her aunt ushered the messenger inside, for a gale blew in.

She read it quickly. "Oh, dear, it seems Mama is very poorly. She is asking for me. I must return home immediately."

"Well, it's too late today. You'll have to wait until the morning, my dear. Does she say what the matter is with her?"

She reread the letter as she went to the bureau to pen a reply for the messenger to take back. "No, she does not. I hope it is nothing too serious."

"Had she been poorly before you came away?" Her aunt took it and handed it to him. "Thank you, sir."

Pulling his jacket around his ears, he bowed and withdrew.

"I had better find Sybil and give her the news." Florence went through to the stairs. "She will be relieved. She finds the countryside very boring."

Her aunt called her back. "You had better send a missive to your lord, Florence, to tell him you won't be able to meet him tomorrow."

Wanting to stamp her foot like a tantrumming child, she cursed, "Yes, damnation." She looked around to check if anyone else could have heard her. "I am sorry, Aunt, I hope none of the children heard me swear, but all my excitement is to no avail, now. He will think I have left in such a hurry to escape from him."

"Not if you explain, my dear. I'm sure he'll understand. His own mother ails from time to time. He must have to hare after her now and again."

Chapter 13

Arriving home after a very chilly journey, she found her mother sitting up in bed, drinking hot chocolate. "I thought you would be at death's door, Mama, from the words in Lizzie's letter. You seem to be perfectly well to me," she berated her as she took off her gloves.

Her mother put down her cup and wiped her brow, a sulky look on her face. "You mean you hoped I would be at death's door." At least she was speaking to her.

"No, I do not mean that. Of course, I am glad you are not." She reached over and kissed her cheek. "It's just that I have put off plans, thinking you much worse than you obviously are."

"Yesterday I thought I had breathed my last, I was so ill." Picking up her cup again, her mother finished her drink. "But today, I feel a little better. The doctor says I must stay in bed for a few days, though."

Florence sat in the armchair next to the bed. "Where is Eliza? Is she not tending to you?"

"She had an engagement with some young buck or other."

So had I.

"I tell you, I cannot keep pace with the girl. Anyway what plans have you cancelled?"

"It matters not, now. I expect everything will come to nought."

"That is fine then, if it does not matter. Seeing as you have brought us to ruin and will never find a suitable husband because of your irresponsible behaviour, you may stay and nurse me."

"Yes, Mama. What would you like me to do?"

"You may read to me. That would be pleasant."

"Very well." She picked up a book that had been discarded upside down on the side table. "This one? What is it? Oh, 'A Christmas Carol' by Charles Dickens. Frederick was reading that. I did not know you liked Dickens."

"My friend, Madame Orgée recommended it to me, but I find reading very hard work, and you read so beautifully, my dear."

"I am surprised a French lady would be able to understand him. She has gone up in my estimation."

Shifting her position to a more comfortable one, her mother pulled her nightcap further onto her head. "She speaks English better than a lot of English people. You should become better acquainted with her. Anyway, I had reached the part where that horrible Mister Scrooge is visited by the ghost."

Florence began to read but had only reached the second sentence when her mother interrupted her.

"Just put another log on the fire for me, my dear. I feel the cold so much."

She did so and wrapped another blanket around her mother's shoulders. "Is that better?"

"Yes, thank you, dear. Now, where were we? Oh, yes, the bad lobster in a dark cellar. What a peculiar saying, do you not think?"

"Yes, Mama, very peculiar. Would you like me to continue, or would you rather criticise the author's words?"

"Now, my dear, there is no need for that. If you do not want to carry on…"

"I did not say that." She took a deep breath and continued with the story. After several minutes, just as she had begun to enjoy the narrative, she realised she had been relating it to deaf ears. Her mother had slipped sideways, fast asleep. Making her more comfortable, she covered her with her blankets and tiptoed out of the room.

The house seemed deserted. Would her sister still be out with her newest 'young buck' as her mother had put it? And had Frederick returned from his visit to his friend? He spent more time away than at home. She smiled at the conversation she had had with her sister before she had gone away, not believing her intimation. Just because he would rather be around men did not signify that he preferred them. Heaven forbid! Once he met the right girl, he would settle down and raise a family. He had not done so, that was all, she felt sure. Not like herself. All her dreams looked as if they would be vanishing into thin air. By the time Luke Lancaster returned to Ambleside—if he ever did—he would have met somebody else with whom to fall in love. Once again she pictured herself sitting in a rocking chair, needles in hand, knitting pretty cardigans for her nieces and nephews, never having married or had children of her own.

Hoping her mother would sleep for a while, she wandered through the house, picking up ornaments and putting them back down, smiling at the misshapen one she had made for her father as a Christmas present when she had been nine—a paper decoupage box, covered with pictures of flowers and animals. *What is the point in keeping it?* she wondered, but could not bring herself to discard it. *It is not as if I shall have anybody to hand it down to.* Walking across to the window, she watched carriages going past, sending spray splashing onto the pavement. Would that one of them contained her lover, coming to whisk her away! A rainbow appeared in the sky, making her smile. What beautiful colours!

Luke read the letter once more. Had Florence been honest, or had she made up an excuse to evade him? She had seemed very acquiescent the previous day, had given him hope that he had not had since…well, ever.

He made his way to the nursery. The little boy would not be disappointed, even though he had told him his future mama would be coming to visit to become acquainted with him. He would be too young to understand. Lucky him!

He picked him up out of his cradle. "Hello, Michael. How are we today?"

His nanny sat darning a sock. "He is very well, sir. He can stand now, if he holds onto the furniture, or my hand."

"Good, good, he is developing normally, then?"

"Oh, yes, sir. In fact, I would say he is advanced for his age." She put down the darning mushroom. "Is the lady still coming?"

"No." He handed her the child. "No, she has been called away on an urgent matter."

"Oh, and I had dressed him in his best dress as well. I may as well remove it, if he is not to be shown off."

Do as you please, he wanted to tell her, but thought she might take umbrage, and went to find his mother.

"I am sure her reason would be genuine," his mother reasoned with him, after he had finished telling her about Florence. "Why would it not be? Have you done anything to scare her off?"

"No, I do not think so." If a kiss were enough to frighten a girl, she would not have entertained speaking to him after they had left the forest.

"So, then, go after her. What is holding you back? You need not worry about me. I have everything I require. Not that I would not miss you. I always enjoy your visits, but if the girl means that much to you, then be gone. Before she changes her mind."

"But I thought you wanted me to walk out with Miss Smith."

"Not any more. Her buck teeth are still too prominent."

He stared out of the window at the rain. The sun came out from behind a cloud and a rainbow appeared, arcing across the sky. He stared at it for several minutes before continuing. "Miss Fisher will not have the opportunity to meet little Michael, though. How can she make up her mind if she has never even seen him?"

"Take him with you."

"What? How could I do that?"

"With his nanny, of course."

He dragged his gaze from the colourful spectacle and sat down in an armchair. "Hm, I had not thought of that. But how would I manage with him at my house? We have no provisions for a baby, no cradle or...or anything."

"Well, it might take some organising, but I am sure you can cope." She stood up and rang for the maid. "Actually, I could come as well. Would that help? Your house is not too far from Ambleside. That is where you said she lives, isn't it?"

Not expecting that, he blinked. "Oh, no, Mother, there is no need."

The maid entered and his mother asked for tea and biscuits. "Any for you, my dear?" she asked him.

He shook his head and picked up an inviting bottle of brandy. "Something stronger would be more welcome." Pouring out a large measure, he tried to ignore his mother's disapproving look.

"It would solve a problem, though, would it not, if I came with you? In fact, why do I not come for Christmas? It is only a month away now. I could assist you with all the preparations, supervise the trimmings and decorate the tree for you. Oh, please, Luke, say I may. I am quite excited now, at the thought of it."

"But what about my sisters? I had thought you would be staying with one of them." Her crest-fallen face stopped him going any further. "Not that I would not love to have your company."

She slumped on the sofa. "I am sure you have other plans. Ignore me. I am being presumptuous."

The maid brought in the refreshments and she shooed her away when she offered to pour out the tea.

He grimaced. Should he allow her to accompany him? It would delay his departure by a few days, for she would want to pack everything, including the sink from the kitchen, if she were allowed, but she would be a great help.

"Very well, Mother, I would appreciate your assistance. When can you be ready?"

She jumped up, almost spilling her drink. "As soon as you would like me to be, son. I shall go now and ask my maid to find my valise."

"Drink your tea, first." He smiled. "A few more minutes will not go amiss."

Missus Fisher made a speedy recovery, giving Florence the idea that she had not been as ill as she had made out. But what would be the point in having words with her? The damage had already been done.

A few days later she wrapped herself against the bitter winter wind and went outside. Eliza called to her as she was about to close the door behind her. When she heard the name Lancaster, she turned and pushed it open. "What? What did you say?"

"I forgot to tell you, this morning I saw your Luke Lancaster in town."

"Are you sure? Maybe it was someone who looked like him." She went back inside, to stop the chill entering the house.

"No, it was definitely him."

"Whereabouts? And why has he not sent me word to say he has returned? Oh, Lizzie, he must think I used Mama as an excuse to flee from him."

"Wait, I'll come with you." Eliza followed her out. "You'll just have to start looking elsewhere, dear sister. Start all over again, like I do."

"Your situation is scarcely the same, Lizzie. You have not fallen in love as deeply as I. Who is this latest beau, by the way?"

"Well, I did not want to tell you, but I may as well. Do you remember Lord March's ball?"

"What about it?"

"You know." She linked arms and they battled against the gale. "The man you fancied, who did not give you his proper name, but called himself Mister A N Other?"

"Yes, he had rather gorgeous eyes."

"Well, even if you do not see Lancaster again, you will not go looking for him. He is mine now."

She pulled her over to a milliner's shop. "Oh, just look at that beautiful stripy satin. Is it not the most divine colour blue you have ever seen?"

Florence clung onto her bonnet. "Yes, maybe, but what did you say?"

"Mister A N Other is actually Mister Arthur Walmsley, and I have been out twice in his carriage. He speaks highly of you, but do not go thinking anything in that, for he has practically declared his love for me now."

"You are welcome to him, my dear. But has he told you why he did not give me his full name?"

"Oh, something to do with a joke. I did not take in what he meant."

"And, anyway, what has he been saying about me?"

"He mentioned something about your abduction. How would he know about that?"

They continued on their way, Florence trying to work out how her sister's friend could be connected to Luke, but they soon gave up battling the elements and returned home. As they entered the house, Crakeplace informed them that Lord Head had arrived. "Oh, no, what can he want? I thought I had made it clear I did not want him."

"He is not here to see you, ma'am."

"No, Flo, he is probably visiting Mama again," her sister told her. "When he heard she had fallen ill, he sent her flowers, and called around once or twice to ask after her."

Flabbergasted, Florence's mouth fell open. "Well, that is a turn up for the books. How amazing."

"You youngsters do not have the monopoly on romance," she heard her mother's voice from behind her. "Why should you think it amazing that I should have a suitor?"

She turned to see her mother, radiant in a new green outfit, descending the stairs. "I did not mean that, Mama. I am just surprised it should be Lord Hair…I mean, Head. Why did you not say anything before?"

"I do not have to tell you everything. I must not keep the good man waiting." She flounced into the parlour, the picture of health. Maybe a 'good man' could perform miracles, and cure her of whatever had been ailing her.

Good luck to her, she thought. *She can have all the fineries she wishes if she marries him.* Her foot on the bottom stair, about to go to her room to pen a letter to a friend, she turned as the front door bell rang. Eliza had preceded her upstairs, so she thought she may as well wait and see who could be calling.

Crakeplace opened the door, and her heart missed a beat when she heard the voice she had been longing to hear. Should she run to him, or play it casually?

Without warning, her legs took over the decision and she flew into his arms, uncaring if the servant witnessed her behaviour. The whole world could watch, for all she cared.

Crakeplace coughed behind her. "Ma'am, please may I close the door?"

Reluctant to leave her haven, she dragged Luke inside, and into the front lounge. "Come in, come in. you cannot imagine how pleased I am to see you, my darling. I thought I would never see you again."

As soon as the door closed, she fell against him, uncaring whether he had not come for that or not, and raised her face for his kiss.

He did not need any encouragement, but enfolded her roughly in his arms, ravishing her mouth with his. Breathless, she yanked him back when he pulled away, but he held her at arm's length. "There will be plenty of time for that, my darling love, much as I am loath to stop, but I have someone in the carriage who would like to meet you."

She straightened her clothes. "Oh, who?"

"A certain little boy." At her raised eyebrows, he added, "I had to bring him. How could we ever come to a conclusion until you met him?"

"Um, do you want to bring him in?"

"Oh, no, no, I thought we could all go for a drive. My mother has come as well."

"Oh." Would the surprises never stop? "I had better put my cloak back on, then." She turned to go but he grabbed her. "Just one more kiss."

Several minutes later, her hair in disarray, and her bodice slipping, she ran out, calling, "I need to tidy myself. Pray, take a seat while you wait."

Blowing out her breath in short pants, she hurried upstairs. Eliza sat on her bed, combing her hair. "My, my, I had not realised the wind to be that strong, Flo. You look as if you have been…"

"Oh, Lizzie, he has come for me. He is here, his mother also. I must make myself presentable to meet her. Where is Sybil? I cannot do justice to my hair without her."

"I think she went out. Would you like me to try?"

Not much later, she took a last look in the mirror. "It will have to do. I would have preferred it loose, but it is tidy, at any rate. Do you think she will like me? But, what if I do not take to the child? What if he is a monster?"

Eliza put her arm around her. "Stop faffing, dear sister. I am sure everything will turn out just fine."

"Maybe I should have worn the brown dress. Should I change?"

"No, go, off with you. You look lovely. Not that you do not do so all the time. You will melt their hearts, so stop worrying."

She rushed downstairs and, before entering the lounge, had another quick peek in the hall mirror.

Taking a deep breath, she went in. "I am so sorry to keep you wai…" Pulling up at the sight before her, she blinked. Her mother, arm in arm with Lord Head, stood chatting to Luke as if they were the best of friends.

"Ah, there you are, my dear," said her mother. "You had not told me about Mister Lancaster. He knows your brother."

"Yes, Mama." She turned to Luke. "I am sorry to have taken so long. Your poor mother will be frozen to her death, and the child. I should have invited them in."

He put his hand on her arm. "Do not concern yourself. I told them to return to my house, and asked the driver to come back for us."

"What's this about a child?" her mother asked, going over to the window.

Florence looked at him, wondering if it should be her position to give her the facts, but Luke took the matter in hand and explained everything. Not quite everything, though, he did not mention the proposal, or the escapade in the forest.

"So we had better be going." She bowed to Lord Head, who seemed to be watching the tableau with interest, not at all heart-broken as she would have imagined. So much for his undying love, but she was pleased he had transferred his affections to her mother. Her plan had worked without any help from her.

She took Luke's arm and steered him towards the door. Once outside, she expected a carriage to be waiting, but, of course, he had sent it away.

"Shall we take a walk while we wait for the carriage?" he asked. "It will pass us by, so will not miss us."

"Well, I suppose the wind has abated, and the rain has stopped. It might be pleasant to walk." Clinging onto his arm, she smiled up at him. The love in his eyes turned her insides to mush, and her legs to honeycomb. She clung to his coat to keep from falling, wanting to pull his head down and kiss him there and then in the middle of the street.

Passing a side alley, he glanced around in each direction and pulled her into it, giving her a sound kiss before stepping back out onto the street. She giggled. How naughty. Her mother would have a fainting fit if she could see her. "Again," she whispered.

"You minx, you temptress," he muttered. "But, alas, there are no more alleyways ahead."

"What a shame." She giggled again. "Where exactly do you live? I can't believe we have not met before, or that I have not even heard of you."

"The other side of Windermere, near Bowness."

"Ah, that's probably why." She drew away and danced around in a circle, her arms in the air. "Oh, Luke, you make me feel so alive. I never thought I could experience such pleasure, merely by being with somebody."

"So, you are saying yes, then?"

"Yes, yes, yes, to whatever you ask. If you wanted me to go to the moon, I would go. If you wanted me to fly in the sky like a bird, I would try."

"Very poetic," he mumbled as he pulled her back into the crook of his arm.

"Hey, that reminds me; I promised Mister Wordsworth I would visit his father. Have you ever met his father, William Wordsworth? He is a very famous poet."

"No, and I do not want you visiting any other men, not now you have agreed to be mine."

"Aw, Luke, he is an old man. Surely you would not begrudge him the presence of my company. Just for an hour or two. I so love his poems. Do you not?"

"Well, yes." They stopped to watch the swans on the lake. "Maybe we could go together?" he suggested.

She rubbed her hands to warm them. "That would be a splendid idea."

"Shall we proceed?" When she hesitated, he added, "I hope you are not deliberately delaying us."

"No, my darling, I just want to spend as much time alone with you as I can."

He laughed, scaring a pair of mallards that flew up into the sky. "This is hardly alone, with all these people milling around us." A man pushed past him, clearly in a hurry. "See?"

"You know what I mean. Anyway, Eliza told me something earlier. Do you know Mister Arthur Wellesley?"

"Yes, he is a very good friend."

"And you told him about kidnapping me?"

He took her hands in his and with his head to one side, grimaced. "It was his idea."

"What?"

"I owed him a favour, and he wanted to become better acquainted with you, so asked if I would stop your carriage and take it to his house."

She pulled her hands away. "And you agreed? What a preposterous suggestion. Why did you not tell me?"

"I did not want you being complimented by his feelings for you since, as you know, it all went wrong, and I ended up falling for you myself."

"Well, he must have soon given up on me for now he is courting my sister."

"I have warned him never to look at you again."

"That will be difficult." She looked around at the lake, shimmering in the weak sunshine that had escaped from behind a cloud. Did it really matter, now she had lost her heart to Luke? No, she did not feel the slightest thing for the man. "Come on, then, lead your lamb to the slaughter."

"Oh, my darling, that is not how you think of it, is it? We could put it off, if you would prefer."

"No, I am resigned to the fact. Actually, I am looking forward to meeting him, and to becoming better acquainted with your mother."

He took her hand and they ran, laughing.

"Here goes, then, my darling. Are you certain you do not want to back out?"

"Luke, I have told you…unless you want me to?" She looked up into his eyes, those gorgeous sapphire blue eyes, now so unsure. When he shook his head, she continued, "I love you, and wish to spend the rest of my life with you, to share the problems and doubts, so yes, I am absolutely certain I am not backing out."

The carriage drew level. He caught her to him. "You do not know how long I have waited to hear you say you love me. Say it again."

She threw her arms in the air, shouting, "I love you, I love you. Listen everybody, I love Luke Lancaster."

He clamped his hand over her mouth. "Very well, shush, now. You will have everyone peeking out from their little windows, wondering who would have the temerity to be so bold."

"Bold. Yes, that's me," she declared as she accepted his hand to help her towards their future together.

Author biography

Married to Don, I have 5 children, 9 grandchildren and one great granddaughter. I live in Derbyshire, England, and enjoy researching my family tree (having found ancestors as far back as 1475), reading, gardening, Scrabble, meals out and family gatherings. I am the treasurer of my writing club, Eastwood Writers' Group. At church I sing in the choir and am an Extraordinary Minister of Holy Communion, a reader, a flower arranger and a member of the fundraising team for Cafod, my favourite charity. I have written hymns, although I cannot read music.

You can see a list of my other books at the front of this book. They are available on Amazon:

https://www.amazon.co.uk/Angela-Rigley/e/B00607O51M/ref=sr_ntt_srch_lnk_1?qid=1540287989&sr=1-1

Find me on Twitter: @angierigley;

Facebook:

https://www.facebook.com/angelarigleyauthor

LinkedIn;

my website

www.nunkynoo.yolasite.com where you can see pictures of lambs and birds, and some of my Thoughts for the Day;

and my blog:

https://wordpress.com/view/authoryantics.wordpress.com.

If you enjoyed reading about Florence – or even if you didn't – I would really appreciate it if you could find the time to post a review on Amazon or Goodreads.

Some reviews of my other books:

Nancie: Fate deals Nancie many hard blows, and Angela takes us on Nancie's journey through a troubled childhood. Nancie takes it all in her stride, without being overly sentimental.Will life ever get better for her? I couldn't wait to find out. This is my favourite Angela Rigley novel. *Lyn*

The Peacock Bottle: The Peacock Bottle is a very entertaining historical novel, with great characters that held my attention. I started it one day and finished it the next as I got caught up in the stories of these lovely girls . I also loved the gentle writing style of the author who wove nature references cleverly into the narrative.

Other books by the author:

Looking for Jamie
A Dilemma for Jamie
School for Jamie
Choices for Jamie
Rewards for Jamie
Nancie
Lea Croft
The Peacock Bottle
Harriet of Hare Street
My Book of Silly Poems and Things

My Silly Poems for Kids
Cal the Caveboy
Cal Saves his sister
Cal's Good Idea
Baarlie the Naughty Lamb
Baarlie and the Snow
Baarlie Wants to Fly
Baarlie and the Star at Christmas
Dotty and Raggy are Lost in the Woods
Dotty is Lost
Dip the Farting Dinosaur
Dinosaurs should Not Eat Cheese
Macnally the Alien
Squidgy and the Fawn

I dedicate this book to my family, my friend, Jasmine, and to The Eastwood Writers' Group.

With acknowledgement to William Wordsworth and his son, William

Printed in Great Britain
by Amazon

10139478R00190